SLEEPERS AND TIES

SEEPERS AND TIES

SLEEPERS AND TIES

A Novel

GAIL KIRKPATRICK

$\lfloor$ N₁ $\lfloor$ O₂ $\lfloor$ N₁

CANADA

*Publisher's note: This book is a work of fiction. Names, characters, places and
incidents are either the product of the author's imagination or are used
fictitiously, and any resemblance to actual persons living or dead
is entirely coincidental.*

Library and Archives Canada Cataloguing in Publication

Title: Sleepers and ties / Gail Kirkpatrick.

Names: Kirkpatrick, Gail (Author of Sleepers and ties), author.

Identifiers: Canadiana (print) 20220482047 | Canadiana (ebook) 2022048208X |
ISBN 9781989689462 (softcover) | ISBN 9781989689509 (EPUB)

Classification: LCC PS8621.I75 S54 2023 | DDC C813/.6—dc23

Printed and bound in Canada on 100% recycled paper.

Now Or Never Publishing
901, 163 Street
Surrey, British Columbia
Canada V4A 9T8

nonpublishing.com
Fighting Words.

We gratefully acknowledge the support of the Canada Council for the Arts
and the British Columbia Arts Council for our publishing program.

Cover design by Shannon Hayward

For Amy and Paul

Plover Station, June 2007

1. Ballast

Yellow wallflowers and purple thistle cover the former Plover railway line, and I wonder why it hasn't been turned into a walking trail. That way at least, a century old route carved from the land would have been preserved. Markers could be placed every ten miles or so with illustrations of the meadowlarks and starlings to be found hereabouts, details of the geography, Métis and First Nations Peoples, maybe the names of the workers who helped build this line, perhaps even sacrificed their lives for it, something akin to the scalloped shells of the Camino that mark the route and distance to Santiago de Compostela, not so much to mark a pilgrimage, but comparable here enlightening the traveler on the path that links one part of the country to another. For the briefest moment, I slip into curator mode finding it ever difficult to shed the professional skin and am grateful for the distraction.

Fool's gold sparkles in the rail bed. The sparrows skulking among the cattails alert with *tschip tschip tschip*. A few feet in front of me, something glints in the sunlight, and leaning forward I recognize a rusty spike, the once t-shaped silver nail now umber and bent into a U. Someone at the museum might make use of it in one of the displays, maybe place it surreptitiously in a coal-mining or ship-building diorama, or repurposed by some enthusiastic junior, label it a coat hook for the gift shop. Just what the museum needs, more trinkets. I turn away, shade my eyes against the platinum sunshine, and wish that I had remembered to bring my shades.

As if I were cleaning my gardening clogs on the back-door boot-scraper, I brush my sole across the rail, but the polished surface of the track rejects the Italian leather and my shoe slips away from the steel. I dig my toe into the salt and pepper quarry, the ballast that neither time nor wind has shifted. Sharp-edged flint, ice-coloured quartz, limestone, and shale, rocks of glacial tills and ancient mountains, once tucked between wooden planks meant to keep the rails from shifting. Now, for the chance passer-by, merely a collection of weathered boards and silent stones interrupting the plain.

The sun warms to the marrow and there is no need of a suit jacket. Before I can decide whether to drape it across my shoulder or drop the jacket onto the grass, my bare right foot shakes off the flat I am wearing, and in one smooth, easy motion prints itself on the sun-warmed steel. I teeter right, left. The other shoe falls away, and with the lightness of a tightrope walker I let the railway track lead me through the tangle of pompous and prickly bloom. The pleats of my skirt fan in the careless breeze.

Overhead, the contrail of a jet vaporizes in the cloudless sky and the thin, white thread being pulled across the firmament spreads into widening vertebrae. Perhaps the very same jet that brought me west to east is now headed back to its home airport. I feel a longing for where I have come from.

Obligation has brought me to this place, but I no longer know how to be here. The pre-dawn espresso urged me on to Plover Station, immediately after I'd crossed the tarmac and picked up the rental, but now I am steeped in abandonment. My heart is staked with Jake, two time zones away, and our three sons, who, from time to time, return from their global wanderings. Jake will be sitting down to his lunch about now, while the bees flit amidst the lavender.

When I reach the yellow and purple wall, I recognize a column of Queen Anne's lace raising their heads to form a rear-guard. As effortlessly as my shoe slipped from the rail, I slip back in time. Dad, when he'd been able to predict down a clean track, had the habit of standing on the platform, looking in this westerly direction. He'd pull at his watch strap, say, 'Right on time,' and then, as if by magic, draw a train out of the horizon for Shirley and me. Not any more, not through this barricade of flora.

Without stepping off the rail, I crouch, slowly maneuver a hundred-and-eighty-degree turn, and heel-toe back towards the car parked in the field where the railway station had once been. Quackgrass, foxtails, and buffalo beans have taken over the place where our home had once been planted. I scan the horizon for anything that used to be ours. A meadowlark whistles its two-part verse and I tip off the rail.

I look from bulrushes to power lines for the yellow breast and black V-collar. *Sturnella neglecta.* Eager to flaunt my book learning, I had recited, 'Named because it had gone unnoticed as being different from its eastern relative. The emblem bird of six American states.' My younger sister would simply turn and point to the bird on its pedestal and say, 'There,' proving her perception an unequivocal match to my memorized recitations. Oft, superior.

A second call sounds behind me. I spin round, imitate a poor response. No answer comes back to me.

Instead, a child's sing-song voice, unheralded, out of the blue, 'Margaret's losing her marvels.' We didn't understand why the adults had laughed. When she was a child, Shirley had switched her b's and v's. And I hadn't been losing my marbles; my collection of misty blues and ribbon swirls had been mischievously hidden in the rail bed by Shirley and her thieving magpie friends. Marbles lost. Marbles never to be found again.

The birthing smell of poplar drifts down the wind, and I breathe in melted snows, muddy cattails, tadpoles, and willow from the late spring slough. I gather up my skirt between my thighs, place my ear on the rail and listen for a train. In the last three decades of living beside the ocean, the sound of the sea in a shell remains a myth, yet, somewhere deep in these rails, I can hear the scrape and huff of Diesel 1416.

In the rail bed, the sun on fool's gold tempts again, and this time I pick up the stone with the most sparkles, blow away the dust, and put it, warm, into my pocket. Our parents, Neal and Jean, are gone, and so now is my sister, Shirley. I have no need to ever return here. The keepsake will join the global assortment of stones in the bowl on the mantle back home.

Ahead of me, the white cross-tie marks the former stop of Plover Station. I knew what to expect. The disappearance of small railway towns is forgotten news, and it matters naught to me. Two decades ago, Shirley showed me videos of the dynamiting of the last grain elevator, and my friend, Massy, had sent a letter when Plover's railway station was jacked up and hauled away—to be re-imagined as a cottage, it was rumoured.

I close my eyes and try to recreate the station from my childhood experience of it as well as my memory pictures. The enclosing caragana hedge, semaphore saluting over the platform, rain barrel overflowing beside the front door, waiting room separated from the office by a customer counter, the dit-dah of the Morris code, the portrait of the Queen on one side, family rooms after, freight shed beyond, and coal bin somewhere there too. Gone now are the four company grain elevators, Pool, Searle, National, and Home—prairie skyscrapers of the 20th century. Gone, the station, Mother's garden, and Adam's section house. All gone.

The wind blows around me, the boarded-up buildings of Plover's main street, and where the hotel and pub stood before the night of the fire. I retrieve the car keys from my jacket pocket, pull at my watch strap, and turn my head one more time for the meadowlark.

'Stop daydreaming and wasting time,' I imagine Shirley whispering. I can't put it off any longer. The lawyer is waiting to dismiss the second and final probate of her will.

2. SIGNALS

The law office is north of 22nd Street, away from the Saskatoon downtown core, in a 1970s-designed building. The single-storey, russet box, with its V-winged roofline is hidden between 21st century apartment towers. I take out my phone to capture the juxtaposition. On the screen, the outline of a man appears ghostly behind the sheer curtains of a front office window. Though we have only corresponded by post and the odd telephone call, I presume it is Gerard Hall, anxious to close the file on Shirley's will and deliver some parting lawyerly words of wisdom, in exchange, of course, for his final payment.

A large arrangement of tiger lilies and oat grasses, more suitable for a hotel foyer, dominate the high counter of the reception area. When I lean over to smell the flowers, a petite woman raises herself to the level of the greenery. I smile and inhale, expecting the sweetness of lilies, but the deceptive papery facsimiles are covered with dust—dust that has sifted down from legal volumes of precedents which serve as the back wall.

'I hope you've come in a car,' the receptionist says.

This was where, years before, we'd been left sitting on the shag carpet with the instruction, 'Mind your sister,' while Hall had taken Mom away to go over Dad's will. I remember handing Shirley one of the jawbreakers we'd been allowed to buy minutes before. We'd taken turns showing each other the changing colours on our tongue. No carpet these many years later, all hardwood. I can't remember meeting Hall then, nor have I seen him since. With a mother and sister dying in quick succession of one another, and he being the lawyer for both of them, it might seem unusual that I am just about to be reacquainted with Hall, but Mom made it known that she had designated Shirley the executor of her estate—'You're too busy with your job and kids,' she'd said. At the time, I'd felt thwarted. After all, I'd been the one responsible in my teens for keeping track of the bills, entering the household accounts in a ledger, and putting into the cocoa tin the pocket money I'd earned delivering newspapers. But, when the time came, I was grateful for Shirley taking on the responsibility, for when Mom passed, as she had predicted, I was busily arranging displays cases for a Japanese Okimono exhibit. Shirley had said we were in it together, but to my surprise she had stepped up and taken care of the tedious paperwork, and I hadn't given much attention to the copies of statements and legalities that she'd cc'd to me. I'd trusted her to do whatever was necessary.

When she passed away, I found Hall's business card and a note in the wooden puzzle box I'd once given her, instructing, 'To whom it may concern,' to contact Hall about her will and any other business that might come up. Up to this point, everything had been handily managed by letter or telephone. Until the second probate was completed, I hadn't seen any reason for dealing with him face to face.

The receptionist knocks on the office door across from her station and announces, 'Margaret has arrived.'

'You've picked some dandy weather,' Hall says, nodding to the window that I'd seen from the street. He takes my right hand in both of his, and then puts one hand on my shoulder. I look into his eyes and notice the grey film of cataracts, wonder if I appear slightly blurry through his eyes, as if through a scrim. I anticipate his reaching out to embrace me, and seeing no reason to be anything less than formal, I let go of his hand and take a seat in one of the captain's chairs across from his desk.

'Yes. Sit. Please,' he says. He takes his place behind the desk, bumps the rollers of his swivel chair over the ribs of a plastic mat as he moves forward, drums his hands on his desk as overture to our appointment.

The man in front of me is nothing like the waist-coated squire I'd created in my mind from his telephone messages and the formal documents and letters he has sent. He appears well past retirement age, rather too casual looking in his polo shirt and brown trousers. I suppose the relationship between client and lawyer, as in doctor and patient, should be one of trust, but I keep up my guard, even perhaps, though I don't know exactly why, decide that I will dislike him. He has a flushed complexion and there are several sunspots on his receding hairline. At first, I mistake them for a continuation of his arm and neck freckles, but then I realize the scaly spots are similar to those on the pate of the commissionaire at the museum. The commissionaire had to have biopsies of similar-looking blemishes. I wonder if Hall has seen a dermatologist.

Legal books and client files are stacked on every flat surface around him and Hall nests himself in the centre. The wastepaper basket beside his desk is empty, as is the shredder that also serves as doorstop. It seems to me these small gestures of order are the allowed limits of the receptionist's duty to make his cluttered space navigable for clients.

His final summary of fees was sent to me and I have a cheque in hand for the exact amount. I am determined to keep track of time and not let chitchat end up costing me extra lawyer hours. If there is one way in which I count myself similar to Shirley, it is in not wasting time. I glance at my watch.

'Shall we begin?' Hall asks.

I signal with a smile.

'This is a copy of the will I sent you many months ago, but since you are finally here in person, let's review everything. In fact, it's probably my legal duty. You can follow along. Let's skip over page one of the legal jargon. Follow me to page two.'

Halfway down page one, I Shirley… being of sound mind and body, in this the year of our Lord. I flip to page—

Hall continues. 'That "1. Robert, Russ, and Ryan"—your sons—"shall each be entitled to $10,000 from my estate. 2. That Jean shall be entitled to $20,000"—but, of course, your mother is deceased and that amount has been dispersed among the beneficiaries.'

I'd sorted both of Shirley's bank accounts; my sons had received their inheritances. This pretty much added up to all the money she had managed to put away—her life savings.

'And "3. That Margaret be entitled to the residue of the estate."'

There was her severance pay, the government's death benefit, but no life insurance, she didn't believe in that. I've already calculated that once Hall's fees are deducted and I've paid the last of Shirley's income taxes, estate taxes, and any unforeseen bills, there will be little left. I have a sneaking suspicion that before all is said and done, expenses of one sort or another will pop up, and I will be paying them out of my own pocket. Many times, over the years, Shirley borrowed small amounts of money and I'd never seen any repayment.

Hall picks at one of his sunspots. 'Do you follow me?'

I've had six months to live with the details. What is there to follow?

'As to the residue of the estate, Margaret, I have calculated that to be approximately eight million, give or take.'

'Pardon me?'

'The rest of her estate is left to you. Eight million dollars.'

'What are you talking about? Please, don't joke. Are you serious?'

'Absolutely.'

'But I've been through her bank accounts. My sister didn't have that kind of money. There was an outstanding mortgage that was paid from the sale of her condo, and our mother had nothing to leave but a bit of jewellery. There were no investments.'

Hall shuffles through some papers. 'Well, actually, there were. Now let me see, which would you prefer to see first, the letter, or the potash valuations and statements?'

'What letter?'

'Your sister left a letter with me which was to be attached to her will. Here it is.'

He hands me a piece of paper. I recognize Shirley's unmistakable intermingling of print and cursive writing.

'She left this letter with you?'

'When she came to settle your mother's business. She asked that if the day should come, I give it to you in person. I saw no urgency in this personal matter, because it holds no legal weight. Tea or coffee?' he asks.

I read:

'*Dear Marvels*, (I stir at the private endearment she'd called me, only a few times in our lives.)

I am writing this letter in case something bad should happen to me.

Many years ago, on the advice of a friend, I was talked into investing some money and forgot about it. Remember the fellow I dated for a while, the one you called a self-centered schemer? Turned out he knew what he was talking about, at least where potash was concerned. I don't know the exact amount that has accumulated in the account. You know money has never meant much to me.

For the last few years, though, I have dreamed of reviving a rail line like the one that Dad believed in. Now, there may be enough money to get the project started, and if you are reading this, it means I have not been able to see it through. Please, Margaret, I know you will finish what I started.

I love you, my bossy marvel. Don't cry. We've had enough tears to last a lifetime. Have a double whiskey. Tell the boys I loved them more than they could ever know.

Sis, Shirley xo

I push away from the chair and make my way to the window, brush my cheek and steady my hands on the sill.

3. Extra

Nothing in Shirley's belongings had hinted at a letter. Why hadn't she left it where I could find it? All those weekends I spent going through her condo, taking clothes to the charity shops, having her neighbours round to help themselves to furniture, books, and CDs. Why hadn't she ever mentioned the money or investment? She had eight million dollars. Eight-million-dollars. And she expects me to—what has she written?—*finish what I started. Reviving a rail line like the one that Dad believed in.* What does that even mean?

'Shall we continue?' Hall clears his throat. 'There are a couple of other important legalities we need to address. Please sign the second probate here, and here, and initial at the x's.'

He hands me a pen, and when I press the cap, a retractable fountain pen nib appears. I examine the reservoir of ink; dad had been fond of fountain pens.

'And the letter regarding the donation of land to the conservancy? Do you have that? The one for The Saskatchewan Very Land Trust, the VLT. That is very important.'

I stop mid-signing. He'd just said a personal matter was of no urgency. 'Why didn't you send me this letter six months ago? Or at least tell me about it. Why did you keep it from me?'

'I didn't exactly keep it from you. You told me that you would be making a trip here with your sister's ashes, and I assumed it would have been sooner than this. As I've noted, her wish was that I give it to you in person.'

'I am the executrix of her estate. This letter should have been delivered with the will, or you could have told me there was an urgent matter that required my attention. You had no right to keep this from me.' I stop short of shrieking my reprimand.

'Please, don't upset yourself. You have it in hand now. The letter is just a sweet farewell. It is not a legally binding document. I also had an obligation to Shirley.'

By her words, my sister is in the room with me, but unable to speak further than the contents of this piece of paper. I am almost physically ill at the thought that before her personal sentiments could be absorbed by her family, they had been discharged by a stranger.

'But the letter forms part of the residue of her estate. Didn't you think that I had the right to know about the money?'

'I assure you, I've been meticulous with the assets. I handed over the accounts to an independent accounting firm when we began this process. It's all documented. Besides, in all of our correspondence, you never implied that you didn't know about her investment.'

How smoothly he has turned this into my oversight. Sun spots or no, I now have reason to dislike Hall.

'We need to discuss the matter of the small parcel of land, the remnant of your grandparents' original homestead, bordering the old rail line. Your mother turned all but these fifty acres over to the land trust, the VLT. You now own this land,' he adds.

Hall waits for me to settle. He takes out a handkerchief and wipes his nose. Something chokes to the surface—nostalgia or perhaps office dust. 'This has been a difficult time for you,' he sniffs.

Difficult time. What a convenient box for something which cannot be contained. What could he know of my *difficult time*? He sees a woman in front of him, dressed in a business suit, perhaps a little tired looking, but he knows nothing of the anguish that I alone own. How I've kept on, barely placing one foot in front of the other.

He leans back in his chair. 'You know, you don't look like your mother or your sister. And you probably don't remember me tending to your father's will. I had just started out on my own then.'

Like I give a fig who he thinks I do or don't resemble. He is diverting from the fact that he's kept from me my sister's letter and her eight million dollars.

'Jean and Shirley both had their wills drawn up here.'

'Marvels. Really?'

'I beg your pardon? You are quite flushed. Are you feeling alright?'

'The VLT, you were saying.' I am still holding the document.

'Right. Let's go back to the terms of the VLT commitment. I am also obligated to make sure you are clear about the details regarding your grandparents' homestead as given over to the land trust.' Hall forces a smile, and then his lips fall back into their acquired judicial frown. 'When we spoke a few months ago, I inferred that you were not fully aware of the donation of land your mother made, before she died, and which Shirley agreed with when she inherited the remnant fifty acres that your mother wished to be kept in the family.'

'I wasn't unaware.' I brush the prairie dust from my skirt. 'I chose not to be involved.'

This again? 'I get how it works.'

'Just to review a few of the particulars then,' Hall continues.

'May I have a glass of water, please?'

'Of course.' He rises to attention. 'Unless you'd prefer tea or coffee?'

'Just water. Thank you.'

I hear whispering; he's left the office door ajar.

I suddenly find it difficult to breathe. The room, all these papers. I look to the office curtains hoping for some fresh air and notice that I've left the rental car windows done up all the way. The car will be a sauna if I don't get out and roll down the windows.

Hall holds out the glass of water. I take a drink.

'I'm suggesting you reverse your mother's donation. I've found a loophole whereby you could take back the land left to the trust, and still put the entire family homestead up for sale. But, that opportunity will quickly pass.'

'I'm sorry.' I gather up my things. 'I will have to come back another time. I need to be somewhere else right now. Do you mind?'

I am almost at the door. Hall is close on my heels. 'But there are several items we must go over.'

I fold my sister's letter and place it in my purse. 'I'm assuming I can keep this.'

'Of course. I have copies.'

'I'll call and make another appointment.'

'You'll be wanting to wrap things up here and get back home. Did I mention I have a buyer interested in that land?'

As I force the outer door open, I look back over my shoulder and see Hall leaning over his secretary.

'I'm sure Mrs. Hall can find an extra time slot for you in the next couple of days.'

Typical. So much for the cheque I've made out for his fees.

4. DIVISION

The phone rings three times. I check my watch, realizing I haven't accounted for the time difference. I've driven away from Hall's office so that he can't come chasing after me. I have to tell Jake the news. I am idling at a bus stop when a parking spot comes available, facing the opposite direction. I drop the phone to my lap, crank a u-ey and pull in front of the Bessborough Hotel. At the fourth ring, I am about to hang up.

'Hello, hello, Jake here.'

'I've just been to see Gerald Hall.'

'Margaret. Did you get everything sorted?'

'You won't believe this. Shirley has left me eight million dollars. Do you hear me? Eight million dollars.'

'What are you talking about? I've seen her will.'

I feel in my purse for the letter. 'There is a letter. Hall had a letter.'

'I don't get it. Someone sent Shirley a letter? Was she in some sort of class action suit?'

'No. She left me a letter, telling me about some potash investment she had that she just let sit and grow.'

'And you didn't know anything about this?'

'Of course I didn't know.'

'I know you cross t's and dot i's, but could you have missed something in her bank accounts?'

Does he think it is my fault for not knowing about her money?

'Where is this money?' he asks.

'I've just left the lawyer's. I don't have the money.'

'That was rather selfish of her. She could have passed on that little financial tip to me—us.'

Jake visits his bank every month, hounds his financial adviser for better, higher paying dividends on our small savings, but he is also averse to risk. I've always just left the financial matters in his hands.

'It was years ago.'

'Well, seems we've got the money now,' he says. 'How soon can Hall transfer it over? I'll go and see my broker this week and get it earning some dividends, or maybe put it in one of our no-risk funds.'

I wonder if all that money will fit in a carry-on. Did Hall tell me there was a cheque for that amount? Does the law office have a safe?

'Dividends? It's eight million dollars. Hang on, I'll just dig the letter out of my purse and read it to you.'

The meter attendant is approaching the car. I wave my purse to indicate I am looking for coins to plug the meter. She gives me the thumbs up. I unbuckle my seatbelt and read the letter to Jake, adding that Hall made it clear that the letter was not legally binding.

'Marvels. I don't think you know she called me that after—'

'I've just gone to your desk, and taken her will out of the file. "The residue of the estate." And here we were worried about paying the last of her taxes out of our pockets.'

'I have to go back to the lawyer's office. I left in a hurry.'

The line goes quiet. While Jake is processing what I've just told him, I peer up at the stone walls of the Bessborough Hotel, stretch my head back looking towards its parapets. Shirley and I had spent the one night here together, when we brought Mom's ashes home. We'd walked along the riverbank together in silence. She might have told me about the money then.

When we were forced to leave the station at Plover, Mom felt claustrophobic in the apartment we'd had to move into and she often brought us to the park adjacent to the stately hotel. 'The Bez', she'd explained, was named after the 9th Earl of Bessborough. It was one of many planned Canadian chateau-style railway hotels meant to entice wealthy travelers, and at times, house the railway's executives and their wives. Shirley and I had pretended it was our castle. The hotel was near the original CNR

station. The present station stop, for the now cross-country passenger train VIA Rail, is west of town.

'I've just had an idea,' Jake says. 'This isn't the best time of
course, with you out there and me here, but I'll start looking
around for one of those river cruises like Reg and Mo went on.
Maybe something along the Rhine. A good long rest from all
that we've had to deal with in the last while.'

I can almost see him rubbing his hands together.

Jake—not we—has been obsessing about river cruises ever
since his retired pals enjoyed the pleasures of cycling and cruising.
As if I have time to piddle away on a boat.

'But what about the rail line?'

'The what?'

'Her letter. She's asked me to revive a rail line.'

'Didn't you say the letter wasn't legally binding?'

'What has that got to do with it?'

'It's a ridiculous request, at best. No one would expect you
to take on that mission. Remember when Shirley first moved out
to the coast and was going to take up scuba diving, hoping to
communicate with whales to see if they could tell her what they
needed?'

Where is this sarcasm coming from? 'Yes, but when she
joined the movement to lobby for tourist boats to keep a greater
distance from whales, there was definitely a change.'

'Well. Apples and oranges.'

'I need time to think about this.'

'Of course we do.'

Jake's suddenly referring to everything as 'we' is beginning
to grate. After Dad died, Shirley, Mom, and I had closed ranks.
A troika of defence had its own consequences. Led to my equat-
ing separation with strength, the ability to endure. Now this we
against Shirley.

'It's a lot to take in. I had this urge to phone her and ask her
what she was thinking.'

'You'll feel that way for a long time. But railways don't make
money. Look, practically speaking, this kind of thing could take
years, and way more than eight million dollars. And where would

you find this little railway in need of reviving? No, the money would be long gone before anything got off the ground. Do you want to throw away our and the boys' futures on a fanciful request left in a letter?'

Just now, I am really needing that whiskey. There's likely a bar fridge in my room.

'I thought you liked my sister.'

'I did. But you have to admit she could be all over the map with plans that never materialized. Given a second thought, I know she'd want you to have the money.'

Six months ago, my sister's age had been cut off at 47. No one, not even a husband, has the right to now criticize her personality, or her bequest.

'Jake, I need to check into the hotel. The attendant is coming back up the street and I haven't put any money in the meter. I'll call you tomorrow and we'll talk about it some more then. Alright?'

'Do you want me to fly out and take care of this side of things? Being back there could stir things up and leave you vulnerable.'

This side of things? Jake had been too busy to help me clean out my mother and sister's condo; even suggested it would be cathartic for me to do it on my own. There had been moments in the division of property, sorting and hauling, when I would have appreciated his presence, his arms to carry a load down to the bins, or gather me up when I felt broken, but his own work obligations with the Ministry of Education have always taken precedence. I suppose I am still feeling resentful.

'No. I can manage just fine.'

'Alright then. You go and have a nice long hot bath. And order up room service. We can afford it now.'

And now, condescension. I could have ordered up room service before Shirley's letter if I bloody well wanted to, but I am in no mood to start something over the phone, and with Jake it is usually less aggravating to let him have the last say.

5. JUNCTION

Over the years, on my travels to meetings and conferences, I've gotten into the habit of taking my own unscented shampoos and lotions, and my own cleaning sponge to counter the malodourous cleaning products they frequently use in hotels. And while the novelty of staying in a hotel has worn off, I still feel a kind of euphoria when I punch my card key into the door. If the hotel is of exceptional ranking, there is an expectation of indulgence. The hair products and wrapped foreign soaps are so unlike my practical pharmacy specials, and a white bath robe on the back of the bathroom door offers up blissful surrender. At this door, though, it isn't euphoria, but fight or flight adrenaline still surging though me from the events of the past few hours.

I open my carry-on, fling open the curtains, wash my hands, and then open the miniature fridge and evaluate the assortment of tiny bottles. They seem less than adequate—not because of my sudden increase in cash flow, but more that they seem to say, 'Here's a little something, for a little something.' More suited to a ladies' night out. The unexpected news, the money, and my sister speaking to me through her letter, added to the day of travel, call for a large pour, over some deep ice, from a substantial bottle.

I slide onto a stool in the hotel's bar. 'A large Bushmills, please.' The barman nods when I raise my glass and say, 'To Shirley.'

If she were here, she would have added something to make us both laugh. She could always size up the moment, and with quick wit, draw a line under the occasion. I think to myself, well planned. A little money always makes the grief go down a little easier. Random. Definitely not funny.

The whiskey jolts and I drink it to quench my thirst. I don't order a second, but one appears, and this time I let each bite of honey sweetness linger on my tongue. There is no one else in the bar. Thankfully, the bartender reads that I am not one for chatter, and spends his time taking bottles off the shelf and giving them a polish. With only an airplane breakfast sandwich in my stomach, I soon feel lightheaded. I could grab something to eat, take a long bath, live dangerously and open one of those bath balms, but that doesn't appeal. I could go back to Hall's, pick a fight, but not that soon; I would just embarrass myself. And I need time. My friend, Massy, isn't expecting me for a day, and although country people don't bother about such things, I don't feel up to driving back to where I've just come from only a few short hours ago.

There is only one place to go. I get into the car and cautiously drive towards the north end of the city, across railroad tracks, through a set of high wrought iron gates, to where I know they will be waiting. Sections of the cemetery are separated by narrow pathways, and I immediately look for section fifty-one. I estimate it to be closer to the gates than it is. Over one crossroad, and then another junction. More to the left side than I recall. Then doubling back when I go too far on a path. I pull the car over and walk along the perimeter of the section where flat stones mark the graves. Stepping carefully between their neighbours, I find my parents', Neal and Jean's, resting place. A tiny bouquet of weather-beaten artificial flowers is nestled in a corner of Mom's stone, the wire ends shoved deep into the earth. I wonder who has placed them here. The edges of the stones have pocketed clippings of mown grass and clumps of mud. A film of dirt dulls the marble and blurs their names and the dates of when their stories started and ended. A car passes by on an easterly access road, but there is no one else in sight. I wish I had a pair of secateurs so that I could trim away the overgrowth. The groundskeeper has mowed the grass, but nobody is keeping up the appearance of headstones, and the ones lying flat on the ground always collect detritus. I take a tissue out of my pocket, dry the tears that alcohol has fetched, and try to wipe away the dirt left by the seasons, but that only makes more of a mess. All is still. Like the museum, before it opens.

A whistle blows and a freight train rattles by on the tracks that run parallel to the place. It is within hearing range of where my railroad father and mother rest. I think it coincidentally pleasing. I am too tired to give way to seeing it as anything more. Then I remember Adam. I have to see Adam.

6. SWITCHMAN

'Tell us again about the soldier,' Shirley would start. I kept track of where the story had left off.

'You told us last time about him camping in England and the long walk across the Netherlands. You were going to tell us about his coming home.'

Even at my young age, I could discern a melancholy in Adam's telling. 'The young man was very tired and when the boat arrived in Canada from across the stormy sea, he had to wait his turn to get on the train.'

'Was it like our train?'

'It was a train with a steam engine. Like the one that used to come to Plover. In that book I showed you.'

'Smoky,' Shirley says.

'Yes, well, that was the best part about the soldier coming home. He heard the whistle—whoo hoooo, hoo whoo—and he was the happiest soldier on the platform.'

He didn't have anyone to come home to, after the Second World War. An only child, his parents died back in Canada, as his Squadron was advancing across the Netherlands. He'd returned to Plover to become the section foreman, and was the first friend Mom and Dad made. He ate dinner with us every Friday night, went to the lake with us on the weekends, and spent the holidays with our family, often buying us presents our parents could not afford. Shirley and I grew up assuming he was family. He'd kept in touch with Mom, dropped by our cramped city home a couple of times when I was a teenager, but decades had gone by since I'd seen him. Shirley mentioned that she'd tracked him down; I think they might have spoken a few times after Mom's passing. I suppose, like so many things I've put off, I thought I'd eventually get around to reconnecting with him, but I never did.

Still, I believe if anyone knows what to do with Shirley's request to revive a rail line, it will be Adam.

'I'm looking for the Adam who once said that a train whistle is the finest sound man ever created.' I knock and enter room 26A of the Robin Mills Retirement Villa.

Adam lowers the newspaper he is reading. 'I'd know that voice anywhere. Is it Marvels?'

His six-foot frame stretches beyond the footrest of his recliner, and from his half-tipped position, he wags his finger at the package in my hands.

'After all this time, that had better be the good stuff.'

I rest my hand on the soft flannel at his shoulder. I kneel beside the chair, manage to get one arm around the front of his chest, the other around his neck. He leans his head on my forearm and I kiss the top of his head. When I let go, he sits up straighter in his chair, seemingly invigorated by the embrace, and when he looks into my eyes, it comes to me that he is the only one left as witness to my childhood. He motions for me to take a seat.

'Nurse said you might be calling today,' he says. His eyes study me from toe to head, marking the years I've grown away. 'You've gone to short hair.' I feel the back of my neck, the lifetime of hair pony-tailed now gone.

Amongst Jean's papers, Shirley and I had found copies of letters Adam had written, but I don't mention them. He'd lobbied the railway, petitioned town mayors to protest at the closure of railway stations in the region, never getting any reply for his efforts. He'd managed to stay on in the section house on the railway property at Plover for a while after the station closed—taking the final curtain call. Jean had saved Adam's letter in which he apologized for having failed Neal, her, us. Maybe Shirley had contacted him because of the letters we'd found.

He'd held Shirley's hand and I'd stood bravely close to him on that autumn day at the cemetery. Then, while Mom and the mourners laid Dad to rest, Adam ushered us away to a leafy hill, sat us down, and told us we'd have to be brave soldiers.

Over the years, Mom had occasionally mentioned getting a post card from him from some place or other. Adam's last note was postmarked from the care home. I'd read, 'I've assigned myself to "the home," but I plan to rouse the rabble.'

'Not a day's gone by I haven't thought of you and Shirley, and now here you are, and it seems as if you've jumped out of the past and into the present, and all those years in between have vanished.'

Except, I reflect, I'm older now than you were then.

'I suppose you've got lots to tell.'

'You always used to say, don't beat around the bush.' I remove my cardigan, fold my hands in my lap, and try to be as gentle as possible. 'I'm sorry, Adam, there is no easy way to say this. Shirley is gone. As quickly as Dad.'

Adam reaches out his shaking hand. I hold it for a moment, and let go. 'I didn't know for certain where you were, until I went through Shirley's things. I wasn't sure if anyone else had told you.' I can hear the excuses in my voice.

'I never wanted to interfere in your lives. After Jean passed, Shirley called and said she would visit. I left it up to her.'

Adam takes a hanky from his back pocket and clears one nostril and then the other. The limit of a public display of grief this soldier gives in to. 'I visit her, them, every now and then. Take flowers.' So, he is the reason for the flowers at the cemetery.

I move to the window that looks out on a small garden. A hummingbird hovers near a feeder hanging from an apple tree. A tree old enough to have survived construction of the building.

'I didn't want to put the news in a letter, and I haven't been able to get here until now.' I want to be considerate.

He shuffles the newspapers he's been reading, puts them aside. 'Don't you ever mind about that. There's a couple of glasses in that cupboard. Why don't you pour us some of whatever you've brought.'

It is late morning. Rum before lunch. Why not.

I open the cupboard and take two glasses from the shelf. Inside are a couple of lager and a half-drunk bottle of red wine. He knows I will notice them, and seems to want to make sure I don't draw the wrong conclusion about octogenarians with time on their hands and drinking.

'Some of the union brothers working on the mainline visit now and then. I save the booze for their visits.'

I can see a troop of young men with picks and shovels following Adam away from the Plover Station. For years, he'd trained section men, teaching them how to repair the ties and how to manage weed burning to keep the tracks clear. If they still visit him, I am glad.

After I pour, Adam picks up the bottle and studies the label. I'd witnessed him and Dad, and the businessmen of the town, Mr. Grewin from the hardware store, Mr. Novakowsky, who owned the hotel and pub, and Mr. Winton, Stan's dad who owned the grocery store, gather in Mr. Grewin's office at the back of the hardware store to empty a bottle of rum. He reads the likely unfamiliar label and says, 'The thing I remember about our little Shirley, she wouldn't back up for a buzz saw. Punched Ron Winton in the face once, as I recall.'

I hand him a glass and Adam toasts, 'To them that was.'

'Yes.' The rum has a heavy, settling taste to it. I take another sip, then tell him about Shirley's plan. I do not want him to feel suspended in sadness.

'She wrote me this letter. Attached it to her will. It seems she had an investment that paid off and she wanted to revive a short-line train or rail system. I don't know. Adam, she's asked me to finish something she hadn't even begun. I think what she wanted is just impossible, but it's my duty to somehow try.'

He gives no answer, seems lost in his thoughts. I soften my tone. 'It does seem like only yesterday you were bringing us Dixie cup ice cream, when we both had the measles. And the stories you could tell.'

'I'm sorry that you were burdened with bringing me sad news.'

'I've come to pick your brain.'

'Slim pickens.' Adam downs his drink. 'Well. Let me think. Some private consortiums have been buying up sections of deregulated railway, oh, since the '80s. I seem to recall a Keewatin Railway in Manitoba and there's the Polar Bear Express to James Bay. Though I think that one may be a joint venture with the major lines.'

The television is on with the sound turned off, and he absentmindedly changes channels until the seven-day weather forecast appears. Miniature smiling suns and crying clouds ahead.

'Don't know all what's come of those, but Shirley might have looked into them.' He rolls the empty glass between his hands. 'One of the fellas in here, he's retired rail too, expat Brit, knows all about the fancy pants trains, the steam and diesel family-day-out type of thing. Santa trains, afternoon excursions through vineyards and the like. He might have mentioned something about a southern train system.'

He shuffles the newspapers beside his chair, pulls out one train magazine after another.

I've almost forgotten about the train crash. 'Adam, there was a train crash in England, and the man in charge of the tracks didn't know when they had been laid or serviced. I forgot to bring the article.'

'Yes, someone showed me that piece at dinner. Tragic, any which way you look at it.'

He fans through one of the magazines.

'Short line rails. Short lines. Britain's doing the best job of resurrecting abandoned lines. Here's something.' He reads:

'From Wales to Leicestershire groups of citizens have gathered funds from grants, charities, trusts, and public donations, and with the sweat of volunteers are restoring former discontinued lines.' He hands me the magazine and continues to look through the others.

'Well, your Vancouver Island's E&N railway line, going up and down the island, was ultimately rescued through public donations and the will of the people. Every person who donated a hundred dollars received their own tie. I think mine is somewhere near Ladysmith.'

Adam motions for another pour. 'I rode it in the old days.'

I take in his weathered face and wonder why, if he had visited the island and ridden the old Esquimalt Nanaimo Railway Line, he never called or visited, but I don't pursue Adam's never contacting me.

'The Lochside Trail was the old rail line from Sidney to downtown Victoria.'

'I know.'

'Unfortunately, lots of old rail beds have been peddled into bicycle paths. The world over. France, Finland, Portugal, you name it. I've got a book somewhere around here about them too. From our Newfoundland to Portland—yup, both the American Portland *and* the Portland of Dorset, to New South Wales and Germany.' Adam sips, relishing the sharing of all he's read, then says into his glass, 'Think I ran across a path called the John Wayne Trail. Damn shame, if you ask me.'

'Rails to trails.' I raise my glass in a toast. 'Walkers and cyclists seem to make good use of them. Horsey folks too.'

'As if some convenient rhyming slogan excuses the deed.' He exhales a chuckle. 'Getting rid of rail lines. A cover-up. Like old Winnie. Remember her? Had more goop on her mug than the Sistine.'

I suspect my memory version of Plover's Avon lady, with her coral cheeks and crayon blue eye shadow, is not far from Adam's.

'Always trying to sell us some of her potions. Your dad couldn't stand her parading through the office.'

'I remember.'

Looking from one wall to the other of the small room, I squeeze in between some bookshelves to closer inspect framed works that appear to be expensive watercolours.

By Rail to Wales, For Speed and Comfort, I read above a Wooton poster, and *Passing the Kish* by Wilkinson, train travel by rail and steamer, drawn to tempt travelers on a luxurious jounney to the seaside through a British landscape of dappled skies or over Irish azure seas.

'I became a bit of a collector,' Adam says. 'Some of those British rail posters are worth a few pennies now. I rotate them with a few of the Canadian Pacific Rail originals I picked up at auctions. They're at this place west of town. A kind of museum.'

He uses his sleeve to brush dust from one of the frames.

'Why, when this colossus of a country was being planned out, did we never allow for footpaths, rights-of-way, as old as Britain's? That way we could've kept our short lines and folks could still have rambled the countryside.' He whispers to the posters, analyzing or arguing with himself.

I veer from the financial or political reasons for rail line closures. 'Adam, I don't think rights-of-way would have saved our railway. As you said, Britain, and other countries as well, have now converted many of their rail tracks to hiking paths.'

'Course they have. I've seen television programs, showing them off. Look at what we've done. Got rid of the tracks, and now we can walk all over the place.' He spreads his arms out like some astronomer presenting the vast universe. 'Still, they've managed to keep a hell of a lot more trains going than we have. Achh, I don't know.'

'Are most of the British railways now privately owned?'

'Privatized, franchised. Who can keep up? Nationalized into the British Railway system, hmm, around about '48, then British Rail privatized, let's say '93, '94? Lost many of their short line trains when the coal mines and quarries shut down and mills closed. Then in, hmmm, maybe '63, after some idiot wrote a report, what the hell was his name, shut down rails and closed over 2,000 stations. Meanwhile, here in Canada the same devastating passenger rail cuts were made under I believe the Hall Commission and that smug transportation minister, Pepin, or was it Lang?'

'How do you know all of this?'

'Was part of my job, and my pastime.'

Adam stares at me. He looks into the distance and then recites, '"No one left and no one came. On the bare platform."'

'Plover.'

'Adlestrop.'

'Who?'

'A place. A poem.'

'Oh.'

'By the English poet, Edward Thomas. His experience of a station stop. It's here too, somewhere. Read it when I was over there.'

'Aren't you full of surprises.'

He runs his finger over the spines of the books on his shelf. 'Prophetic. Written around 1917. Adlestrop station closed. As did many others.'

'I guess it all comes down to making money. VIA rail seems to make a profit on some of the Canadian Rocky Mountains trips. Banff, Jasper. Hot springs and an icefield. Then there's the Eurostar and of course the Orient Express. Or is that just a movie now? Anyway, British railways must make a profit. How else could they keep running?'

'Some of the franchises likely, prices going through the roof, but let's not kid ourselves, some of their rail lines are going to pot over there too. Increasing rates, infrastructure in disrepair, disruptions, routes backed up, but you can still take a train into London from the smallest seaside village or the northern most tip of Scotland.'

'We can go across Canada. Well, those who can afford it.'

'And up and down the island now, don't forget.'

'True.'

'But, aside from Winnipeg to Churchill, though, who knows how long with that wearing track, and commuters—in and out of Vancouver, Toronto, and into Quebec and the like, it's mostly mainline freight routes. I wonder if that train still runs from Montreal to Halifax?'

'There are still tracks running through Plover Station,' I offer.

'Damn right. Canada's CN and CP had more tracks than Carter had liver pills. There was grain freight through Plover up until, well, not that long ago.'

As we sip, a nurse enters. She tsk tsks, and then places pills on the small table next to Adam.

'This is Margaret,' Adam says proudly, 'an adopted daughter.'

'If you say so,' the nurse nods at Adam, and then says to me, 'his limit is two before lunch.'

I wink at Adam. 'Sounds adequate.'

Adam spills the pills into his mouth, throws his head back, and swallows. 'I've been reading about a fascinating plan for a rail line over Baffin Island to haul out the iron ore.' From the stack of magazines he's rifled through, he picks up *Global Trains*, searching for the article. 'Going to be a helluva thing, building track over permafrost.'

'I'm pretty sure Shirley wanted the money to go to a railway line around here. I suppose, well, Dad and all that.'

He drops the magazines onto his chair. 'You know,' he says, knocking on his skull, 'must be the rum stimulating the old brain cells. Maybe someone did tell me about buying shares on a southern short-line, resurrected so farmers could ship their grain direct—bypass the grain elevators. I'll ask the fellas, next time we chew the fat.'

I wonder if I should make the time to travel to southern Saskatchewan and investigate. I've never seen the Cypress Hills.

'Complicated now with a disintegrating grain board and multinational corporation politics,' Adam says.

'I'll bet.'

The smell of sour soup drifts down the corridor.

'Lunch.' Adam raises his eyebrows. 'Too bad.'

Above a small bar fridge is a single sink, and above it, a cupboard that might hold a few groceries, but there is no stove. No cooking allowed in the rooms. If the food is terrible, a resident couldn't manage on cold snacks.

'Do you have to have all your meals here?' It occurs to me that he may not often get taken out for lunch.

'Huh?'

'Can I take you out for lunch?'

He laughs. 'No, no. The food is fine. I meant too bad there isn't more incentive or subsidies for more local rural passenger service. Freight has always been the priority. Cities need efficient people movers, but shouldn't rural transportation matter? Wouldn't that help cut pollution?'

I've heard all this before—the questions haven't changed, and so it seems, neither have the answers.

He rubs his hands together as if to warm them, and I note the arthritic nodules along his finger joints. I've seen him remove railway ties and hammer in new stakes, work in freezing temperatures to keep the tracks clear and in good repair. The industry of the younger Adam now present in these hands.

'Bravo, Shirley,' he sighs. 'Ace idea. Maybe you'll just have to sit with this for a while. Maybe take a trip to Britain, or somewhere else where they are actually taking back rail lines. I'll give it some more thought. I know you'll do the best you can.' He squints. 'You look good, grown up, nice, I mean. Oh heck. Never learned how to pay a grown woman a compliment.'

'That was all right.' I move to the bookshelf. 'Does this bug still work?'

'Geez. Yeah. I used to hook it up to a 12-volt battery every now and then. Your Dad gave it to me, after he taught me the Morse. The dit-dahing drove the staff crazy, all my sending and receiving to myself, so I disconnected it. You still able to read Morris?'

'Oh, no.'

He moves to the right side of his chair and takes up a cane that has been laying on the floor.

'You got wheels?' He waves the cane in the air. 'Don't really need this. It's for when the old hip tires. I gotta use the john, and then how about you and me go for a little drive? I'll ask them to save my lunch.'

He directs me east of the city. We drive for about twenty minutes, and then turn onto a side road and go through a gate. He tells me to park directly in front of the entrance to a building.

'You go on in,' he urges, reaching for the car door handle, before I turn off the motor. 'I'll get this.'

In the middle of a field, a locomotive sits idle on a short track going nowhere. Three other rail cars are positioned one behind the other on a side track. They resemble a discarded big boys train set.

Adam walks up to a narrow window of a building painted in the familiar brick colour of many stations. An overhead sign reads, 'Train Museum.' I smile, wondering if he remembers what I do for a living.

A man reaches through the ticket window for Adam's hand. 'Adam. I've been wondering when you'd show up.'

I open the door to the so-called museum and step inside. 'Don't stand out there,' he says to Adam. 'Come in, come in.'

'This joker's name is Gib,' Adam says. 'You get those guys I sent to help with siding and switch installation?'

'Yupper, and a high school is bringing some shop students out to take on a few repairs and the polishing of the passenger car.' Adam hands him a ten-dollar bill, the recommended donation entrance fee. 'Put that away. Your money's no good here.'

'The kid been out?'

Gib points across the yard. 'Can't keep him away.'

The open room is meant to invoke a railway station, but is really just a few tables of memorabilia. There is a model train set up in one corner, and Gib flips a switch to bring some rattling train sounds and flashing lights to the room. There are several Morse code keys, a CN phone, a mailbag, wooden and rubber stamps, a yellowed Waghorn's Guide. The slim, 160-page 1949 guide lists the names of post offices and railway stations with to-the-minute arrival and departure times of Canadian National and Canadian Pacific Railway trains right across Canada. It feels like a well-worn pocketbook, and when I lift it to my nose, I smell creosote. Here and there are cross-tie town signs, bits of cutlery with CPR engraved on the handles—haven't I set some in a museum display?—buttons from uniforms with the same insignia, a signal lamp, a few boxcar seals on a key ring. Along the wall, Canadian Pacific Railway vintage posters show off the vast Canadian landscape behind black monoliths of power and promise. A bench along the wall sits near a table with a kettle and some cups and saucers.

'Where did you ever find this old book of tariffs? "Canadian National Railway. Canadian Freight Association. C.F.A Tariff No.5-J 10th Revised Page 158D cancels 9th Revised Page 158D. Commodity application and Rates. Wood. Build Up (Plywood) for Storage and Shipment."'

I had once filed tariffs. I'd read the titles on the pages, but I hadn't understood any of it. I only knew I had to take out the '9th revised page 158D' and replace it with the '10th revised page 158D.'

While I worked at the smaller side desk, Dad sat at his captain's chair, facing the platform at the front desk. Di-dah-di-dit—the Morse code clicked and clacked while we worked. He'd decipher the messages, without ever looking up.

'You'd always be in a hurry to get through those,' Adam observes. 'Back then you were making a scrap book of John Glenn. Your uncle used to send out the paper as I recall. Couldn't get your hands on the Toronto Sun fast enough for the latest pictures.'

'Did you know John Glenn actually steered the Friendship 7 'cause the automatic pilot was making it steer to the right?'

'So you reminded us many times. I'm not surprised you can still quote chapter and verse.'

'Back at Adam's home, there's a girl who brings busloads of folks out here, and they take a little tour around the yard.' Gib says. 'Gets them out, and it works on their memory.'

I walk around the room, run my hand over the old cast iron bench arms, and look through train schedules.

It takes a few moments before I tune in to the ticking of the wall clock.

'This looks like the one that we had in the station.'

'Might have been. Can't remember which place I pulled it out of. Arthur Pequegnat wall clocks were in most railway stations. Neal was a stickler for time. Refused to switch his watch to daylight savings. Always said his watch would run on Standard Time.'

'Railway Time, Greenwich Mean Time, was invented in England so that all the trains could run on time,' Gib adds.

'How did all of this come about?' I ask.

'We began with a donation of some land,' Gib says, as he follows me around the room. 'Volunteer section men laid down the first switch and couple of sections of track—you can't see it from here, but it connects to an old line—and we rescued cars going to the crusher. Well, with the exception of that 44-tonner.' He whispers, 'His nibs paid for that one.'

I look through the window to where the ticket agent is pointing. I see now that the locomotive is laid out like a cadaver. Someone was either attempting a repair or removing parts. Waste of time and money.

'We haven't opened up for the season yet, but last summer we had over five hundred visitors. By the way,' Gib says to Adam, 'that company still hasn't come out to cut the grass.'

Adam points to the book Gib is carrying around under his arm. 'Whatcha readin?'

'This? Something I found in a stack of donations. A biography by the grandson of a fella who was the horse drawn delivery driver and worked at the stables they used to have under St Pancreas station in London.'

'I'd like to have a look at that when you're done.'

'I also put aside a dog-eared Bradshaw's Hand-Book of Great Britain and Ireland for you. I know you've lost yours.'

Adam and I browse around the room, and then saunter outdoors and climb up the stairs into the first car on the tracks, an old buildings and bridges, B&B, crew bunk car. It contains a stove for cooking, bunk beds, a toilet.

Adam says, 'A couple of the men's wives are planning to gussy up the interior. Someone has suggested that the B&B car and the rusty passenger car might be rented out overnight as a moneymaker. Get that? A B&B in a B&B on rails, but with a catered breakfast.' He chuckles at this marketing alliteration. 'Gib's wife's sewing up some curtains.'

It is cold in the car, and I realize that Adam is wearing only a thin sweater. His agility in moving around the grounds is impressive, but now he appears to be shivering.

'Are you cold? Do you want to go back inside?'

'No, I'm good.'

As he opens a cupboard door, I ask, 'Did you get to go on many train journeys, Adam?'

'I couldn't afford anything like the Orient Express, and yes it was/is a film and an excursion. The film is a who-done-it. I guess the highlight, back when you were kids, would have been Penn Station. Imagine me, Plover lad, making my way to New York, just to stand around Penn Station.' He looks away, makes a 'whew' sound, as if he were once again standing in that grand building, looking up at the glass ceiling. 'But that was before Plover shut down. You were too young to remember. Let's see. Managed a trip on the Royal Scotsman, then won a raffle ticket to spend a month at the National Railway Museum in York, volunteering in their workshop. You ever been?'

I shake my head.

'Oh, man. Train heaven. Never thought I'd go back over-seas, but I couldn't turn down that opportunity. Only one bridge on my old line, so, after York, I went on a tour they had going of Irish railway bridges. What else? Train trips. Let's see.' His eyes glisten as his arms swing out like a semaphore. One points west and the other south. 'I took Amtrak from Vancouver right to Florida—saw some of the American south. And, though it's more bus than train, the Chiva Express, which ran through Ecuador. As I recall, a lively Spanish dancer was aboard.'

'Adam!'

He meanders through the back and down the stairs of the bunk car, pausing on the last step.

'Dreamed of tracing Paul Theroux's footsteps, after I read *The Great Railway Bazaar*, but in the end the book was adventure enough. Sure wouldn't mind inspecting that track on Baffin Island, if they ever finish it.'

I make a mental note to find out what I can when I get back home, and to send Adam updates.

We skip a tour of the passenger car; the box car is mainly used for storage. I stroll on, as he stops to talk to a young man who is working under the locomotive. However loose the definition, the curator in me can't see in this labour of love either museum or train station. As we make our way towards the car, he puts his arm around my shoulder.

'I invited Jean, once, to go on a train vacation with me.'

I questioningly look up at him.

'Just as friends. Course, by then she had moved out to Vancouver with Shirley, said she was busy with grandkids. I guess your kids.'

We arrive at the car. He gives a salute in the direction of the museum window. I am surprised when he opens the driver's door for me. I recall the warmth of childhood protection in this small courtesy.

'Any of your lads take an interest in trains?'

'No. Not really. Although Shirley often read train books to them when they were little.'

When he has settled himself in the passenger seat, he says, 'I need to tell you this now. Because I've regretted not doing so. I'm sorry I let all of you down.'

'Adam, you didn't.'

'I loved all of you. Neal, Jean, Shirley, and you.' He gently touches my hand on the steering wheel, then leans in to look at my wrist. 'Neal's watch? It's still running?'

'Never stopped.' He slightly lifts the face.

'The last thing he did was put that on your wrist.'

'When I told Mom to have it, she wouldn't take it.'

'That was the hardest day of my life. Seeing you kneeling over him, Neal collapsed on the platform like that. You were so young, and that frightened, shocked look on his face. Broke my heart.'

The scene plays out in front of me, how I was sent to find Shirley, and Adam and Mom stayed by Dad's side as he took his last breaths.

'You never said. Was it an aneurysm took Shirley too?'

'No. They said it was her heart. You know, I didn't know for the longest time that all I had to do was move the watch to keep it running.'

'I always thought Neal had placed it over your hand as something to remember him by. Over the years, I wondered if perhaps he meant it as a symbol to look ahead. A twist of the wrist, so small a gesture needed to wind the spring and keep time ticking.'

I start the car, turn up the heat.

'You were all my family. When I looked over and saw the lights on in the station, it made a difference in my life, and I daresay the lives of many around Plover.'

'And you tried to save the station, even after Dad.'

'Well, I owed it to Neal. Poor Jean. She just fell apart.'

'So long ago.'

'Past, present, eventually it all just rolls into one time. Of course, the War dates I remember, but the other memories aren't dates, they're events, pictures. Neal and I unloading grain doors, the tornado that went through town, you and Shirley playing on the tracks one minute, then arguing the next, Jean in her rollers in the office.'

'*Saving* her hair for later.'

'Well, they didn't have all the paraphernalia that's about now for spur of the moment do's.' He warms his hands over the air vents.

Gib comes running out towards the car. 'Hang on there. I forgot to mention the trip. We've got a party of seven now, eight if you decide to go, but you better let me know soon. The travel agent needs to book everything.'

'I dunno.'

'You said you wanted to ride The Ghan and the camels outside Alice Springs. Could be our last chance.'

'Wait. Why would there be camels in Australia?' I ask.

Gib looks at Adam, and when he doesn't quickly offer an explanation, Gib effuses. 'Too hot for horses. In the mid/late 1800s they brought camels to the outback to haul supplies and people to build the railway, The Afghan Express. Brought drivers from the Middle East and Asia. The train's called The Ghan, runs from Darwin to Adelaide. We get a deal with a tour for eight.'

'Wouldn't mind seeing how those tracks hold up. Long, long, flight though. I'll get back to you next week.'

Gib turns and gives a wave over his shoulder.

'What am I going to do about this rail line business?' I ask.

'I don't know. Shirley had her schemes, you were always the details one.'

Next time, next time, I'll ask him to tell me what else he remembers about us. 'I'm sorry I let so many years pass,' I say to him. 'I was probably wrapped up in self-preservation. Just up and moved away.'

'Shhh.' Adam waves away the rest of my intended words.

'People who have cared about one another can just pick up where they left off.' He looks away to the 44-tonner parked in the grass that needs cutting. 'He should have that baby up and running any day now.'

7. Drag

While the coffee brews, I lie on the bed and flip through one of the hotel's tourist brochures. Bright orange prairie lilies, as they are commonly known, bloom over the top of all the pages. I read:

> *The province of Saskatchewan received its name from the Cree word kisiskâciwan, which describes the 'fast-flowing' Saskatchewan River. The province was once home to Archibald Belaney, author and conservationist, the affluent Englishman who came to the province at seventeen and who is better known as Grey Owl. Saskatoon received its name from the purple berries that grew along the riverbank.*

Saskatoon berries.

There is a whole section on the Riders football team, where to buy season tickets and jerseys. Near the back of the brochure, spread over two pages, a picture of a tent at the river's edge, the home of 'Shakespeare on the Saskatchewan.' 'Directed again this summer by Henry Woolf, longtime friend and collaborator of Harold Pinter, Head of the University of Saskatchewan's Drama Department, the oldest degree-granting drama department of the British Commonwealth.' History, rough stuff, theatre. I would add more pictures, switch the order, as I often contribute to museum brochures before they go to the printer, but brochures are the least of my concerns. I reach for the glass of water beside the bed.

The coffee beeps ready, and after I pour, I stand at the open window, looking out over the South Saskatchewan River. Five floors below me in the hotel's sunny enclosed garden, a stage is being set for the Jazz Festival. The waiters are setting up tables and chairs. From some part of my brain, which hides things you can't recall when you need them, but at unexpected moments launches upward unbidden minutiae, comes, '*Now is the winter of our discontent made glorious summer by this sun of York.*' How did the following line go? And all, something, something.

'...UNNY DAY OUT THERE, *SASKATOOOOON*,' the bedside radio blares. I scramble for the alarm that the previous occupant had likely set, and wonder if housekeeping checks such things when they finish cleaning the room, or perhaps in trickster mood, themselves go about setting the alarms.

I reposition the down quilt and six pillows. The sheets are still warm, and despite having had almost ten hours sleep, I so want to crawl back under the covers and have a lie-in. The exhaustion of the last few months is finally catching up with me. Not long after Shirley passed, I moved into the spare room, unable now to deflect the radiation of energy and heat from Jake's body, but the airy, solitary room emphasizes my loss, and for months I've averaged only around four hours of sleep a night. Maybe the day before I leave for home, I'll reward myself with a leisurely day, then suggest a king-size mattress to Jake. As I come around the opposite side of the bed, I notice that I've left on the floor near the door the small carry-on bag with Shirley's ashes. I take up the small box of ashes, still surprised at the weight of them, place them on a chair, and turn the chair to face the fresh air and garden below.

It isn't as if this is something I have been doing regularly. Shirley's ashes have waited six months in the china cabinet. Over that period, I've begun to feel closer to her than I have for most of our grown-up lives, but it isn't because of the ashes. Ashamedly, it is as if I've finally appreciated her, grasped the arc of her adult life, through the disposing of her possessions. In the things that are left over. The miniature fairy lit village in her living room, the wheat hull snacks in her cupboard, the half tube of Nivea hand lotion at her bedside, and the children's books and movies still on the shelves, bought for her nephews' visits.

Before training as a curator, I had similar experiences, years ago, as a novice archivist/conservator at the museum. Because we are a small museum, many of our tasks still overlap. Then, I could-n't help filling in an historical life story around the objects that had come into the museum's possession. My boss, Hetty, was more patient then and had said it wasn't an unusual thing to do. A healthy connection to artifacts, from their origin to their donor, instilled diligence in their management and preservation, but Hetty had cautioned on losing objectivity. Observing me, she'd said that it could be time consuming, unproductive, and distracting at best. In the extreme, in the cleaning, researching, documenting, and placing of museum artifacts, there was the possibility that conser-vators might temporarily lose themselves in objects if they didn't pay attention to their own lives. Even misrepresent displays. She'd given the rare example of art restorers. After working on a painting for a long time, they could begin to think of it as their own cre-ation, and perhaps subconsciously modify the colours or shading, ever so slightly, to leave their own mark. Best to maintain some distance. I know I have tried to cope with the grief of losing my only sibling, to try to connect, and give meaning to Shirley's short-ened life story through the objects with which she had surrounded herself. It is the only way I know how to lessen the guilt of not seeing fully who she was when she was alive.

I top up my coffee, sit in the chair opposite, close my eyes, and try to put some context into the last few days. I've had half a year to get to Saskatchewan to settle my sister's estate. I've told myself that, once here, I'd just have to sign a bunch of papers, blow through like the wind, and maybe then I could get back to the life I've put on hold.

My sister died in British Columbia, while owning the last fifty acres of our grandparents' Saskatchewan homestead; the law dic-tates the will probate has to be settled in the provincial court of her last residence, and then resealed in the province where the land was owned. It doesn't have anything to do with beneficiaries. It is the land that has held up my ridding myself of all attachments to our shared past.

That, and now the letter that is sitting next to an empty glass of water. I've read it so many times now that I can nearly recite it from memory.

I am writing this letter in case something bad should happen to me. Did she expect something 'bad' to happen? Are there other things she's kept from me? Is there medical information that she'd known about, but didn't tell anyone? Something that might affect me or the boys?

For the last few years. Last few years? Hadn't she only mentioned it when we were sorting mom's things? *I have dreamed of reviving a rail line like the one that Dad believed in.* What did she remember that I didn't about the kind of railway Dad believed in? Why now?

Many years ago, I was talked into investing some money on the advice of a friend and forgot about it. You don't say? *Remember the fellow you called a self-centered schemer?* What the heck was his name? *Turned out he knew what he was talking about, at least where potash was concerned.* Did he ever? *I don't know the exact amount that has accumulated in the account.* Well, it's over eight million. *If you are reading this, it means I have not been able to see it through. I know you will finish what I started.* How do you know? This was your crazy idea. It has nothing to do with me.

There is a knock on the door. I open it fiercely, and then both the housekeeping person and I jump back, each of us surprised by the other. I apologize, she apologizes, and then asks if now is a convenient time to make up the room. I send the young woman away with a twenty-dollar bill, saying that for as long as I occupy the room, she needn't check on me, cleaning isn't necessary, and that I will ring for fresh towels if I need them. She hands me the complimentary newspaper.

June 12, 2007. The front-page headline is all about the province's boom. POW, bold, large font across the page. Potash, Oil, Wheat: 'How The Have-Not Province Came to be The Have-Province.' The second page contains a comparison of property prices throughout the province over the past century.

In the papers I've brought with me, just in case, is the original land title for my grandparents' land. They had bravely left Great Britain never to return, and bought their homestead from the Canadian Government in 1910 for $100.00. Land as far as the eye could see.

As is my habit, I turn first to the international section. There is more on yesterday's story about the train crash in the Lake District in England, and the train owners blaming the ageing railways, stating there was nothing wrong with the train. It was a 'points' failure. The spokesman for the rail line didn't know when the tracks had been laid or last inspected. I cut out the piece for Adam. It has never occurred to me that the people who own the trains don't also take care of the tracks. The writer of the piece explains that 'points' are also known as 'switches,' the place where the train can move from one line of track to another.

Music from the hotel's garden distracts me. A band is now setting up and tuning their instruments. If the weather stays warm, there might be a good turnout. I take my coffee cup from the windowsill, rinse it, and put it back on the tray where the coffee cups are meant to be. In the desk drawer, I find a notepad, its letterhead a replica of the hotel, and begin to make a list. *Land taxes, Massy, Adam, go back to Hall, ashes.* I number the items in order of importance, scratch them out and renumber, draw a few arrows pointing off the page, and then write, *long hot bath, sleep.* I step over one shoe, and am looking for the other under the bed skirt when the telephone rings.

'Miss me already?' I ask, anticipating Jake wanting to continue the discussion about the money.

'Hey, you.'

'Massy.' I look out of the window, as if my old friend is in the garden looking up. 'How are you? How did you reach me here?'

'Had a hunch you might stay there,' Massy says. 'I half expected you last night.'

Her voice still retains the quality of being on the dolce edge of laughter. Everything else about a person changes, I believe, but not their voice. Every voice has its own individual pitch, scale, and tempo. Effected as much by the amplification through the heart or stirred with gall, as by the size of vocal chords or body mass. 'I didn't say I would be out there first thing, did I?'

'No, no. Just thought you might be. It was a great sunset and we could have watched it from the deck.'

I smile, wonder if anyone ever turns away lamenting, *what a crappy sunset.* 'I was tired after the trip and had several things to do here, so I've had early nights. I didn't know the Jazz Festival was on.'

'Yes. Tis the festival season. Jazz, book, folk, fringe. Think that's the order.'

I walk over to the room-service tray of the night before and pick up a sliver of celery, all that remains of last night's salad.

'What are your plans?' Massy asks.

'I've seen the lawyer, but I've got to go back.'

'Is he dragging another visit out of you? That greedy bastard.'

'No, it was my fault. Something unexpected came up and it threw me for a loop. We have to finish up a couple of things. I think he said something about me taking back the land from the land trust and selling it.'

'Of course, and then he could collect a tidy finder's fee.'

'What do you mean?'

'Nothing. Forget it. So, what else do you have to do in the city, and when can I expect you?'

'I've just been reading the paper.'

'It's a gorgeous day. Why are you holed up in that hotel room? Wait. What am I saying? You have a hotel room all to yourself? I'll see you in a few days. Order room service.'

I've missed Massy's chattiness. Her breezy company always pulls me into the present. How she stayed so upbeat married to Stan, I'll never understand. I brush my hand over the Damask curtains.

'I'm not going to spend days in this room.'

The newspaper is spread open on the bed. I turn the pages. I don't know why I lie.

'I've just had a bath, and I was looking through the real estate section of the paper. I can't believe the jump in house prices—*anyone who wants to come home will be welcomed with open arms.* Lots of jobs, and the farmers' market will be open now every Saturday and Wednesday evenings.'

'Don't get the paper out here. What else?'

'More on yesterday's train crash. In England. Not good. Arguments on whose fault it was. What are you up to today?'

'My daughter-in-law just brought over two flats of strawberries and I am up to my elbows red. You eaten yet? There is a great breakfast buffet downstairs. My usual Mother's Day spread.'

The smell of bacon and toast wafts from several floors below. 'The kitchen must be on the same side as my room.' The band is tuning their instruments.

'How are the boys?' Massy asks. 'I suppose you've asked if they'd like the last bit of land.'

I picture my sons' faces. I wish that one of them had expressed interest in overseeing stewardship of their great-grand-parents homestead. But that option was never presented. When I disagreed with Mom on donating the land to the Very Land Trust, that was the end of the talk about the land. When I joined Shirley to place our mother's ashes next to our father's, Jake had been too busy to accompany us, and my three sons had given their own reasons for not being unable to make a pilgrimage to their grandmother's final resting place.

Robert had phoned. 'The company is sending me to Japan. Not the best time.'

'It's crunch time with the PhD, and I'd like to remember Jean the way she was,'—this in a Skype from Russ, studying environmental politics in Montreal.

And Ryan, our youngest, happily following his latest girl-friend around the globe, discovering cultures, and picking up work when he could find it, had offered, 'I miss Gran, but she made the right decision giving the land over to conservation, so now you can, too. Let it go, Mom. Post some pictures.'

My sons are looking forward through a telescope. How clear the present and future is for them. It seems to me that all I've done lately is look back through a magnifying glass.

'And Jake, how's Jake?' Massy shouts, sounding as if she has switched to the speakerphone.

'They're all fine.' I consider telling her about Shirley's letter, but think it better to do so in person.

The band below is improvising, but I can't make out the song.

'Can you hear that?' I hold the phone to the open window. 'The band is warming up.'

'Might be noisy tonight. After the berries, I'm going to pull some weeds. Get out my binoculars and scan the horizon for the lovely Mr. Oak's return.'

'Every year, you tell me the Englishman has returned, but somehow your paths never cross. I'm beginning to think he is just a figment of your literary imagination.'

'Oh, he's real alright. I saw the backside of him interviewed on our local television station, came into the room too late to see his face. Looks very fit. He was pointing out the pelicans at Plover Lake.'

'Just drive out there. Plant yourself at the water's edge and wait.'

'I couldn't do that. When might you arrive?'

'Maybe later today, maybe tomorrow?'

'I can't wait. I thought you'd prefer the guestroom downstairs. It will be cool for sleeping.'

'Please, don't fuss.' She is expecting me to spend the night. I leave off saying that I am uncomfortable with the idea of staying in the house that Massy and Stan shared. I am reserving my right to change my mind at the last minute.

'Okay. See you whenever then. If I'm not here, the dogs are nosy, but friendly.'

'I forgot about the dogs.'

There is a long pause, and I'm not sure if I should hang up or wait for Massy to do so.

'We'll be all right, Margaret.'

I assume Massy is referring to our both coming through grief and not an observation after all these years that our relationship has managed along because we have both avoided talk or analysis about the past.

'I know.'

'Margaret.'

'Yes?'

'Get outside. Go breathe the land. Don't put things off, like you usually do.'

'I am heading down to breakfast, right now.'

'I've missed you. Bye then.'

'See you soon.'

My eye catches the room service menu. My stomach growls. I find the luncheon offerings and run my finger over the selections. A blast of cool air comes down from the ceiling, then hiccoughs to a rhythmic flow of air. The rehearsal on the old Earl's lawn is a burst of drumbeats, the guitarist repeating a riff, and the bass player cranking his amplifier. Nothing poncy. I close the window, gather up the box of ashes, and gently place them back into the carry-on. Then I slip back under the covers.

8. TOKEN

There is no getting around it. After a quick phone call, Hall is more than anxious to fit me in between appointments.

'We won't be charging for this one,' his secretary assures.

A good-will token, or a bargaining chip?

This time Hall is wearing a navy blazer, over what appears to be the same shirt and trousers as when we first met.

In a pitiful tone, he almost whispers, 'I imagine the news of the residue of Shirley's estate, and the letter she wrote to you were quite a bit to take in.'

I don't get an apology. He is perched on his desk with a folder in his hand.

'I had the accounting firm send over all of the details of the eight million since it was deposited. You'll find everything in order.'

I quickly skim the columns of dates and monthly deposits of interest. What they say is true, it takes money to make money.

'I'd like you to think about something regarding the land your mother gave over to the land trust. I've studied the fine print, and there is the possibility of your taking it back and putting it on the market.'

This makes absolutely no sense to me. 'My understanding is that I cannot take back the land my mother donated to an organization which seeks to leave fertile land dormant and unproductive. It was handed over to this organization with no obligation for accountability. I've gotten used to the idea.'

I shrug and smile, try to counteract my churlish tone, but all this back and forth is just slowing everything down.

'Technically, dormant would be inaccurate. It's more about preservation, restoration, protecting the natural diversity. But as your mother donated the land such a short time ago, and you and your sister were the direct heirs, there is a time sensitive provision for heirs to reconsider the donation.'

I lean over the desk to a heavy block of potash holding down several folders, scrape my fingernail over the surface, and rub the salt between my thumb and forefinger.

'I don't think I want to go there.'

'Well, land prices are good, and if you combine it with the left over fifty acres your mother retained that runs beside the old railway line, you could have a tidy sum of money.'

'You've just handed me the accounts for eight million dollars.'

'You used the words dormant and unproductive. Contributing to the breadbasket of the world, sort of thing, I sense is something that is meaningful to you. If the land were sold to a good farmer, it could go back to being productive.'

He's partially correct. I love the wildness of the West Coast forests, but too late I had disagreed with Mom giving away the land and allowing nature to take its course. My grandparents had turned sod into fertile fields, picked rocks, pulled out stumps to create wheat fields—bread—survived the Dirty Thirties. Undoing that process seemed to make their lives, their work mis-spent or meaningless. I'd always judged my mother as someone more attached to the past, but she must have had a good reason for her actions.

'I have a farmer interested in that entire property. Excellent operation. I've done some work for him and his brother in the past. In fact, he probably would have bought it from your moth-er, if she hadn't donated it to The Saskatchewan Very Land Trust. Or the VLT as it is referred to for short.'

I wonder if Hall would find this amusing. When Jean first spoke of the VLT, the acronym also for video lottery terminal, I assumed she was about to summarize another afternoon at the casino. She'd won small amounts of pocket money and had taken to going one or two afternoons a week. Hence, my initial igno-rance. My mind had strayed to the events of my own work day. I didn't pay attention, and I never suspected she might want to open a discussion on land conservancy. I had heard, but I had not listened.

Hall pages through an address book, and then tries to wake his computer. 'Would you like me to get him on the phone?'

'Him?'

'The fella interested in the land.'

I wonder if Shirley hadn't passed, if she would have gotten rid of that last fifty acres. They just seem like unfinished business, more paperwork left over from mom's estate. I certainly don't want the boys to have to deal with it in the future.

'I don't know,' I defer. 'What about that other business? Do you know of anyone resurrecting a short-line railway? Anything will do.'

'One of my legal interns carried out the obligatory inquiry. Oh, and before I forget.'

Hall leans back in his chair and his feet manipulate a box under his desk to where he can pick it up. He places it on the desk and slides it across to me.

'Might as well have all of this back too.'

It is a box like the museum uses for storing archival material. I'd given a few to Shirley over the years. I wonder where Hall would have gotten such a box.

He begins laying out articles onto the desk, as if they are archeological finds.

'On one of Shirley's trips out to deal with Jean's estate, she brought me this box. She told me she had printed copies of some of the files she had on her laptop. She even mailed news items to me. You must be familiar with some of this.'

He sets down printed copies of magazine and online articles, reports, newspaper clippings, and notes, train schedules, and what looks like a petition. Bits and pieces of items not unlike several I'd seen in my sister's condo and piled up for recycle.

'She was impatient with the fact that I was ignorant of railway lines in the province. Well, the whole country, for that matter. I'm sorry to say, I haven't been able to get through much of this material.

'Look at this.' Hall pulls more cuttings from a brown envelope, 'The Toronto Star—57 million commuters per year. And here, someone—likely your sister—has written something about… looks like… privatization.' He holds the paper at arm's length. 'I can't read this.'

I open a ledger in Shirley's handwriting. It is a journal of some sort, but with dates and names, and beside each name a series of numbers with north and south designation.

'I'm sure she didn't really intend for me to keep this.' Hall continues, 'Not after all the research she'd done.'

I see my desk back home inundated with the past months' worth of executorship correspondence and updated letters dealing with my sister's estate. Everything from utility cancellations and reimbursements to tax statements and condo inspection details. I've looked at Shirley's computer files, placed several in a folder and transferred them to my own computer, but have, for tax purposes, only accessed spreadsheets having to do with day-to-day bank accounts and items I felt relevant to the estate. I had glanced at only a few emails. It hadn't felt right going through Shirley's personal email, but trashing everything seemed wrong, too. Other documents, letters and journals, more personal matters, I briefly scanned. As the keeper of my sister's unfinished life, I believe one of my duties is to seal her privacy. My chest tightens at the weight of more papers to sort through.

In desperation, Shirley had turned to a lawyer for guidance. 'I don't understand,' I say. 'Why you?'

'I may have let it slip that I once sat on a possible CN–CP rail amalgamation board. Shirley may have assumed I must, pardon the pun, have some sort of inside track. At first, I just thought it was part of your dad's memorabilia. But a lot of the stuff is more recent. Look at this.'

He holds up articles and notes, turns one side to face me, and then the other, unsure of which is the more relevant, reminds me of an optometrist saying, 'This one or this one?'

'Rolling Stock Auctions, "Operating License Granted to North Yorkshire Moors Railway," statistics on'—he struggles to read—'carbon footprints. "Overlooked Colonial Railways Expand Transportation in Africa." Letters to an MP.'

Amongst Shirley's keepsakes, along with several of Dad's employee rail passes, I had found a tattered Eurail pass, a brochure for the Ocean, a Montreal-to-Halifax train excursion, and a schedule of trains leaving Victoria Station in London. Souvenirs of vacation trips Shirley had taken over the years.

'Did you say, when she came to settle Mom's estate?' I calculate that Mom might also have contributed to, or at least perhaps known about some of this research, but there is no way of knowing.

Hall nods. 'Quite a hodgepodge. Yes, your mom's estate. Shirley seemed to be in a hurry to gather as much information about railways as she could.' He pushes back into his chair and mutters, as if I weren't here. 'All of this must have given her fantastical notions. I don't think she knew what she was doing.'

'Shirley always knew exactly what she was doing.' Old habit, must defend family.

Hall sneezes into his handkerchief. 'Of course. You knew her best.' He picks up a yellow notepad. 'According to this— now these look like my intern's posts—"there is a company whose purpose is to carry out feasibility studies on whether or not the train tracks in a particular area, and the communities around it, as well as the potential business opportunities, would support a rail service. They do cost-analysis, write up reports, and then help certain individuals organize themselves to support an independent rail service."'

He squints. 'Says here, "there is a short-line freight co-op in southern Saskatchewan. One starting up in northern." Question mark.'

A few scraps are one thing, but all of this material is substantial. Who knows what might have eventually come about if Shirley had lived? From what is in front of me, and taking in the items from the condo, with the right annotations, the material might accentuate an historical museum display.

'I moved some of her files to my laptop,' I say. 'I just haven't gotten around to looking through all of them. My work keeps me very busy.'

Hall takes back the items that he's placed in front of me, slowly turns them over in his hand again, and puts each one carefully back into the box. I think again about my sister's desperation at handing over so many personal things to a lawyer, and stare at the bent flaps of the container.

I remember a call, one that had come in the middle of the night. I'd left a snoring Jake to run and answer the phone before it woke him.

'I'm telling you, it can be done, and it will be done,' Shirley had announced, oblivious to the time, and knowing I would be the one who'd pick up the phone. 'We are going to put back the railway they pulled out from under Dad.'

I'd looked at the kitchen clock, heard my sister take a drag of cigarette, and a gulp of something, and then I'd said my piece. 'You're still upset about Mom, and thinking too much. I've worked all day, got soaked walking home, made dinner, reviewed department budgets, and I need to get some sleep.' I'd taken the handset to the next room and whispered, 'I don't have time for this.'

Hall waves a book in my face. 'What do you know? An old paperback of Pierre Berton's *The Last Spike.*'

I lift my gaze from the oak floor to Hall and the book. Wonder if it might be the copy, the last book Dad had likely read, that he'd kept next to the telegraph key called 'the bug.' I'd tackled the book in my late teens. Might have been part of the Canadian high school canon. Hardly a book to capture the imagination of a teenage girl, but at a time when Jean was struggling to make ends meet, and seemed to be all resentment and rules, I'd found my father's copy and tried to reach, through what he had been reading, the uncomplicated Dad I missed.

The box is too full to close, and Hall begins to remove items, sort, and repack them in a more orderly fashion.

'I am sorry.' He throws his hands up. 'Shirley kept calling to see if I'd made any headway with this material. I told her I was getting to it, but really, it is out of my scope.'

An image flashes of my office shelves of binders on researched Canadian heritage, from the 17th century Upper Canada sculptures and carvings to the finest hand-engraved jewellery by Bill Reid. I can recognize the weave and tagging of an original Hudson's Bay blanket from five meters, but had been useless to my sister. I let Hall off the hook. 'I suppose I am as guilty as you are. I never paid much attention to her train mumblings.'

Hall opens a file and hands me a receipt from the Canadian Government. 'See now, this—this we did separate from the other material because it is a copy of an official government receipt. In 1914, they paid your grandfather $400 for right-of-way land to run the tracks between his quarter sections.'

I check my watch—shake my wrist, advancing the time from 1914.

'There is also a copy of a letter from Shirley to Canadian National Railway requesting the option to buy back that land. My intern didn't find any reply. There was no point in pursuing it. As I was saying, that parcel really belongs with the acreage from the Very Land Trust.'

I thank him for his assistance, and tell him I'll get back to him in a day or two about the fifty acres bordering the jurisdiction of the Very Land Trust, as well as the land trust property itself. However, I know I won't reverse the decision my mother made during the last year of her life. To me that is tantamount to not following the behests in a will.

Hall folds his arms across his chest, purses his lips, and drives home the point he wanted to make all along. 'It was not in the will, Margaret. I have to say this one last time. The letter to you that she attached to her will does not hold any legal weight.'

'You've said this—'

'It is a lot of money.' Hall is determined to give me an accounting lesson.

'Shirley bought that potash stock when it was fifty cents a share, got in on an initial scheme that allowed shares to buy shares—good God, half the province wishes they'd done the same—sold her seventy thousand shares at over $200 per. No one walks away from that kind of money.' He turns and claws open the Venetian blind, to preview who might next be entering his den. 'Her will stated you are the recipient of the residue of her estate. Trust me on this, though it might sound harsh. Your sister's letter of appeal, summing up her dreams of resurrecting a short-line rail system, goes beyond your responsibilities as executor of her will. I am sure she'd want you to enjoy the benefits that this kind of money brings.'

How dare this outsider pontificate on Shirley's private financial affairs, nay, her life, and summarize what she may or may not have wanted. I clasp my hands, put a knuckle to my mouth.

He comes back to face me, leans against his desk, and then realizes that his backside is pressing on something. He reaches around for the Berton book that hasn't been put back into the box.

He looks for a long time at the back cover 19th century photo of the men assembled around the track, the ceremonial photo taken to mark the Canadian Pacific Railway's completion of the transcontinental railway, all grey coats and beards, except for the boy, and then slaps the book against his thigh before tossing it into the box.

'This venture is best left to the kind of men who drove the last spike.'

I pull the box towards me, hug it close. In a flash of pique, almost ask, 'And what kind of men would they be?' but my mind settles instead on the word that has become my mantra.

'Complicated word, that.'

'Which? Venture or spike?' he asks.

'Executor. From the French, *execucion*, a carrying out of orders'—I feel a pain in my temple—'and the Latin *executionem*, an accomplishing.' I sigh. 'Don't suppose you've lately had to look it up.'

The computer fan whirrs. Hall squeezes his eyes open and shut, as if trying to blink away the cloud of cataracts. I catch his eye, and wink. 'And people used to say I look like Neal.'

'Neal?' It is Hall's turn to look surprised, and then it comes back to him, what he'd said. 'Oh. Yes. Well. Everyone tells children they look like one or the other parent. Who else would they look like? It doesn't mean anything.'

He raises his index finger, as if to instruct, but then rubs a spot on his head instead. I take out the cheque I owe him for his services.

The cheque hangs in the air. Hall takes a step back.

'If you could just leave that with Sheila. She looks after the paper work.'

I smile, thank Hall again, and step into the doorway. I've almost exited, when I stop, pause, then, balancing the box on a raised knee, reach inside and hand over *The Last Spike*—not Neal's, not the one I'd dog-eared. The words come tumbling out. 'A keepsake. From my poor recollection, it gives a pretty good account of who won and who lost with a syndicate in control of building a railroad.'

I regret the words as soon as I've spoken them. I had planned an agreeable follow-up meeting. I could have left off the historical criticism, and how many had that been—three, or four acerbic remarks within five minutes of leaving?

I slip past Hall, drop the payment for services rendered at the receptionist's desk with instructions for Sheila to mail my receipt, and push the exterior door open with my hip. My goal had been to lighten my load, and, despite the folder I'd brought with me being one piece of paper lighter, I am leaving with a box full of papers. There is no room in my suitcase for any of this.

'Do you need a hand out to the car?' Mrs. Hall half-heartedly asks, as she sips her tea.

The sunshine hits me in the face as I leave the lawyer's office, and I am reminded, yet again, that I have forgotten to bring my shades.

9. Buffer

I try to call Jake when I get back to the hotel, but the line is either busy, or he isn't picking up. I hope he isn't sitting in some travel agent's office, or worse, on his way to me. I want my time here for myself, to quickly sort things out on my own, and, however well-intentioned, his past half measures of support often slow my process. Hall has left a message asking me if I want him to drive me out to the old homestead and have a last look around. I erase the message and don't return his call. I use the car's GPS. The flashing red arrow on the four-inch screen declares, 'You-are-here,' with an accent of universality, and I follow the instructions through downtown and onto the highway heading north.

It was a quick trip, flying directly from the West Coast. Plugged into a language course repeating Italian phrases, I'd immediately fallen asleep on the short flight and woken somewhere over the province, disoriented, and half dreaming that I was returning from a curators' conference in Florence. It takes me a lot longer to get over jet lag traveling east to west, Europe back to Canada, sleep eventually overwhelming—like an anesthetic. But hardly anyone gets jet lag from a hop-skip-and-a jump across Canada. West to east, once over the Rockies, from 30,000 feet in the air, you can count the quarter-section squares between provinces. Almost measure the distance home. It's much different when you are driving across the plain and everything seems unreachable.

In contrast to my hurrying out to Plover on my day of arrival, I notice that fields of spring wheat and canola catch the air, quick proof of the existence of wind, and without mountains or forests to obstruct, the horizon is an infinite tease, the cars, mirages that never seemed to arrive. I've fallen into a Rothko painting, the pavement just a lead line drawn between blue and green halves. For miles along the highway, worn shoes have been placed over fence posts.

On a couple of quarter sections of land, billboards display the Saskatchewan Very Land Trust logo, but I pass by so quickly that I can't read the fine print. When I roll down the window, dust grit flies to my hairline, into my ears and nose. When a semi passes, the tires of the rental car shimmy and I tighten my grip on the steering wheel as the car veers to the right.

Once off the highway, the roads grow narrower. The farm access road to Massy's is newly graveled. The thick crush of stone scrapes the underside of the car, and like a rogue wave, sucks and drags the tires. When I enter her driveway, I see her up on the wrap-around deck surrounded by pansy seedlings. She must have seen the gravel dust, but for just a second, I think she looks surprised. I open the car door and wave at my friend. She quickly throws off her gardening gloves and takes hold of the collars of her barking dogs, preventing them from charging down the steps. She shouts something to me or them and I smile as if I understand.

I reach into the back seat for the gift of smoked salmon pâté and Rogers' chocolates that I've brought from the West Coast, not truly original, but the requisite standard treats, not readily available in the local grocer. The same gifts I've taken to curators in Florence and Japan. Gifts that say, *here is a taste of the land I've come from.* I remind myself to take Saskatoon berry jam in the opposite direction to some of my co-workers. Massy maneuvers her way between the Labs as they galumph down the stairs. They wag and busily sniff around the car that has brought a different world to them.

'I'm so happy to see you.' She unabashedly wraps her arms around me and encloses me, so different from the quick squeeze and pecks on the cheek my mom and sister preferred. 'They graveled the road yesterday, and you're the first one to drive over it.'

'I'd forgotten about no traction on loose gravel, but I stayed in the centre as much as I could.' I step back, can't resist the tease. 'How are the parts, combine?'

'You're the only one left who can still ask me that. Really, how drunk do you have to be on the night of your child's birth to come up with a name like that?'

Massy's father had taken great pride in confessing that when she was born, he loved her as much as his combine, and wanted to name her Massey Harris, but Massy's mother had said there would be no Harris, and they would drop the 'e' if they were to name her Massy. Mr. Kasha had agreed, but said that if they had a boy, he would insist on calling him Harris Ferguson, after the farm equipment companies, Massey Harris and Massey Ferguson. Perhaps that was why Massy's mother had never given her a sibling.

'I'll tell you how this combine is. Can't get replacement parts anymore.' Massy fluffs the short hair I am trying out. 'You've cut your hair.'

She gives me a second hug, and I rest my head on her shoulder. 'Still smoking, I smell.'

'Yup.' She pulls the half cigarette butt from a pocket and flicks it onto the grass. 'Only half as much.'

I hold out the salmon and chocolates.

'Ooh, thanks. I was secretly hoping for even just one of these.'

She is ready for summer, in cropped trousers and a loose floral cotton shirt and sandals. Her blond ponytail is highlighted by only a few silver streaks, despite her being three years older than me, and she has lost some weight, but when she smiles, the Lauren Hutton space between her two top teeth will forever rule that she is the same Massy I grew up with.

Why I am still wearing the skirt, minus the jacket I arrived in, I have no idea.

Arm in arm, we walk towards the farmhouse that overlooks the Saskatchewan River. Massy's husband, Stan, or Stash, as we'd sometimes called him, dragged the 1940s farmhouse Massy had coveted from ten miles up the road. Deserted for decades, it had been infested with mice, the windows long gone. In a year of bumper crops and high cattle prices, Stash had given up on the idea of building a new home and instead laid a cement foundation and resettled the Sears catalogue mail-order home Massy had dreamed of owning.

Along with milking cows, keeping chickens and ducks, managing a vegetable and flower garden, raising children, preserving and canning food the way her mother had taught her, and acting as farm hand, Massy had gone about the business of restoring the house into a modern working farm home, worthy of the cover of *Country House Beautiful*. She insisted on an Aga, and with the exception of twin lemon-coloured leather sofas, furnished the rooms with rescued antiques. It was to be the home where she and Stash would welcome grandchildren. Then, just after they had moved in, Stash had had a heart attack while fishing in a remote area near Hudson Bay.

'I love this house.' I walk from the kitchen to the living room and back, absorbing the tranquility of space and and the green hills beyond the bank of nine-paned windows.

'I'm sorry I didn't call first.'

'You've arrived,' Massy says. 'That's all that matters. Hungry?'

'I ate a sandwich on the drive out, but what have you got in mind?'

She points to a basket. 'I have a picnic ready to go. Pee if you have to.'

'Sounds like a plan.' I step into the bathroom, where a clawfoot tub overlooks the river. I could spend the whole day soaking and gazing.

Massy is waiting at the bathroom door as I exit, the radio on in the background. 'You're staying the night?'

'I've got lots of territory to cover. I've done with the lawyer, but tomorrow I've got to go into Winging town office and pay the land taxes on the fifty acres.'

Eggs hang from a wire basket along one side of the Aga range. A quart of amber honey, and a collection of various salt and pepper shakers, roosters and hens, bread and butter, outhouses, and cabbages stand in handy reach on the other side. The Aga and the south facing windows are just the right dose of cozy for when the winters hit -30. I picture Stash at the kitchen table, tipping salt from a cabbage or rooster into a bowl of soup, and wonder if anything left of him confines what is now only Massy's house.

'What is it with having to do two probates in one country? Is that why it's taken you so long to settle the estate?' Massy asks.

'Sort of. Canadian law. You have to probate in the province in which the deceased lived, and then reseal in the province in which they owned property. It's been an eye opener.'

'As if once isn't enough. I wonder if other countries have the same complicated legal process.'

'So, where to?' I roll up my cardigan sleeves, trying to adapt my choice of clothing for a sunny day's adventures.

'Well, I thought we'd head down the grid road.' Massy throws the picnic basket and mosquito repellent into the trunk of her car, tells the Labs 'stay' and 'be good.'

'My neighbour found some wild strawberries not far from here. She swears she saw the handsome English birder out there, monitoring birds.'

'Out where, specifically?' I ask.

'Out there.' Massy waves conductor hands in a westerly direction.

'Wouldn't it be handier to find another bird watcher who lives here year-round?'

'Shame on you, Margaret. He is not a *bird watcher*. According to Dr. Simpson's newspaper column, this Dr. Merell is famous.'

'Dr. Simpson is still alive? The Dr. Simpson that once came to our school with samples of bird poop?'

'Yes ma'am. He was, is, and long may he always be, THE bird man of Saskatchewan.' She does an elaborate bow.

'Are there meadowlarks about?' I ask. 'A couple of years ago, you told me they seemed to have disappeared.'

'Oh, yes, Dr. Simpson reported their return months ago.'

We drive back along the gravel road that earlier challenged me, and then turn off onto a narrower side road. Massy has driven these roads all of her life, and she negotiates the gravel with ease. Every now and then, we pass a field where a farmer is mowing hay grass. I wonder if I should again apologize for not seeing

Massy two years ago, when Shirley and I delivered Mom's ashes to the cemetery in Saskatoon. Then, I had made the excuse that it was to be just a sisters' time for goodbye, an overnighter. Since then, I've often wondered if I should have been honest and told Massy that Shirley and I presumed our mother wouldn't want a Winton at her being laid to rest.

Our parents had been close, and Mom and Shirley had accepted that Massy would always be my friend, but it was understood from the time we left Plover that Mom wanted nothing ever to do with Stan or any of the Wintons. And when Massy married Stan Winton, she became one of them. Mom blamed Stan for our being stuck in an apartment in the city, instead of living out our lives in the station. Nothing in the papers about countrywide rail line abandonment would have convinced her otherwise. Nor would the physician's report that Neal had had a longstanding undiagnosed brain aneurysm. When Stan passed away, some of Mom's anger diffused, and Mom had said, not completely unkindly, that she hoped Massy would soon get over her grief, and that I could tell her so. After Mom was gone, Shirley said she'd never had anything against Stan or Massy, had been too young to remember the events of so long ago; only went along with everyone, because I was the one who had insisted that family loyalty came first, though I am pretty sure those had been Mom's words and not mine.

I breathe in the fragrant newly mown hay. Every now and then, with a dip in the road, or upon coming to a windbreak of trees, I experience a déjà vu. I had likely been down these roads when I was learning to drive. Dad had let me practice driving in the autumn, as he flushed out game.

The June afternoon is still and warm, but Massy points at mares' tails—clouds signaling a coming change in the weather. She makes a series of turns from one farm access road to another and before long we come upon a Tara-like spread. I count two houses, one old and one new, three huge barns, and thirty metal grain bins back and beyond.

'What is that?' I ask.

'*That* is the Wheeler farm,' Massy answers. 'The brothers consolidated their whole operation after their dad passed away. With his inheritance, one of the sons built this house.'

It stands on the open prairie like an out-of-place legislative building. There are four pillars at the front entrance. A four-car garage is at a right angle to the house, twin Hummers are parked in front of the entry, and opposite, seen through a cast-iron fence, a water slide appears to wrap around the back and connect to a swimming pool. An extravagant luxury that might, at best, get used two months of the year. I never imagined this kind of opulence on prairie farmland.

'I thought it was tough times for farmers.'

'Not for some, buying up the smaller ones.' Massy points with her head. 'Last count was… I think, they're up to owning 125 quarters of land, just in the immediate vicinity. No idea how many quarters they rent on top of that. A big corporation.'

I take out my cell phone—use the calculator—125 quarters times 160 acres a quarter.

'That's… 20,000 acres of land.'

'Is that all? I must be wrong. It's probably double that. There's talk of them being able to form their own municipality. Not unlike the Vatican.' She laughs. 'Your friend Hall keeps an eye out for estates, passes along potential sales to them, seals the deal, and receives a nice brown envelope for his handiwork.'

She hands me a bottle of water to open.

'He's not my friend.'

'The government has started this plan of bringing in Mexican workers through seeding and harvest. Over there are the workers' quarters,' Massy points, as the road curves. I see the building a ways behind the main house, low and spreading back into a hill, configured to fit in with the estate's entire design.

'And are they known as Lord and Lady Wheeler?' I ask.

'Their "charitable work,"' she air-quotes with one hand, 'often lands their faces on the front page of the paper. I was invited to a Christmas thing once. They had valet parking.'

'Really?' I can't read Massy's face to tell if she is joking. The prairie spreads away as one open-air parking lot.

'I don't know if I've ever told you that our son, Carl, convinced Stash to make the transition to organic farming. It's on ten years now since Carl and Stash began sustainable farming—no herbicides, switching mostly to oats and alfalfa. These guys keep pumping all kinds of chemicals into the land to force it to produce.'

The radio crackles off station and Massy gives it a punch. 'Course, they still have to wait on the weather like the rest of us peasants.' She drives on.

'Are both of your kids still farming?'

Massy nods. 'For now. Don't ask me why. They're determined to make a go of it. Luckily, both kids have partners who also feel connected to the land, and have jobs that pay a regular salary.' Massy pushes aside the visor that keeps dropping down in front of the driver's window.

'They seem to think that small homesteads are still feasible. Even coming back in a fashion. I don't know what the realities are anymore. Carl's wife is in charge of the local farmers' market. It has a regular clientele of city day-trippers.'

'Stop.' I throw my hands onto the dash.

Massy's tires spit gravel. 'What's the matter? Are you carsick?'

I open the passenger door and stand beside the car to take a better look.

'What's going on here?'

'Going on?

I look to where an operation of machinery and a dozen men are going back and forth in the field. A bulldozer pushes dirt into a valley, while several men load branches and other greenery onto one-ton trucks. All noise and a hurried tearing away, as if to carry out the deed before being caught.

'They can't get the monster equipment around the sloughs, so they've cut down the aspens, and they're filling them in,' Massy explains.

'Are you kidding?' I lean against the car in silence, as birds squawk above.

Over the years, I've followed the news as West Coast environmentalists chained themselves to old growth firs in Cathedral

Grove, and I've even signed a petition for a Garry Oak bylaw—the teenager with the petition enthusing the spiritual importance of the foundational natural species. I've even read somewhere that plants send signals to each other when they're being pruned.

I look on in stunned disbelief. Clear-cutting forests is one thing; everyone knows who is guilty, but I didn't think trees in this part of the country were threatened. I have the urge to call out, the way I might if I happened upon an owner mistreating their dog. I am not so foolish by half, though, to think that a cry of, 'Hey, what do you think you're doing?' will get this lot to reconsider the effects of what they have just done. I'm not even entirely sure myself what those effects are. I am an outsider. All I can do is stand and stare, and wonder if the law of diminishing returns applies here.

Massy pats the passenger seat for me to get back into the car. 'Ron, Stan's younger brother, wrote a piece for the national magazine, *Take Back the Farm*. Remind me to show it to you.'

Massy drives on, as if what we've seen is nothing new. 'Do you remember him?'

'He was quiet is all I remember. That, and how upset he was the night Stash disappeared.'

The memory of him does not have a face. He is a small boy seen from a distance, holding something in his hand.

'He started out with hopes of going into law, but switched to ethics.'

I scan the fields, looking for evidence of missing trees and sloughs.

'He's got a great girlfriend. Makes pots. Pottery ones.'

'Did he go back to farming too?'

'Stan left him a section of land near Shell Lake. He's keeping bees now. Every once in a while, he sends Carl something he has written about native species or farming. And he always shows up at Carl's door, come rock picking, seeding, and harvest. He's been a great uncle, especially since Stan died.'

She turns right, and after a short distance, pulls the car over to a barely noticeable trail. I follow Massy up a hill through the tall grasses. The land spreads out in bucolic fields of young grain and hills of green, dotted by algae-covered ponds and dugouts, and white farm buildings. The odd metal roof reflects the sun, and cattle graze in the fields. Windbreakers of aspen and birch, planted decades ago, buffer farmyards against the weather, but there are also sloughs circled by native brush that perhaps have never been cut.

Clouds pass through the sun's path, and for brief moments, the light over valleys and fields dims. I squint and focus on a familiar sight. We are within sight of my grandparents' homestead. From this vantage point, I see the frame of my grand-parents' log farmhouse. A grey shell, with only scant whitewash visible in the joists. It tips on its side, as if it is being swallowed into the earth. I look back in the direction of the Wheeler farm, still thinking of the trees being ripped away.

We spray our arms and legs with mosquito repellant, and stand quietly looking to the land that now belongs to the Very Land Trust.

'You know Hall told me I could undo my mother's donation to the land trust. He also said he has a buyer.'

'Of course he does.'

Massy puts her arm on my shoulder.

'How am I supposed to tell where the fifty acres that they retained starts or ends?'

'Just along there. Either side, where the train tracks curve. I'm not supposed to ask, but Carl wondered if he might buy it,' Massy says, 'if you want it organically maintained. But, I don't know how you'd feel about that.'

Looking down on the land, it seems as if it already is a part of the Very Land Trust. At least none of the sloughs has been covered.

'Here's some news. Shirley made a small investment without my knowing.'

'Yeah?'

'It's ballooned into a small fortune.'

'Really?'

Massy lifts the old barbwire, and we crawl under from one property to the other. Now we are at the far reach of the VLT land.

'She also left a letter. Not with me. Hall had it.'

'He never sent it to you?'

'He said he was ordered to give it to me in person.' The field at my feet is a confusion of weeds and wild grasses. A young grasshopper jumps up ahead of me.

'The old scoundrel. Look, this is fireweed.'

'No, I see his point now.'

'What was in the letter?'

'She's asked me to revive a rail line.'

Massy pulls her chin back into her throat, makes a "What?" face. 'I've heard of odd demands in a will, money left to a pet, a brooch that must be kept in the family, but seems to me that reviving a rail line is a bit much to ask.'

'I've been going over and over it in my head. Why would it have been so important to her?'

'So. How big is this balloon?'

'Balloon. Oh, the money. A few million.'

Massy's raised eyebrows seem to be asking for a precise amount, but I want to keep this to myself for now.

'And she wants you to build a railway?'

'Revive.'

'Pardon me. Listen, of course, I'll support whatever decision you make. But you also have to think of the future and what is best for everyone.'

'Now you're starting to sound like Jake.'

A flock of pelicans fly around us in a circle. A lone figure walking in the distance stops and then ambles away. Could be the illusive Dr. Merell.

'So, tell me, what's with you wanting to meet the pelican man?' I grab handfuls of oat grass and let them go, the top seeds exfoliating my palms.

'I should have given you a pair of walking shorts to wear,' Massy says.

'It's alright. I thought you were happy being a hermit now.'

'It wasn't always easy loving Stan, you know that. He called me his crutch for a reason. I miss him, but in all of our life together, I wish, well, let's just say my current day-to-day calm was rare. So, yes, I do like to drift to the hermit end of the social scale.'

She pulls up a piece of couch grass, placing it between her thumbs and whistles through the blade. 'Lately, I'm starting to think it would be nice to have someone to shovel the snow and bring in the wood.'

I suspect my friend, still vibrant and attractive, misses more than having someone to shovel snow.

'How is the museum world?' Massy asks.

'Always changing. We have an elaborate traveling Renaissance display on the books and I have to get back to move stuff around, make room for it, make nice to visiting curators and benefactors. You should come.'

'I just might.'

Only twice has Massy used the egg money and splurged to visit me, but I had inferred at the time that she was desperate for respite from Stan or the farm. 'If things had been different,' she'd once said, 'I probably would have run away to the West Coast too.'

Massy looks towards the car. 'Do you want to drive into Plover first, and then maybe swing around and have our cider on a dock someone has built at the far end of the lake? Check out the Buffalo Berries in bloom.'

'I've already had a look at Plover Station. Can we just head over to the dock?'

'The lake it is. Look over your shoulder. You can see it from here.'

I turn, and above the tree line a silver crescent edges the fields. Dad took us swimming every afternoon in the summer, and often pointed in this direction, trying to get us to see the farm from the lake.

We walk back to the car, but one of the windows has been left open and now the car buzzes with mosquitoes. Massy lights a cigarette, hoping the smoke will drive them away.

'I don't think it's fair that Shirley dropped this on you. But if you aren't going to take the money and run, or if you change your mind and decide to, I'm here either way.

'Thanks.'

'Three years this October that Stan is gone. What, nearly two for your mom, and not quite a year since Shirley. And now here we are.' She exhales smoke up and over her shoulder.

A momentary flash, I think, reminds me of Beckett's *Waiting for Godot*. 'They give birth astride of a grave. The light gleams an instant, then it's night once more.'

10. TURNTABLE

We are into our second bottle of wine. The sunset glows beyond the sage-coloured hills, and Massy has promised the northern lights.

'If you're getting chilly, we could go inside,' she offers. She's given me a pair of jeans and a sweater to wear. Teased me for forgetting to bring an overnight bag.

'No, this is good. Amazing dinner.'

'I'm so glad you decided to stay. It's been a long time since I got drunk with a friend.'

'We aren't drunk.'

Massy pours. 'Oh, but we are going to be.'

I like the buzz I'm beginning to feel from the wine, but at the same time I try to hold myself in check, taking in deep breaths of sobering night air. It doesn't seem the right time to be letting my hair down. I have to stay on top of things and try to figure out what to do with Shirley's request. At the same time, her leaving and still imposing further demands on me makes me angry as well. I seem to be losing the force to keep myself focused in the way I've been able to, before I arrived here. Alcohol can also lead to loose tongues and a picking of scars. We had a companionable day out by the lake, seemed to make up for the years and distance that has separated Massy and me, and I want it to stay that way.

The alyssum and marigold boxes on the porch are recently planted, and the young plants scent the night air with old-fashioned fragrance. The wild baby's breath and Saskatoon Berry blossoms that we picked are in a vase on the table. Prairie flowers. They are a world away from the West Coast temperate zone—blooming rhododendrons and hydrangeas. How varied and vast this country is that we are so lucky to live in. Now and then, between the robin's evensong, a cow's bellow drifts from the neighbouring pasture.

Flowers were an extravagance in the railway station garden. Aside from a few lilac bushes, it had been a black patch of dirt until Mom and Dad filled it with every vegetable you could possibly grow. The railway expected its agents to keep the station grounds well groomed, a duty left over from the time when passengers would descend from steam trains and take a turn in the cool of the railway gardens, but my mother preferred the kind of plants you could eat.

This side of the exterior of Massy's house has a couple of broken eaves, and the dogs have scratched away the finish on some of the deck boards. It takes at least two strong people to maintain a farm house. Perhaps it is too much for Massy now, or maybe she just doesn't notice or care. Our house could use an exterior paint job, and something should have been done years ago about the cracked driveway.

'Jake's never been much good at house repairs. Says he doesn't notice. Everything is fine.'

Massy slips off her sandals. 'Stan could fix anything. My son used to have more time. He and his friends did the roof a couple of years ago, but the wind tore some of the tiles off last year and the attic leaks. That is a cost-cutting risk you take when you employ your progeny.' She slurs her words slightly. 'You just get used to things breaking down on a farm.'

'How are they?'

'If it's not the wind, then it's the frost. They? Oh, you mean the progeny.' She places her hands on her shoulders, rotates her neck. 'The kids, who aren't kids anymore, have their hands full with work and farming.'

'I thought everyone wants to move to the city now.'

'Like I said before, they are trying to balance both worlds. Outside jobs pay some of the farm bills. Carl's wife does the farmers' market, and works the odd clerical shift in the hospital, and Kelly's man does a bit of accounting, income tax returns, that sort of thing to supplement the farm.' She undoes her ponytail, combs her fingers through her hair, then pulls her hair back into the elastic.

'Funny. I never expected they would be the future generation of next-year-things-will-be-better farmers. But, they help
each other out. And they're happy. That's the most a parent can
hope for.'

It's my fault that my boys haven't shown any interest in their
great-grandparents' homestead. Of course, it's different when
you are born and raised with malls and movie theatres, and the
farm is three generations away. I should have done more to plant
part of them in the prairie. They return to the West Coast to visit
because we still live in the house the boys were raised in, but our
sons see themselves as citizens of the world. They are convinced
that you can make home anywhere, and, to them, we are just a
flight away.

'Keep this between us. They haven't told anyone else. It's
early days, but Kelly is expecting. Next trip to the city, I've got
to buy some wool.'

'How long will you keep living out here?'

Massy thinks for a moment. 'I just have this house now, and
the pasture around it. I am tired of the winters, but so far, I'm
still managing. Music. That's what we need. CBC Saturday night
jazz, or do you trust me to pick an old record to throw on the
record player?'

The image of Neal and Jean moving to the fiddle strains of
Pat Shaw's 'Margaret's Waltz' dances across my memory. Was it
in the town hall after a fall supper, or did Neal gather Jean up on
the station platform? It is Connie Kaldor's lyrics set to that tune
that I sing to myself.

"I close my eyes and I see the lights of town twinkling at
night. They say that home is where your heart is. I guess they're
right."

'They're called vinyl and turntable,' I call after Massy.
'Remember how we used to listen to Peter Gzowski on CBC,
and you'd call me with spoilers two hours ahead of when his
show was broadcast on the coast?'

A voice, not a railway, had connected the people of St.
John's, Newfoundland, to Vancouver Island, Massy to me, while
we raised our children. From the collapse of the cod industry to

the raging grannies protesting nuclear subs, radio had kept us in touch with the world and each other, even while we were absorbed in the details of our own families. The inimitable host is gone now, too. Obviously, Massy is still a keen listener if she is referring to Saturday night jazz. Jake has never forgiven the CBC for dissolving their radio drama, and has moved on to BBC4. Though I couldn't tell you what we last listened to, something about the Arches or Archies?

From inside the house, the Beatles, 'Ob-La-Di, Ob-La-Da' blasts, and then goes quieter as Massy plays with the volume. I stand and walk the wraparound deck. On the south side is an old creamer covered with sandpaper and cloths. The dogs' water bowls have drowned a few mosquitoes. I page through a magazine that has been left on an old recliner, a good place for morning sun and coffee. Beyond the rustling poplars, the creek trickles merrily on to its way to the confluence with the South Saskatchewan.

Massy calls, 'Can you hear this?'

She cranks up the music and then her hips belly dance through the kitchen screen door with a plate of lemon squares held high away from the Labs.

'If I look around here, I might be able to find a joint that one of the kids has stashed.'

I lift my wine glass. 'I'm good.'

'That's another thing I miss about Stan, he was some dancer.'

'I did Jazzercise for a while, but all that jumping up and down kills the knees. Tried tai chi too, but lately I've let my fitness slip.'

'You're still in a grief fog. Tai chi. What is that anyway? Is that like slow-motion karate?' With lemon squares set on the railing of the deck, Massy steps back, lunges onto one knee, points her chin, and then does a slow bird-wing flap with one arm and then the other.

I nod. 'Yeah. Like that.'

Stevie Wonder is into 'For Once in my Life.' Has to be one of those decade compilations, *Best* of hits I've often seen advertised on late-night TV. Massy goes through a combination of dance moves, picks crumbs off the plate of squares and stares into the sunset. 'A Stan song,' she says.

She points to the trees behind me. 'Look. A hawk.'

I turn and in the poplars see the crown of a red-tailed hawk, its head slowly surveying left to right for prey.

'That's why I don't keep chickens anymore,' Massy says. 'That, and after twenty-five years I realized I was sick of the smell of them.' She falls into a deck chair, draws her finger across her throat.

'People back home have started keeping chickens in their back yards.'

Massy rolls her eyes. 'City folk. You have a lot of eagles out there.'

A dim lamp shines from inside the house. Dusk settles around us. I am sleepy from the day spent outdoors, walking through the fields and then along the west side of the lake, followed by the full dinner and wine.

'See that?' Massy observes. 'Sometimes, when the lights flicker like they just did, or when I enter a room, I wonder if it's Stan.'

'I could have sworn I saw Shirley the other day. I was behind a woman at an ATM. She was wearing a denim jacket and her hair was very short, like Shirley's. She had the same slightly protruding thyroid. When she turned to leave, she didn't look anything like Shirley, but standing behind her, I sensed my sister's presence.'

'I lie in bed at night and imagine Stan locking up. Patting the dogs one last time, and saying something ridiculous to them, the way he always did, like, "Help yourselves to the dog treats on the bottom shelf. I won't tell." '

She turns the wedding ring that she still wears. 'I was too young back then to know what I was getting myself into.'

I see the two of them as sweethearts in public school, faces pressed to each other before and after the school bell. They started out together very young.

'Can you still hear his voice? I mean imagine the way it sounded?'

Massy closes her eyes and does not reply.

'Why is that? It hasn't been that long,' I say. 'Yet, I can't recall, or imagine, or, or conjure up, whatever you want to call it, the sound of their voices. I imagine what they might say, but not the unique tonal quality or timbre of the voice that was theirs. I can't *hear them*.'

Massy lights the citronella candle, and the air fills with moths batting blindly at the night. 'You probably haven't been still enough for their voices to come through. Your life right now is just making too much noise.'

She's missed the point.

'I'm pretty sure I saw Shirley filling up her rental car, maybe on one of her last trips out here. She was two lanes over. I was going to speak to her. I wish I had. I really wanted to call your mother too, after Stan passed away. Was it selfish of me wanting to connect with her, hear her admit it wasn't his fault? That Stan made a mistake.'

I try to accommodate. 'Maybe she realized that at the end. She'd just lost so much.'

Massy rises from her chair. 'I better change the record.'

I haven't noticed that the music has stopped. I am appreciating the quiet. Our first time together in years has been easy, and I really don't want to bring down the mood by a rehashing of old wounds or talk of illnesses. I need an oasis in my life right now.

'At least you were able to get away from all of that.'

And there it is. That ever so unsubtle dig at the past.

Massy bites into a lemon square, as she settles back in her chair.

'He messed up. Who doesn't? But the rest of his life made up for it. He set himself challenges, goals, I suppose, and he accomplished a lot of them.'

This sounds to me more like affirmation to herself than defense. She tops up our glasses, and I wonder if wine has numbed her own grief.

We sit in silence. I watch her eyes shut and her chin drift to her chest. She can't help the adenoidal snort, begs pardon, and continues her train of thought.

'I know how demanding settling an estate can be. I hope you will be done soon. You're looking worn out.'

'I'm just tired. I was counting on wrapping up with the lawyer, and maybe just sleeping for 24 hours before I went home. Now this all feels like a puzzle with the pieces scattered everywhere.'

Massy twists the strand of hair that has fallen over her cheek, yawns. Her words come slowly. 'Stan was sooo—organized—but wills will always take more time than you think they will. Did I just say wills, will, will?'

'Shirley's will was straightforward. The money was a shock. And the letter. How the heck am I supposed to build a railway?'

'Resuscitate,' she pointedly miscorrects. 'When I am gone, Stan's belt buckle goes to Carl's future son, and my Royal Doulton goes to Kelly's future daughter. My kids want nothing of the old stuff.' She waves her intentions off, towards the east. 'Nice and simple. Why don't you go to the library or the university, or contact, I don't know, someone in a government transportation department. They'd know if there was anything in the way of a rail system that you could just hand some money over to.'

'It would be easier if she had said any rail system. But she said—a rail line like the one that Dad believed in.' I am getting sleepier too, losing focus.

'Too bad she couldn't have finished. That.' Massy mumbles. 'The spare room downstairs is ready when you are. Need anything more?'

She tips the stain of red from her glass, reaches for the Pinot, and evenly settles our glasses with the bottle's dregs.

'After the fire, when Stan came back from the *boys' school*, he didn't want anything to do with formal education. Mr. Winton, senior, and Stan, took on the grandparents' farms. Good thing too. When the station closed, and their grocery store had to close, they sowed their frustration into the land. Our son seems to have reaped a transformation of love.' Massy tries to stifle a yawn, then adds, 'Course we are the *have* blah blah blah now.' She puts up her arm and throws me a high five. 'Gold, potash, and a sh-nynchrotron.'

'So I've heard.'

The phone rings. Massy slowly makes her way to it. I realize the cushion I thought I was sitting on is actually a tightly folded blanket. I open it and drape it over my legs and shoulders. The muffled conversation goes on inside for a few minutes, until Massy calls out, 'It's Jake,' and then brings the receiver out and hands it to me.

'How you doin?' he asks.

'Not too bad. I think we're into our—Massy, is that our third bottle of wine? No, it can't be.'

'Good ol' Massy,' Jake says.

'She barbequed bison steaks.'

'Lucky you. I noticed that you'd called. Have you been back to see Hall?'

'Yes, I have. There are just a couple of loose ends. But that should be easy.'

I don't have the energy to go into detail.

'I guess you really can't talk.'

'No, not really.'

'Okay. I just called to let you know that Hetty telephoned asking if you took your cell phone with you, and she needs you to call her.'

'She knows I am unavailable.'

'That's never stopped you before.'

'Heard from the kids?' I ask.

'No. I'm going to try an email to see if they're doing alright.'

'Good idea.' Jake is still getting used to our sons' preferred methods of communication. I can see him sitting at the computer waiting for a reply. 'Anything new there?'

'I've been asked to do a ten-year summary paper for the ministry on the results of integration of special needs children in middle school. And I'm still thinking of going to Toronto for that conference. What do you think?'

'That's going to be an enormous amount of work.' I am used to Jake taking on extra work. He has always felt his work is a call-ing, and there aren't many calls he hasn't answered. At least he isn't making plans with Shirley's money.

'How does the farm look?'

'The house is collapsing. Lots of mallards in the sloughs. Prices are good, like you said.'

'Well, there you go.'

I can hear the news channel behind Jake's words... 'dissidents surrounded... the United Nations will... and now back to... reporting from...' Jake is a news junkie, and now that his hearing is declining, the television blares in the background from the time he arrives home. Now sirens. Now small explosions. Advertisers paying for repetitive sensationalism. Oceans and tides. So far away.

'Margaret?'

'Yes, I'm here. Okay. I'll call Hetty in a day or two. You alright?'

'I'm sorry.' His voice becomes softer. 'Margaret, you know I was only thinking of you when I said Shirley would want you to keep the money. And that you don't need another project.'

Is he really thinking of me? After so many years of marriage, what the other wants or needs has become blurred, or perhaps muted is the better word.

'I understand.'

He might have said, I love you, but I hear his cut off reply as 'choo,' as I press end call.

Massy isn't in a deck chair when I look out on the porch. I walk through Massy and Stash's house, quiet now except for the wind shushing the long grass and poplar trees. Feeling quite woozy, I step carefully over the creaking hardwood planks, feeling my way among the antiques. I take in the expressions in the framed pictures, young Mr. and Mrs. Winton of the Plover grocery store. Stash too, surrounded by his family, looking proud and happy. Collages of school photos.

I slowly make my way back outside to gather up the wine glasses and bottles. The candle flickers and puffs its ending. I find Massy, legs curled under her, head fallen to one side, snoring softly in the tatty recliner. She holds a cloth in her hand, as if at any moment she might take up polishing the old churn. The dogs at her feet prick up their ears at the stranger in their midst, roll their eyes lazily at me, and then heave a sigh. I'm not a threat to their widowed owner. I stroke her forehead. After only semi-regular phone calls over the years, the day and night of reconnecting and taking inventory has been uncomplicated and pleasing. We've taken up our friendship from where we left off. I am grateful.

I go back and forth on whether it is kinder to let her sleep or to wake her and send her to bed. My eyes drift from the dogs to the roofline and then to the star-filled sky. There, moving in a green, pulsating motion, fading and reappearing, moving from south to north in front of the Milky Way, on its way to the Arctic, is a train.

11. Gauge

I awaken, parched and in need of strong coffee. The evening at Massy's has been a respite, but after a large glass of water, I leave early with the excuse that this isn't a vacation, and I have matters to attend to, and after all, my things are back at the hotel. Massy, groggy, still in pajamas, is disappointed and covers her ears when I pull the imaginary train whistle and shrill its sound.

'No. Please.' And in between her gulps of water, 'Keep in touch.'

I still have no idea how to make a start at Shirley's wish of reviving a working, short line railway, and I need time on my own to think, and convince myself that this isn't just a waste of money and energy. Maybe I should go back to see Hall. That will just be costly. Perhaps I'd get some ideas, as Massy has suggested, from a visit to the university, to have a look through their archives on the historical regional prairie railway lines. I wouldn't mind seeing Adam again, but I decide there are limits to his resources. First things first, though. After a hot bath, looking out of my hotel room at the late morning rainfall, tea in hand, I listen, as speed dial rings Hetty's office at the museum.

Despite our pattern of calling each other at home in off hours if there is an issue that needs sorting, I am slightly irritated that Hetty has asserted herself through Jake. I made it clear to my boss that finishing up the business with my sister's will had to take precedence now over everything else, and she'd agreed. She'd expressed appreciation of my working the entire time I handled my sister's estate business, foregoing compassionate leave, delaying my vacation time. She even offered, 'You can take time off, you know, if you need to.'

Of course, she'd made the offer in the way that people do when their raised voice pitch is really asking a question. Calling

Jake is once again her way of showing me she is the boss. I've always complied with her demands, and she's taken advantage of the fact that my curiosity and need to control aspects of my job, even if I'm away, will always get the better of me. Despite the time change, I know she will be at her desk.

The phone rings twice. Hetty recognizes the number and starts right in.

'The collection is arriving sooner than we expected, and with it the entourage of Italian curators and translators.'

I hold the phone away from my ear.

'I need you to take down the current display in the Dunsmuir Gallery and store all of that collection ASAP. They're sending an advance delegate, and your Italian is better than mine. It is imperative that you work with him to see how we can best display some of the small Medici pieces. You're better with the lighting people. Security is protesting everything I've asked of them. Need I say more?'

'I'm fine, thank you.'

'Good. Me too.'

I can picture Hetty leaning into her ergonomic chair and sliding her too large glasses over her forehead onto her haystack of black hair.

'Just a sec, luv.' Unexpectedly, I am put on hold and sent to the museum's automatic infomercial, reciting the hours, and what to see and do at the museum.

How I wish things hadn't become complicated, and I could just take the escalator down to Hetty's office and have this conversation. We get along best face to face.

We started working together at the museum almost 25 years ago. Modelled after the Victoria and Albert Museum in London, in terms of rooms of collections, it is a museum much smaller in scale, dedicated to Canadian and First Nations' culture, industry, and history, amplified by dioramas of nature. Being a museum where everyone was expected to learn how to do many jobs, when I was first hired, my task was simply to list and number acquisitions for curator Hetty. Over the years, I've moved through cataloging, archiving, conserving, and curating works

Canadian and Canadiana. Larger pieces especially of artwork still go through Hetty, but heritage collections of smaller items, Depression glass, Eaton's paraphernalia, settlers' implements and dishes, as well as items of industry, now all come under my stewardship. As a young assistant, it had sometimes taken me months to date and place a piece, but over the years I've acquired over two hundred books and countless spreadsheets of dates and exhibit objects, and now I can feel the difference between a scrap of tartan brought over by the Scottish Selkirk settlers in the 1800s and a bit of Fortrel tartan rescued from a patchwork skirt made and sold in Kensington market in the 1960s.

My first duty is to check the overall condition of items, record the source of the contribution, and any relevant history, research sources to properly date the items, and situate them in linear timelines with period pieces in glass displays, after an assistant has done any restoring that might be needed. Duplicates or pieces of lesser value that can't be repaired and displayed in good condition, or sold or traded to other museums, are intermittently given over to thrift shops. At times, I work closely in consultation with the First Nations' elder curator and with the museum's auxiliary foundation.

It isn't as if there is a never-ending source of artifacts the way it is in England or Italy, but for now, the museum helps dispel the idea that Canada is all Arctic ice and snowshoes, and tourists like to go home and brag about discovering this. The Europeans, especially, are fascinated by First Nations' lives and their artifacts. The last two decades have seen a decline in unique new collections that significantly represent Canada's past; everything is needing an overhaul. The board of governors has proposed the museum collections need to give a deeper representation of authenticity, diversity, and story. How this will look, is still being defined. The First Peoples of the West Coast will take charge of their galleries, and Hetty and I have been assigned to a task force to meet with interested immigration groups, to hear their stories and encourage them to share and perhaps lend items brought from their countries of origin. One young staffer in charge of boosting gift shop sales has also taken up a lot of my time, asking for my consult on objects that can be reproduced and sold.

'It's come down to trying to figure out which pieces would best replicate as retro house décor and or jewellery,' I've told Jake. 'When I suggested an Avro Arrow brooch, the young man said he would get permission from the First Nations' curator. He took umbrage when I told him that wasn't necessary and I haven't seen the young man since. '

Within the next few weeks much care will be needed to set up the Florentine collection for the Renaissance display. This is to be our most prestigious exhibit since the traveling Tutankhamen collection, and normally I'd be anxious to start work on the project. But, I've spent the last months disposing of my sister's estate and the remnants of my mother's. Anticipating the Renaissance, though obviously prestigious, along with my day-to-day duties, has started to feel like just more shifting of someone else's paraphernalia.

'I believe I am booked off for another week,' I jump in, when the infomercial stops.

'Listen to this,' Hetty continues. 'They want—why, I can't get my head around this—to know if we can pick two unique Canadian pieces to send back to Florence. The Uffizi is putting together a one-time, international display and are requesting one or two pieces from very select museums around the world. Ooooh, we might get to go.'

Out in the hotel garden, people are running in and out taking in flower arrangements from the outdoor tables to protect them against a possible downpour.

'Hang on Margaret,' Hetty says, 'just have to deal with this.'

'Don't put me on hold.'

Then, without placing her hand over the receiver, she recites a list to whomever has come into her office.

I was used to making meticulous lists of museum items that went into storage. When Mom died, I resorted to a list, but Shirley said, 'Why are you making a list. Are you worried something will go missing? I don't want anything, so you don't need to make a list. You're just doing this so that you can accuse me of taking something if it goes missing. Just like you always have.'

'Come on. You've always borrowed or taken my things and never given them back. It's who you are. Just admit it. Not a big deal.'

'I have not.'

'I think we should divide everything, and then see how we feel in a year,' I'd mitigated. I'd brought museum storage boxes over to the condo that Shirley and Mom had shared in Vancouver.

We were in Mom's bedroom trying to sort through her belongings. Shirley set Jean's jewellery boxes on the bed, and I began an inventory, separating the costume jewellery from the 'good stuff' Dad had given her. 'Do you want the pearls or the Alaska Black Diamond?'

'I don't think those are pearls. They look like painted glass beads.'

'We always called them pearls.'

'Remember Dad secretly looking at the jewellery whenever the new, wholesale catalogue arrived? Poor mom, for every birthday and Christmas for years she had to look surprised. So. Which do you want?'

'Neither,' Shirley said, 'but, if they'd kept it, I would have loved to have had one more look through the Sterling Wholesale Catalogue with its folded corners and circled items.' She'd left to put the kettle on.

'You must want some keepsakes,' I called.

'No.'

'What am I going to do with six boxes of jewellery?'

'Why are you writing everything down?' Shirley demanded. 'I just said I don't want anything. Choose a couple of items for your boys to give to their future wives and grandchildren.'

'What about her antique side table? I'll post-note it and this plant stand as Arts and Craft.' Shirley left to answer the whistling kettle.

It wasn't all sad, sorting Mom's things, but two items especially affected me. One was the first rental receipt for the apartment we'd had to move to after Dad passed. We'd gone from the freedom of a country station to a crowded apartment block, and having to listen to the family above us walking over our heads and arguing or shouting at each other several times a day. I realized later that we three had been afraid, afraid of how we would ever manage without Neal to protect us. The other was a picture of Shirley and me wearing matching skorts, and both of us clinging to the puppy that Dad had brought home from Kasha's farm. Such ecstasy in our faces. Our whole lives ahead of us.

There were envelopes of letters and cards the boys had made, postcards from Jake, and an angry consumer letter Neal had written to a wholesale distributor.

I'm going to tell everyone I know not to buy another diamond ring from you, one of Neal's—dad's—letters read. *This is the third time I've had to ship this back and exchange it for one without a flaw.*

'Do you think Dad really knew the difference between a diamond that had a flaw and one that didn't?' Shirley had wondered.

'Especially one that came shipped in the mail. Nah, not really. Maybe.'

'Bless him.'

After Shirley passed away, and I was alone in her condo, I was grateful for the two days we'd spent reminiscing among Mom's possessions. While friends' siblings quarreled over estates, marking or bidding on items left in parental homes, and later fell out over who-did-or-didn't-get-what, Shirley kept reminding me that Mom's will had specified, *take only what is needed*. In the end, I'd convinced Shirley that we should wait a bit, in case she changed her mind about some of the china, jewellery, or bric-à-brac. I wish now that I'd listened to Shirley, taken *only what was needed*. There was so much sadness going back all alone, touching all of those objects again, and in the emotional weight of them, as the keeper of our collective history, having to discharge it all.

Hetty laughs into the receiver, even as she is carrying on a long-distance conversation with me.

'Sorry. Do you get what I'm saying?' Hetty asks, but I can't tell if she is speaking to me or the person or persons in her office. I very nearly hang up on her.

'Now, where was I?' Hetty asks.

'Hetty. Wait. I need to tell you something,' I interject. 'I might need more time. My sister left a bequest I wasn't previously made aware of.'

'What do you mean?'

'She had some money I didn't know about, and asked that I use it to revive a rail line.'

'She'd really lost the plot, hadn't she?'

'I beg your pardon?'

'I mean, seriously? That could take years. I need you here now. Listen, you need to gauge the best items to go back to Florence. They have to be examples of the far-reaching influence of the Italian Renaissance on colonial cultures down through time. You know better than anyone what is in storage for appropriate representation.'

'But why can't you or Isabel do it?' I ask.

'The co-op student?' Hetty asks. 'Let's not get ahead of ourselves.'

'But Isabel knows everything Canadian, from the mid-eighteenth century on. She's been on digs from the Viking settlement of L'Anse aux Meadows in Newfoundland to the shores of Haida Gwaii.'

'I know she doesn't mind getting her hands dirty,' Hetty says, 'but I need someone fast on this. Not someone at the "picks-up-a-milk-jug-meditates-on-its-journey, and tries to figure out the message the piece is sending her" stage.'

I think that is cruel, even for Hetty, a jab at my own apprenticeship. Sure, Isabel is a bit eccentric, but the museum business thrives on its eccentricity.

I pause long enough for Hetty to consider the effect of her sarcasm.

'I take that back,' Hetty tries to convey humility. 'Isabel will be very good, when she has had a bit more training.'

'When do they arrive?'

'The advance man, in a couple of days. The delegation in less than a week.'

'We went through all of the calendars before I left.' I try to be assertive. It's sometimes easier over the telephone. 'You know how long I've put off this trip. I need to be here, and once this is done, I will give you all of my attention.'

It isn't the first time Hetty goes straight to the dollars. 'Getting placement in an international display could guarantee more funding. We cannot compromise on this.'

'You insisted I could take time off.'

'Hold on there, my little munchkin. That was for sorting out real estate, not for some prolonged adventure in some back-woods. One of our museum dictums is "Expect the Unexpected." Get back here and once this is done, maybe we can figure out your railway thingy over a lunch.'

I hold the phone away from my ear.

'Your job and mine may depend on this exhibit. I'll be gen-erous. I'll expect you day after tomorrow.'

The last thing I hear Hetty say is, 'Can you grab me a coffee, luv.'

Hetty is right, and she knows I'll start packing.

'There is no one now who knows everything about me,' Shirley had said. 'Well, except you, sort of, but Mom was always the keeper of our lives. She knew our birthmarks.'

'When I'm gone,' Shirley had said, 'give all my stuff to the women's shelter. Cremation. Scatter my ashes on the prairies.'

'Don't talk about that now,' I remember saying. 'It's hard enough with Mom gone.'

'Let's go back home,' Shirley had suggested.

'This is my home,' I had answered.

'You haven't been back in years.'

'We were just there to leave Mom's ashes with Dad's.'

'Is that it then?'

'What are you talking about?'

'Something should signify they passed this way. So that years from now, it will still be standing, no matter who has forgotten.'

'You mean like a bench or something?'

'You of all people, a collections curator, with all those artifacts representing that someone was somewhere at a particular point in time.'

'Do you want me to take some of this over to the museum?'

'God, you can be thick. Yes, take the black Alaska and put it in a window with the caption, "Neal gave this to Jean in 1967. Ordered from the Sterling Catalogue. Worn to the Plover Fish and Game League Dance." Yes, that should do it.'

Shirley could be wickedly sharp. 'You know what I'm talking about.'

'Are you back on about trains? Let's not talk about that either.'

'At some point in time, can you stop treating me like the younger sib who doesn't know anything?'

When had we, or perhaps I, decided what we should or shouldn't talk about?

Then, a call in the night from the neighbour Shirley had invited for dinner, and the letter. A one-way conversation that I am obligated to listen to now.

I refill the teapot with hot water and read the headlines of the newspaper that has been slipped under the door. The Mendel Art Gallery is going to put on an addition and the permanent collections are going to be put into storage. The Joni Mitchell permanent collection. I think I'd like to see that. Perhaps a half-day to gain some perspective.

I hum one of her tunes.

When my cell phone rings, I think it will be Hetty continuing to bulldoze her way. I take a defensive tone. 'Yes?'

'Oh,' Massy says. 'It's me.'

'Sorry, I thought it was my boss. I've just had the most irritating phone call.'

'I probably had too much wine last night,' Massy says. 'I didn't say a proper good-bye. What are you going to do today?'

'I was going to go and check out the Joni Mitchell self-portrait at the Mendel.' I don't have the nerve to tell her that my boss has changed my plans.

'There are two now. The Van Gogh, she-cut-off-her-ear spoof, and the *Hoppers Nighthawks* imitation of herself at the bar.'

Helnwein's poster of the *Boulevard of Broken Dreams* had hung in Shirley's bathroom. The sales agent asked if I could leave it. 'Part of the staging.' The painting with James Dean, Marilyn Monroe, Humphrey Bogart, and Elvis behind the bar. On one of the nights I'd stayed over to clean up Shirley's place, after five trips up and down the elevator to the recycle bins, I had taken a long bath and lost myself in the painting. The empty street, the five bar stools with no customers, Phillies bar, endless cups of coffee, the only woman at the bar. Shirley would have spent hours looking at the work. Had she felt like one of those at the bar. Wondered what her legacy would be? The buyers asked if it could stay with the place. I had fallen back on 'take what is needed.'

Shirley had had a succession of boyfriends over the years, a few better than others. I'd assumed she was happiest on her own. She had a good job, had worked her way up to an assistant deputy in the Ministry of Housing. When the rare opportunity for a lateral move had presented itself, she had moved herself and Mom to Vancouver.

'If she won't come back to us, we will go to her,' Shirley had joked. 'Those boys need their grandmother,' she had convinced, when Mom at first refused to leave her prairie home. And so, somehow together, they had made a deposit on a condo, and I had helped pay for their move.

When they were young, she'd taken my boys for the weekend, bought them new outfits and anything else they wanted; video games, the latest sneakers, skateboards, and then they'd come home to me, the mom who told them they had to make do with the jeans they had, that homework came before hanging out with friends. The one thing that I did find in her condo, which I wouldn't share with anyone, was a series of rejected adoption applications.

'You don't understand how some things are for her,' Mom had once said, refusing to elaborate. I had always assumed that Shirley had everything she wanted.

'It's really only her,' Massy says.

'Her?'

'The take on *Hoppers Nighthawks*. It always reminds me of the other painting, you know, the one with James Dean and Marilyn Monroe. Anyway, I just wanted to say it's good to have you back here, and I hope I didn't go off on some rant. You really can stay with me, you know.'

I can't bring myself to say that it felt strange waking up in Stan's house. I'd driven away seeing Massy and our long friendship fading down the years in the diminishing exchange of Christmas cards.

'Thank you,' I tell her. 'I might just do that. And, we had just the right amount of wine.'

I take a deep breath and look at my speed dial. Out of guilt, I almost call Hetty back. I am getting nowhere. I might as well be back at the museum. My eye catches the list I scribbled on the note pad a few days ago. *Ashes*.

Maybe I can't build a railway, but as soon as I get home, I'll find the box containing the black Alaskan diamond and it will be going into one of the museum's displays. Surely Isabel should be able to locate a copy of the Sterling wholesale catalogue.

12. BRANCH LINE

I telephone Jake.

'What do you think?'

'Do you really want to know what I think?'

We don't talk about cruises or investments. He mentions something about Toronto. I forget to tell him I am looking into changing my flight.

I doodle again on the hotel notepad, draw arrows every which way. Write, *Shirley's money + savings account > donate funds? charity*. I turn to her ashes. She would have been properly fed up with my stalling.

'Which prairies?' I ask.

Plover Lake comes the answer. Of course, it makes perfect sense. Dad driving down to the lake, the two of us in bathing suits sticking to the plastic front seat and eating penny candy. Window down, sun hot, music loud. Dad singing along with Roger Miller's 'King of the Road.'

The prairie fields surround the lake, seagulls and pelicans will fly overhead and perhaps the odd sailboat will appear. Why hasn't it occurred to me before? The prairie of Plover Lake will be Shirley's final resting place. If I have to get back to the museum, I'd at least better get on with this duty.

As I am getting myself organized, Hall calls.

'Have you come to a decision on the fifty acres?'

He has driven out to Plover and vicinity on business and taken a look at the trust land. He hesitates. I wonder if there is something he is unwilling to share, but he only says, 'Check your bank account tomorrow. All of Shirley's money, your money, will be transferred over to the account set up in your name only.'

'Thank you. I'll confirm in the next day or two.' I don't add that I'm pretty sure I'll be submitting the last fifty acres to the whole of the land trust property.

He is getting to be like one of these mosquitos, I say to myself, as I scratch the bites on my arms and the back of my knees.

I try to call Massy and invite her to a final supper in the city, but there is no answer. Probably out doing some chore. I leave a message that I am driving out to the lake. Who knows when we will see each other again, once I've finished my duties in Saskatchewan. I am scheduled for another museum conference abroad next year and the year after that.

I turn off the GPS, certain now, having been back and forth to Plover, that I can find my way. About forty minutes into the drive, my cell phone rings. At first, fearing it might be Hetty, I ignore it, but it keeps on, and I pull over to a farmer's roadway and answer.

'Mom, Mom, where are you?'

'Ryan?'

'Finally bought a mobile, Mom. How are you?'

His voice fades in and out. I step out of the car, circle-8 my phone through the air, as if some passing satellite might improve the connection.

'I miss you,' I shout. 'Where are you? Is everything okay?'

'Fine. I just wanted to tell you that I got a job on a film set, here in the Lake District.'

'Lake District. In England? Last postcard was from Prague.'

'That was weeks ago. Anyway, we met this film producer. He's my age, and he said he had this project about to start and if we were interested—'

'Are you acting?' I think of my youngest son, how he had wanted a video camera in high school so that he could film his friends for a school project. I'd said no, but of course Shirley had promptly presented him with one. He had even cast his grandmother as a wealthy recluse. She had taken to the part, sitting in her Queen Anne chair, arms on the rests, improvising scripted reminiscences like a tsarina.

'Just a bit part. Have to learn how to hold a cigarette like a soldier in World War I, but I'm not really supposed to give out any exact details. We took the train up from Euston Station. I was thinking about Auntie Shirl the whole time, and how she once told me about taking the train from there when she was my age. You and Dad have got to get back over here.'

I catch the enthusiasm in his voice and I try to picture the station. It makes me happy to hear that in the midst of his travels, he'd thought of the aunt who'd loved him so dearly. I almost mention that I am going to spread Shirley's ashes, but choose not to dampen his mood.

'Well, gotta go. Tell Dad I emailed. We'll probably stay on until Christmas, and then you could come and visit. By then, I'll know my way around and can give you a tour.'

'I love you, Ryan. Take care.' I want to ask after his girlfriend, and how he is fixed for money, but he has hung up.

I get back into the car and onto the road. I feel a rush of excitement at my son experiencing the green hills and drystone walls of England. He will have seen the lights on Tower Bridge, heard the bells of Westminster, drunk bitter in a rowdy pub. Christmas he said. Yes, I'd like that. I look to the ashes next to me.

'That was Ryan.'

I park the car at the top of a hill, very near where we used to park the car when Dad took us down to the lake. I am a little hesitant, all by myself, with no one around, but I rationalize that being alone is better than coming upon some stranger. We had always planned to walk east to west, from Plover Station around the lake and up to the farm. If we'd followed the railway tracks, as Dad had always wanted us to do, we could have walked directly to it. Adam made the journey on the jigger, inspecting the tracks, hundreds of times.

When I open the car door, I am pleased with myself for recognizing the wild garlic that Massy pointed out. I pinch the leaves and squeeze them between my fingers, rub them back and forth, taking in the scent. If I look, I might be able to find wild sage and mustard too.

I unlock the trunk, place the ashes carefully inside. I'll come back for them once I've located an appropriate spot. I grab my bottle of water, pull a granola bar out of my purse, and in a city gesture of precaution, throw the purse in the trunk too. I make sure the car windows are turned up in defense against mosquitoes and slam the door shut.

As I walk along the stubble of last year's crop, the resting field scratches my shins. How many cycles have there been of waist-high wheat to summer fallow and stubble? I consciously plant each foot into the earth, thinking of the Yoga practice I've neglected. 'Root to rise.' Closer to the lake now, the sun shines down and the lake glistens silver. I have never been to the Sea of Galilee, but I imagine it looking like Plover Lake does just now, calm, a surface deceptively willing to be walked upon. As I make my way through the aspen and birch, the soil turns to fine gravel and then loamy sand as I come out onto the shore of the lake. A red-winged blackbird whistles overhead and flutters off. I inhale deeply and take in the length and breadth of Plover Lake. A perfect lake, and yet neither a boat nor fisherman in sight.

In the years Dad was the station agent, and Mr. Novakovsky the hotel owner, a small sailing club had discovered the lake, and the town's business men proposed that regattas on the lake would turn Plover into a booming summer town, be a reason for the railway to keep the station open. Of course, that never happened. How many other seaside, or lakeside towns and villages had visitors arrived in by way of train? How many places had dreams of prosperity until the trains stopped?

There is a small bay down along the shore. I walk back and forth, assessing its suitability as the particular place to leave Shirley. I can't bring myself to say the words sprinkle or scatter. Scatter especially sounds chaotic. A couple of gulls glide overhead, their breasts glowing an iridescent white. There is no one else here to witness this end of the line, and so I begin to organize my thoughts to say a few gentle words of farewell. Words feel inadequate. The song of the lake and the whispers of wind are the praises and prayers attending the vignettes of Shirley down the years. I thought I was finished with tears.

I think of phantom limbs, the sensation of something still being there when it isn't, and in a way, this is what I am most afraid of, that soon I will never remember what it really felt like to have a sister, only the knowledge that it had once been so. Someone occupies a space in your life for a time, and then they don't. I've carried on without father, mother, but Shirley's going leaves a wound that may never completely heal. Lost, a chum, a confidant, and yes, at times an adversary. Someone with whom I shared a genetic code, so that at times simply by looking across the room we would know what the other was thinking.

The lake is tranquil, with only the occasional brush of wave against the shore. The water reaches for the toe of my shoe. I crouch and take in the peace all around me. A fine spray of mist caresses my face. I inhale the lake. A wave suddenly slaps the shore, and an urge comes over me. I want to be in the water—I *need* to be in the water—to know again what it feels like to float in the alkaline.

I scan the hills for tractors or farmers, but everywhere is deserted. With seeding finished and haying just starting, it is an in-between time for farmers. They are tending to machinery, buying hail insurance. No farmhouses, no people. It is secluded and private. Who will pay any notice to a 50-year old woman? I'll be so quick, it won't matter that I don't have a bathing suit. I haven't looked at myself naked in a mirror in ages. I shaved my legs in the hotel this morning. My hair is short now, it will dry quickly. From afar, I might be mistaken for a heron.

For God's sake, would you just jump in. Shirley's words.

There is no one to see me. This is Plover Lake, where I learned how to swim, where we buried each other in the sand, and once dug up what we thought was a Bison's skull. If I don't do this, I know I'll regret it when I get home.

I carefully remove my shoes and socks. The sand is warm. I glance over both shoulders, remove my sweater, then pull off my T-shirt. I step out of my trousers and underwear in one motion, unclip my bra, and place everything on my sweater on a nearby rock.

The water is cool—'huh'—but not as cold as the ocean. I breathe in the brackish water, not entirely dissimilar to Pacific low tide. Blue dragonflies dart over the surface. Arms wrapped over my breasts, I wade out into the shallow water for a long way, then, fearful of a sudden drop, I get down on my knees, touch the lakebed, lean forward and slip my chest under the water. My chin skims the surface. At first, out of habit of ocean swimming and watching for jellyfish and rogue waves, I keep looking away from shore, facing potential waves. But this isn't the ocean, and the only fish that have ever been here were called whitefish. Once oriented in the cool water, I flip over, spread my arms, and lay my head back.

I wait for it, and then exhale a giggle at my buoyancy.

The water reflects the dome above. Seagulls appear, and one after another plop down on the water, not far from where I float. This close, they seem massive, these descendants of small flying dinosaurs. A few ducks bob on the surface near the shore, unbothered by my sudden appearance. I reach down, pull up some mud, and brush a smudge across my cheek, wonder if it might have anti-aging properties, like those I've seen in infomercials of the black mud of the Dead Sea.

As I float, the temperature of the water changes, warming in intermittent sloshing. I frog-kick, but that makes for too much splashing and drives the birds away. When I lie still and breathe in, my breasts and stomach rise above the surface of the water. I close my eyes and let my arms go until I can't sense their presence at my sides. I let my legs drop down, touch the floor of the lake, and then, ten feet from shore, my bottom hits a sand bar, and when I stand, the water level drops to my knees. The air is chilly. Much warmer to be in the water. I dive into the lake and dog-paddle back and forth, parallel to the shore. Jump up, and fall backwards. When we were kids, Dad would bring us here during his lunch break, or after the station office shut for the day. He loved the water as much as we did. And when it seemed the station would close permanently, I suppose he needed to float weightless on his back too.

A pair of whooping cranes settle at the shore briefly, and then take off. The sun glares off the water and I look towards the silvery bay. If this is where I am going to leave Shirley to rest, it is the right place.

I get back onto my knees, throw some water over my shoulders to try to wash away the salt, and pull up handfuls of lake-bottom mud and throw them away into the lake. They break across the water in small pellets. I look back to shore, half expecting all of the townsfolk who had once played here to come running into the water. I swirl the surface in small arcs of sprays, stare into the distance, and then, when it is just too cold to tolerate, hug my arms close again and scamper across the sand to where I've left my clothes. I dry myself off with my T-shirt, put on my bra and panties, and then sit down on the rock. I brush my feet back and forth through the coarse sand, rubbing one over the other, to remove the lakebed mud. Now I know, in some esoteric impression, what it will be like for Shirley to be joined to Plover Lake.

There is a loud rustling in the tree line down the shore. I spring up expecting a fox or coyote. I look to where I've parked the car, and wonder if I should dash up towards the hill, when, from the bushes, a man emerges with a branch as a walking stick, and a backpack over his shoulder. I quickly pull on my trousers and sweater.

He looks harmless, but still I calculate how long it will take to run to the car. He is jotting something on a notepad and seems completely unaware of my presence. As he comes closer, his dark green hunting vest stands out. Could he be a park naturalist or inspector? No name tag or pin. A bird watcher? Might he be Massy's birdman? What is his name?

He calls out in an English accent. 'Hello there. I hope I'm not intruding?'

Has to be him.

'No, no, not at all. I was just uhh,' I mutter, gathering up my socks and shoes. 'Are you by any chance the British ornithologist?' Surely, it would be crude to say, 'birdman.'

'Have we met?' he asks.

I stand and brush my hands on my trousers. Up close, I note that he has a day's growth of beard, but otherwise is well-groomed. His eyes are the colour of the grey sand and his slim build makes it difficult to judge his age. His salt-and-peppered coloured hair is buzzed. Massy calls him the good-looking British birdman. She is right. The pockets of his vest are stuffed with notepapers. I fluff my wet hair away from my ears, extend my hand.

'Margaret.'

'Dr. Merell.' He puts down his walking stick and takes my hand, 'George.'

As if I might not believe him, or perhaps to waylay further discomfort, he reaches first into one of his vest's pockets, and then another, and hands me a card. 'Here for the annual Breeding Bird Survey, but I'm also doing my own bird check-ups.'

I turn the card over in my hand. It is the first time I've ever seen a business card in the shape of a bird.

'Green heron,' he points out.

It is the shape of a green heron in flight. The russet neck and chest lead, while the wings fan out below and behind the chest. One side of the card is the unadorned likeness of the bird, but when I turn the card over, in discreet cursive font over the wingspan, are the words, 'George Merell, PhD, Ethnoornithology.' I repeatedly turn the card over in my hand, amused by the bird changing direction from one side to the other, and then I just embarrass myself and say, 'So, you're interested in birds?'

'Just a little.'

Trying to sound slightly more intelligent, 'And, anthropology?'

'I study humans and birds. At present, how their migration and breeding has been affected by interference with their habitat, and how their changing patterns might affect us.' He crosses one foot over the other once, twice, as if tracing a pattern on the sand, and then adds, 'You might have seen me in documentaries, or perhaps my book.'

I shrug. 'I'm sorry, I don't think so.'

'I'm meant to be counting the plovers, but I'm also checking up on the Plover Lake pelicans. See if they are the ones a colleague banded along the coast of Mexico. Count their numbers, eggs. That sort of thing. I assist the local conservation society.'

I wrap my sweater close. 'Did you see me?'

'When?'

'Just a few minutes ago. I was out there—swimming.'

'Oh, I see. You'll be all right.' He reads the questioning look on my face.

'I'm also going to take some water samples. Before the environmental laws, a few of the older farmers had to be reminded not to dispose of the insecticide containers near the lake.' I must pale at the thought of swimming in polluted waters. 'Oh, no, rare, years and years ago. Last testing it was pristine. Just making sure.'

I look to the aspen stand behind him. I didn't hear a motor, and I hadn't seen a vehicle anywhere in the fields on my walk down to the lake.

'How did you get here?' I ask.

'Walked.'

'Walked? From where?'

'I've been out here for a couple of days. Walking the circumference of the lake. You've got a bit of lake mud, just there. Do you mind?' I must not mind, as I point my chin out towards him. He reaches out and gently touches my right cheek. It is the reflexive action a parent might make, or the familiar light attention of a lover. I bring up my hand and rub at the spot where he's touched.

'Gone.'

We look towards the bay. I sit down, wipe my feet with my socks and put on my shoes.

'I'm knackered,' he says. 'I'm about to make my way back to the city. Sometimes, I'm lucky enough to catch a ride with a local, or by strange coincidence, Dr. Simpson will often show up when I am ready to leave.' He stands his stick in the sand, puts his notepad into his backpack.

'May I drop you somewhere? I mean, I have my rental car parked just up in the stubble field.'

'Perhaps a lift to the main road? I don't carry a mobile, but after this many years, most of the farmers around here know me and let me into their kitchens to use their telephones.'

We walk back up to the car. I reach into my pocket for my keys. I look behind me, down at the grass at my feet, and then feel in my pockets again.

'Oh, no.'

George has pulled his camera from his pack and is photographing the panorama below.

'What is it?'

'Damn.'

I walk around the car, check all the doors, and try to retrace my steps. I'd opened the door, squeezed the garlic, and looked at the ashes in the trunk. I don't see the keys in the front or back seat. I knock on the trunk.

'Are you in there? I'm so sorry,' I say to him. 'It seems I may have gone and locked my keys in the trunk of the car.'

'Most inconvenient.'

We stand looking at the car as if will offer up an answer. I can't think of what to do next.

'Tea?' George proposes. 'You're starting to shiver.'

'Tea would be lovely.'

He motions for me to go ahead.

'Careful,' he says. 'The stubble can be slippy.'

When we get back down to the lake, I apologize yet again for my absentmindedness. 'I guess I was preoccupied. It isn't like me to lock the keys in the car.'

He reaches into his backpack and assembles a single propane burner. He presses it down into the sand and ignites the fuel. Then, he takes out a thermos that has two varied cups which telescope out of the top of a metal lid. 'Water.' He shakes the thermos to determine the contents, but I offer up the bottled water wrapped in my wet T-shirt. He pours the water into the lid and sets it on the small burner to boil. From one of his thigh trouser pockets he pulls a plastic baggie containing tea bags, shakes them out in the air.

We sit and wait for the water to heat, both observing the earth blowing away in the wind from someone ploughing on a hillside beyond.

'There's a sight you don't see much anymore,' George nods.

'No,' I say, thinking of the contrasting skyline of my city.

'They discovered that the nutrients disappear with ploughing, so they leave the stubble. They have seeders now that can penetrate the stubble, and so they plant right over it.'

I don't know anything about agriculture any more, if I ever did, but I wonder who this farmer might be, and why he hasn't kept up on the advances in farming practices, still does things the old way. Hopefully, he isn't farming in the manner of the Wheelers. The small stove gives out a little heat, and I stretch my hands out to the warmth.

'Course, the birds don't know that, and any nests they've built low to the ground—well I'm sure you can figure out the rest.'

I imagine small birds building nests in the warmed stubble, only to be driven to their burial by iron spikes surprising them from above. Why did such a basic improvement also have such consequences? I stretch and look in the direction of the VLT land, which will never be ploughed again, where now the nutrients will be renewed and the small birds safe.

'How did you meet Dr. Simpson?' I ask. 'You mentioned that he sometimes picks you up. Everyone around here believes him to be the keeper of all prairie birds.'

'Still is. Quite incidentally, it was back in the nineties when he came up to the Lake District on holiday. I was living over there then. He met with the local birders, and one day, I took him over to Morecambe Bay to show him the quicksands. He was well chuffed.'

'Synchronicity,' I say.

'Pardon me?'

'On the drive out, my son rang me from England.'

'Ah.'

The water is steaming, and I realize I am parched.

'Darjeeling,' George says.

I pull the twisted granola bar from my pocket and offer it to him.

'And biccies.' He smiles.

13. BOILER

George makes a small fire. 'It'll ward off some of your chill.'

Having used my T-shirt as a towel, after the spontaneous skinny dip, I am left wearing a holey fashion statement of a sweater until the tee dries. With the keys locked in the car, there is nothing else to do but stay put near the fire and sip tea. George arranges some sticks in the ground near the fire, so that I can drape my T-shirt over, and every so often I wave it in the air and turn it over. George does not sit long with his tea.

'Mind if I carry on with some work?'

'Of course not.' I hold the cup to my lips, hiding my amusement as I watch him become the object of his studies.

He crouches and waddles duck-like to get closer to the birds, and then flaps his arms until they take off and he can observe the movements of this particular species when it rises in flight, circles, floats on the currents, and then lands again.

When he comes back towards me and reaches for the cup he has twisted into the sand, he exclaims, 'Wordsworth wrote, "The birds pour forth their souls in notes," before adding, 'I've always envied poets' expediency.' He pulls a notebook from his hunting-vest pocket, curls himself around the journal and jots down a series of letters and numbers that sum up, in code, birds' names and population.

The one time I attempt to be knowledgeable, 'There—eight white seagulls,' moves George to answer, without looking up, 'Herring gulls.'

I don't pay much attention to birds. I mark the arrival of the fall robins to the backyard rowan tree, and I enjoy watching the seagulls float on the air stream behind the ferries that run between Vancouver Island and the mainland of Canada, but my bird observations, of late, mostly run to those of the wooden kind.

The totems at the museum include some of the birds of coastal First Nations' legends, stories, song, and mythology: eagles, ravens, thunderbirds, magpies, hawks. Those tall cedar logs, meticulously carved, join eagle to whale and thunderbird. After Shirley died, I was inexplicably drawn to their stillness. I made a point of slowing my steps when I came into work. The Coast Salish elder liaison for the museum rarely speaks to anyone, but one day, when he caught me standing among the totem poles, he nodded and asked, 'How is your heart today?' It was so quick, I didn't have time to respond. He'd left me in peace among these symbolic representations of protection, strength, romance, and community.

From the little I know of shore birds, it seems to me that some of the West Coast birds are also the birds of Plover Lake.

There is George, sitting in meditative pose, leaping like a frog, then standing facing the water with his head turning into the wind, as if his ear is a cup and he is trying to fill it with distant callings. There is a youthful playfulness about him, and when he straightens, tall, he appears prayerful. It gratifies me in no small measure that eventually, unbeknownst to him, he will also be visiting Shirley with his regular duties.

The changing sky begins to forecast the weather with grey puffs at the horizon. A pelican flies reconnaissance, skimming the surface of the lake, and then flies higher and dives, piercing the water with its long bill. George hands me a compact pair of binoculars, takes his camera from another vest pocket, then stretches out on his stomach and points to a frenzy among the rocks down the beach.

'Plovers building nests,' he notes. A book flutters open in his backpack. It is minus a few graph charts that he tore out to start the fire.

'Their numbers are up elsewhere, but seem to be declining here.'

I focus the binoculars, first on the small island where the scavengers have flown.

Birds cross my view and I guess. 'Cormorants, I think?'
'Certainly are.'

'And way out there. White-winged... scoters?'

'How did you know?'

Perhaps I've recognized the cormorants as similar to the ones
along the shore back home, where I used to run each morning.
The scoters and gulls share the lake, one unbothered by the
other.

'Would these cormorants and scoters fly between here and
the West Coast?'

'Not likely. A variant flock may winter there.'

George whispers like a commentator in a documentary, as
the camera shutter clicks in quick succession. 'The male Plover
has the thicker chest band.'

As I zoom in on the plovers, I take in the orange beak and
legs, and black neck-ring that prevents complete camouflage of
the sandy-coloured bird. Their quick orange legs dance like pen-
cils across the sand. The plovers toss small stones in the air and
into a depression in the sand that will become their nest. George
turns onto his side and scribbles another series of letters in his
book.

'I wish I had last year's notes. It's late for breeding.
Something has changed here, and I can't quite figure out what it
is. No predators about.'

He jots quickly and then slips the book into his back pocket. I wonder if farmers, whose property cannot contain the
overabundance of rocks they pick from their land, have
deposited them here. I can't recall ever seeing so many rocks on
this shore, but why would my memory have retained that
detail? The plovers whistle, and I realize they were here when
I was swimming.

I point. 'Pipers?'

'Pectorals,' he corrects, and clicks away at them. They seem,
at first, to almost sink into the shallow mud, then stretch up and
lean forward, their wings larger than their bodies, beating like an
eggbeater that whirls into action as soon as it is plugged in. They
take off into the wind, circle some five-hundred feet away, the

formation bending and twisting like a ribbon in the breeze, and then they glide back onto the surface of the water. Over and over they repeat their ballet.

A wind eddy swirls near the fire and ashes fly up into George's face. He jumps up, runs his hands over his head, spits into the sand, and brushes his shirtfront. He points to the gathering cumulous. 'They're on the move.' He then stretches and reaches down to swig the last of his tea. Looking to sky again, he gathers a few twisted twigs and branches, and throws them down beside the fire, bundles up a few and shoves them into his pack. It seems an odd thing to do, but I assume he has his reasons. In the distance, lightning flashes. I realize then that the rain might soon be upon us. I shake my arm to wind the watch, and am baffled that two hours has gone by since George made our tea.

The fire is dying down, and while George has his back turned, I quickly remove my sweater, put on my T-shirt, still damp, and then slip my sweater back over my head. The wind over the waves is chilling, and I smell prairie rain in the wind gusts. The silver day disappears into the lake as a growing blanket of grey spreads under the cumulous clouds. Stripes of rain are falling through sunrays on the horizon, and lightning flashes and thunder rumblings grow closer by the minute.

The seagulls screech and skip in frenzy along the shore, as if to warn of the approaching scowl. George points to the clouds rolling towards the northeast.

'It's approaching pretty fast. Did you want to run up along the farm road and try to find shelter?'

A farmhouse could be miles away. It's been a long time since I've been this close to a prairie thunderstorm; I want to see what the birds will do next. I look up at George's six-foot frame as he zips up his pockets, cropped hair standing on end like small antennas analyzing the approaching weather.

'I think I'd prefer to stay here, somehow.'

'Do you really *think* everything over, never just spontaneously commit to something?'

He says this smiling, rhetorically, a neutral observation, with no hostility in his voice, as if he is just observing some quirkiness in a species. Without expecting an answer, he wanders a few hundred feet down the lake and into the stand of aspen from which he first appeared. I assume he needs to relieve himself in the woods, but after a few minutes, he quickly reappears. He is saying something to me, but the wind scoops up his words and tosses them out onto the lake. I make exaggerated, shrugging motions with my palms high in the air. He slips back into the trees.

California gulls, like daring children, dart towards the water, and then away from the waves that are splashing more fiercely on the shore. Then, with a last warning shriek, they lift and fly inland, seconds before a sharp crack of lightening plunges into the lake.

I look to where George has disappeared, wondering if he has abandoned me and headed in some direction in search of bird storm behaviours. I gather up his propane boiler and tea supplies, and put them loosely into his backpack. If he isn't coming back, I'd better find shelter. When I look up, George is waving me over to him. I throw the backpack over my shoulder and run along the shore towards the trees.

As I approach, I see that he is pulling a nylon disc from a duffel bag.

'I keep a small tent hitched up in the trees so that I can spend the night out here. It will keep us dry.'

He moves back a few feet into a clearing in the bush, and tosses the disc towards the ground. The tent springs to life, and with his foot, he quickly pushes the thick plastic stakes down to secure it all. He does all of this with quick, capable precision.

The thunder cracks overhead, and I suddenly feel afraid. If I hadn't lost track of time sitting around watching gulls and plovers and sipping tea, I might now be in a warm dry farmhouse, or at least in the car where there is protection. Lightning is supposed to be rare near the seashore, but the flashes thrown from above seem to make anything and anyone a target. There is nowhere to hide. I have to trust this stranger.

George throws the duffle bag into the tent. 'Don't worry. We'll be safe under this canopy of trees.'

'Oh, it's not that. I was meant to be spreading my sister's ashes is all. At least they are safe and dry in the trunk.' Flummoxed. Totally out of context.

George runs down the beach, kicks sand onto the fire, races back, and holds the tent flap open for me to climb inside. 'Wouldn't want a fire to spread.'

We just manage to climb inside before small hailstones pelt the roof of the tent. I catch myself hoping that hailstones of this size won't affect the crops that are just beginning to show themselves.

The hail lasts for about ten minutes, and then the rain comes down heavy and hard. The walls of the tent suck in and out. We are both sitting on our knees along one side of the tent, as far apart as is possible in the enclosed space. Inches. The roof touches the tops of our heads. I open the tent flap slightly to witness the squall, and take a spit of rain in the face. Seaside rain rarely pours down. Most of the time, it is either a mist in the fog or a leaking tap. The storm is passing over us in a swirl of dark clouds and torrents of rain. I shiver, pull my legs out from under me, and wrap my arms around my knees, only slightly apprehensive of being in such close proximity to someone I only met a few hours ago.

'Here, at least put this vest around you.' He wraps it over my shoulders.

The rain pours down and we sit in silence, listening.

'Ever wonder how birds know there is going to be a storm?' George points to his ear. 'They have a little receptor in their middle ear, called the Vitali organ, which is sensitive to changes in air pressure. When birds get the signal that air pressure is plunging, they take off and look for shelter.'

I bend my ear to my shoulder. 'I always thought it was instinct.'

'Mmm. Some say instinct is tied to characteristics of bodily structures. Maybe that is why birds also have wings.'

'I didn't know that. I mean, the part about characteristics and bodily structures.'

'And here endeth the lesson.'

He hangs his head, perhaps embarrassed that he might be lecturing. I don't mind him sharing his expertise. 'But, how does that explain—till the cows come home?'

'Good one. You tell me.' His eyes twinkle at my quick come back.

I stretch my cramped legs out and then draw them back in. 'If we move, we'll have a little more leg room,' George observes.

We shift so that we are now closely side-by-side, but can sit with our legs stretched out and facing the opening of the tent. The rain slows to a steady thrum, I glance at George sitting serenely and looking straight ahead, staring at the entrance, and yet seemingly taking in everything beyond the nylon wall. Our shoulders touch, and I am grateful for the warmth emanating from his body. The thunder and lightning are moving away, and as the chaos of the storm subsides, I feel as if an energy has been cleared. We turn and face each other. I don't know anyone with grey eyes. Like pebbles seen under water. Cool and still. I am drawn to him in a way that completely catches me off guard.

'Have you found what you came out to find?' I ask. 'Did you find the pelicans that your colleague tagged? Or is it banded?'

'Banded. No, not yet. But my counts show fewer of each population than in previous years.'

I slip to one side, and something sharp pokes into my backside. I rock into George. I've been half sitting on the tent's duffle bag.

He reaches around behind me, and as he does so his face brushes my left ear. He pulls some rations from the duffle bag. He lays out a package of dried fruit, a juice box, and a bag of potato chips, offering me first choice.

'The chips,' I point, 'or, as you say, crisps?'

'Potayto, potahto,' George says. 'I believe the important thing is they are,' and he reads the packet, 'Bar-B-Q flavoured.'

I couldn't begin to guess by his accent from which part of England he hails.

'Does it make you angry, that we have encroached on birds' habitat, or destroyed it entirely?' I tear open the bag of chippy crisps.

'Am I an angry ethnoornithologist?' He pokes the straw into the juice pack. 'Not so much anymore. My anger's diminished with age.' He offers me a first sip from the straw, but I decline.

'It's not that simple. Now I try to put my energy into where my choices lie. You have a lot of birds in your province that still need protecting. And, you may be surprised at the increasing number of folks wanting them to thrive.'

I offer the bag of chips and he takes two.

'I was born here,' I tell him, 'but I've actually lived on the West Coast longer than I lived here. I don't know anything about birds. Not really. We were just over in Plover Station. My father was the station agent.' I expect questions, but none come.

'No station there anymore. Some nice little starlings there-abouts. Nothing like the murmurations I've seen in Somerset, but I've walked the rails past Plover many times, and then caught an old Bison trail to get down here.'

'Do you ever see any sailboats on the lake?' I ask.

'Rarely. The occasional skiff.'

'When I was a little girl we used to watch regattas from some ways up, nearer the island. The residents of Plover had hopes that the lake would turn into a resort of sorts, with the winds on the lake, and the birds and everything. Put our little town on the map.'

'Maybe it just hasn't been found out yet. Seems a likely spot.'

'No. It's too late.'

'Puts me in mind of Windermere.'

'Where?'

'In the Lake District. Like so many of your lakes, formed by a receding glacier.'

'Is that home?'

'It was for a bit.'

'I'm curious about what brought you to this corner of Canada. Great Britain has been blessed with more than its share of beautiful lakes and green hills, moors, highlands, and birds to count.'

'I had a Canadian schoolteacher who made me very curious about this land. And, of course, after I met Dr. Simpson, I wanted to be a part of what he was doing. Birders love to check out each other's patch. I came over on holiday, and then another.' He slurps from the juice box, and then wiggles the straw in his mouth to reposition it in the juice. 'Who knows why we become attached to a particular place. I suppose it planted itself in me. Now, I follow my own migration route.'

I picture again the way his supple body moved along the shore. I'd looked at his hands by the fire. No rings. Not that that means anything. I'm not even sure why I checked.

'You're thinking I look like one of those pelicans. Or maybe a heron?' He pokes his head back and forth in a pecking motion. 'Let me see, hmm, if *you* were a bird, what would it be?'

I know someone who once owned a cockatiel. Don't they mime? I could be a flamingo, all pink and exotic. No, that is just fantasizing. If I were a bird, maybe I'd be one that had forgotten how to migrate. Just built a big nest, and every year keep packing more things in.

'You strike me as a kind of lark. Careful, but adventurous. After all, you were swimming in the cold June water.'

I pull the sides of the vest up over my face in embarrassment. 'You did see me!'

'Only the porcelain bits.' He smirks and helps himself to the bag of chips.

It is fleetingly unsettling, but at the same time slightly erotic that he had noticed, and in his fashion, been discreet.

'Have you ever?'

'Swum here in the buff?' He purses his lips, shakes his head no, but says, 'All the time.'

'Well, just so you know. That isn't really like me.'

'Oh? I suspect it is very much like you.'

Another species observation? 'Instinct and characteristics?'

'Most journeys terminate in a bathing ritual of some sort.'

The rain slows, then stops as quickly, as if a switch has been turned off. Branches above shake droplets down onto the tent. The thunder in the distance is a weakened grumbling.

'Won't drone on, but this bit about being like a bird,' George crunches down on a chip, licks the salt from his lips, and passes the bag back to me. 'I feel extremely fortunate to be able to fly between two landscapes. And I do think of it as migrating between the two. Stay for as long as the air and sun tell me to stay, and when I hear the fells calling me, I fly back.'

'What about work, or don't you have to worry about that?' I instantly regret asking. I should know better; the British consider it poor taste to bring up money. 'I'm sorry. It's none of my business.'

'Not at all. Lots of demand for publications, and I do some conferences, lead the occasional birdwatching tour, the odd local BBC special. Though Sir David seems to have sewn up that department.'

'Sir David?'

'Attenborough.

'Of course.'

'Brilliant man. His is the final word on bird studies. Still calls on me, though, now and then, to compare notes.' He drops his head in humility again, as if to distance himself from the name-dropping. 'Anyway, I manage on very little. But, I have been doing all of the talking.'

He opens the tent flap to let in fresh air. Neither of us are in a hurry to leave the protection of the tent, or perhaps each other's close company.

'You said you grew up at Plover Station, and you aren't entirely correct about not knowing anything about birds. You certainly know this lake and its inhabitants. If I may. You said you don't live here. What brought you here today?'

Where to begin? Simply put, it was to leave Shirley behind in this peaceful lake. I could have said I was hoping to leave my grief along this shore too.

I take a deep breath and point to the pair of returned whooping cranes, each balancing on one leg near the small bay.

'My grandparents came from Great Britain, their homestead was just over that hill. Growing up, I swam here in the summer. My father taught us the names of the birds. I suppose some of that is resurfacing.'

He doesn't reply. I've never been one for small talk.

'I came here today to lay my sister's ashes to rest, just over in that bay.' I let out a deep sigh, and book-end my obligations. 'And, I've stayed on longer than I intended, because in her last will and testament my dear mercurial sister asked me to revive a railway.' I've said too much. Brits hate the way we go on.

He studies me for a few moments, and then motions towards the bay.

'At dusk, that bay can take on the most serene aquamarine hue.' And after a moment's thought, looks into my eyes and says. 'I don't know a birder who hasn't walked a greenway or railroad right-of-way, and many of my birder friends are also railway buffs. They might be able to offer some advice, if that would help.'

The thunder and lightning give way to sunshine again, and through the whips of clouds, tubes of light fall down onto the surface of the lake. George picks up the sticks he brought into the tent before the rain and tries to get another fire going.

'Unfortunately, Margaret, there will be no tea,' he calls out.

He announces 'tea,' ending in an upward slide, but it is hearing him say my name, Margaret, that stirs me. Saying someone's name is an intimate thing. The emotional response to Shirley's voice calling my name down the years is forever gone.

The lake comes alive again. Flocks of resident ducks and gulls land on the lake and bounce along on the waves. Then each scavenger takes its turn rising and skidding near George, squawking for crumbs, or perhaps communicating to him their surviving the storm.

'Take your time. There's no need to hurry,' he calls back to the tent. 'We'll figure out what to do next.'

In these enveloping words, I feel tranquil and unencumbered, released from the responsibility of having to sort anything out. And after months of running between work and estate business, peace comes over me. I let myself be where I am.

I stretch, then curl myself up inside the tent, with his duffle bag as pillow. I will have to move soon, and try to get into the car, or at least up the road to find someone with some tools to open the trunk. But, for now, I have to lay my head down. If only for a short while. The wet leaves of the trees, the soil on the hills, and the sand along the shore are collectively exhaling their perfumes. I breathe deep the after-rain air. George is blowing out his lips in a whispered whistle. I murmur a once used Yoga sutra and can't resist the pull towards sleep. It could have been five minutes, it could have been five hours.

The storm clouds are ragged mountains along the horizon. In the distance, a truck spits gravel along a grid road. A boat motor sputters to life on the far side of the lake, and men's voices echo across its surface. In the boat's wake, a wave splashes the shore. Colourful sails come across the lake, and I am floating again on my back, weightless, without bone, or skin, or arms, or legs. The tent opening flaps. The air brushes against my lips. I taste salt. Shirley waves from down the beach. On the brome grass Jean unwraps sandwiches, and Neal is making a fire. Shadows of townsfolk fill the background. I can smell the smoke. The Grewins, and the Wintons, and the Novakovskys, Winnie, Massy, and Adam are sitting on the sand, drinking beer and laughing in the sun.

A dog barks and licks my face. I hear Stash's voice, meek and apologetic, just as on the day I found him hiding in the skating hut. He says, 'Massy.'

A dog pants in my ear and twin silhouettes tower above him at the tent opening. Stash is talking to George.

'Here we are.' George kneels to meet my blinking eyes. 'This young man has been sent to find you.'

The young man lightly brushes the pup away and it runs barking down to the water. 'Mom called, said she was worried about you,' he says.

I rub my eyes, 'Stash?'

'Carl, his son,' he answers, taking off his cap. 'You probably don't remember me.' He also hangs his head as if it is somehow his fault. The gesture is familiar. 'Mom slipped and sprained her ankle, or she would have come looking herself. I spotted the car. Some storm, eh?' he says to George.

Although I haven't seen him since he was a child, Carl looks exactly like his father did as a young man. A hulk of muscle, blonde-haired, and farmer tanned.

'Is, is Massy alright?' I stumble from the tent, stiff and drowsy, straighten my trousers, and smooth my sweater.

Carl offers his hand. 'Mom does this all the time. She's a bit of a klutz. I mean, slips and falls, or looks away and cuts herself while she's slicing bread.'

'Oh, no.' In that instant, the little girl is looking at the boy of long ago, but now she is older than the boy.

'I've locked my keys in the trunk.'

'I've got some tools on me,' Carl says. 'I can probably spring the lock though the window.'

It takes Carl all of a minute to pull up the lock, flip the latch, so that keys and purse can be retrieved from the trunk. The urn with Shirley's ashes is still propped against my computer bag.

The young man shifts awkwardly, now that he has done what he was sent to do, his eyes moving between George and me, and I realize that finding me with my hair all over the place and my clothes in a twist might be suspect.

'Well, better get moving.' Carl tips his cap at George from the cab of his truck. 'Got a guy comin' to fix the baler. You're more than welcome to come back to Mom's with Margaret. Looks like you could use a bit of drying out too.' Then he turns, waves his cap from the window, and goes down the grid road, still damp with rain.

With only a quick, 'maybe I will come along,' George dashes down to the lake, takes the tent apart, and slips it somewhere back up into the trees. He pours some water on the embers, and we drive to Massy's house.

14. Siding

'We're here,' I announce, entering the kitchen. Massy's face flushes from neck to Lauren Hutton smile; the last thing she's expecting is a man accompanying me. I have delivered the handsome British birder to her door.

A bottle of acetaminophen sits in front of her on the kitchen table.

'I think I've reached my quota for today.' She pushes them away towards the sill. Her foot is elevated on a chair, ice draped around her ankle. I introduce Dr. George Merell, and between us Massy and I quickly draw the line of our friendship back to childhood, leaving out the gaps. George takes Massy's hand to introduce himself.

'I hope you don't mind. Your son extended an invitation.' Massy's eyes flicker. Definitely not the painkillers.

'Quite the storm. I was worried about you.'

'I haven't seen anything like it in years,' I say.

'There's a shower just at the bottom of the stairs, if you'd like to freshen up.' Massy nods towards the bathroom. 'Or the tub through there, if you prefer.'

George turns to me. 'Would you like to go first?'

'Thank you, you go ahead.' My hand is on the refrigerator freezer. 'I'll make the G&Ts. Massy always has the makings at the ready. Am I right?'

She nods approvingly. 'And always an extra Bombay in the basement freezer.' She calls to George, 'Fresh towels in the cupboard, just outside the door.'

When we hear the shower running, I crouch down beside her and our whispered words collide in the space between us.

'Where did you find him?'

'He is lovely.'

'What's going on? How? Have you?'

'What? Course not. The storm waylaid us. I was settling Shirley's ashes at Plover Lake, when he came down the shore. I stupidly locked my keys in the trunk. Who knew he'd have a tent?'

'You were alone with him in a tent.'

'Well, but—'

'Alone. Just the two of you in a tent? How do I look?'

'Fine.' I pull the gin from the freezer compartment and stick three glasses in to chill. There are lemons in the crisper, and I twist the peel.

'What about your ankle? Are you alright?'

'Talk about stupid. I'd planted some tomatoes and was skipping along with the dogs, when one of them stepped in front of me, and I tripped going up the stairs.' She holds up her hands to show me the scrapes on her palms. 'I've told you, warranty is up, and sometimes I forget about the maintenance on this ole vehicle.'

'Combine.'

I lift the ice from Massy's foot. Her ankle is bruised and swollen, but I keep a neutral face.

'Not too bad, eh?' she asks.

'No. Not too.'

'Quick, go downstairs and see if the spare room is tidy.'

'Why?'

She makes a shooing motion with her hands. 'So he has somewhere to put his things.'

I tiptoe down the squeaky stairs to the lower level bedroom, straighten the duvet, fluff the pillows, and open the window to let some air in. The room is as I left it a few days ago. The shower shuts off, just as I tiptoe back up.

Massy is massaging her leg.

'Sore?' I ask.

'Could I have broken a bone?'

'Anything is possible at your age.' I stir the gin and tonics and add lemon peel.

Then, suddenly, there is George.

'Thank you,' he says, as he places his backpack at the door. 'That is lovely tasting and bathing well-water.' His buzzed hair glistens, and he's changed into a long-sleeved black T-shirt. He smells of Massy's Neutrogena soap as he passes close by me.

'How is your foot?' he asks. 'Carl said that you sprained your ankle. Would you like us to drive you to a clinic to have it checked?'

'I think it'll be fine.'

I hand round the G&Ts.

George offers up, 'To weathering storms, old friends, and new.'

We move our chairs around Massy into a close circle, rather than sit across from one another at the table. We each thank her for sending out the search party, and talk about the much needed rain interrupting haying, and Carl's broken baler. George lounges back in the chair, as easily as if he were still on the sandy shore. The gin soothes. For a moment, it feels as if we are all on holiday.

Massy downs the last of her drink, clears her throat and announces, 'As we've been sitting here, over these perfect G&Ts—thank you, Margaret—an idea has come to me. I want to ask a favour.'

George raises his eyebrows. I look from George to Massy, and then I realize that this whole time George's left hand hasn't just been draped over the back of my chair, but gently resting on the angel wing of my right shoulder.

'I want you to stay here for the rest of the week.' She holds up her hand, knowing I'll protest. 'Please, hear me out. Stay and keep me company, until I get over the worst of this stupid sprain. I have a freezer full of food. Can't remember when I last had houseguests. You can finish your business from here, and we could finally have a proper visit. I hope that doesn't sound too selfish.'

It is the 'proper visit' that causes me to bristle. I take it to mean a novel look at the past, which, up to now, I've avoided as skillfully as Rambert avoided cholera in Camus's book. Massy continues.

'Of course, I am including you as well, George. I'd love to hear more about your adventures.' She sweetens the offer. 'And you're welcome to the use of my car.'

My mouth moves to my list of responsibilities. Loose ends to
tie up, Hetty, Jake, land to sell, finding a railway that needs reviving, and now of course, still Shirley's ashes. But I can't bring
myself to say that someone with a possible broken ankle doesn't
figure in the mix.

George doesn't hesitate. 'If you're certain it is not an impo-
sition, I enthusiastically accept. On the condition that you let me
do the cooking.'

His response surprises me. Here is a man who keeps tents in
trees, and seems to spring from lakes. He looks towards me, grey
eyes twinkling, with a look on his face that seems to ask, are you
staying or leaving?

'I wouldn't take advantage of a guest,' Massy says, liquor-
flush this time.

'Please.' George scans the kitchen. 'I love exploring kitchens
as much as poking away at birds' nests.'

'Well, then. The kitchen is all yours.'

My excuses have been outplayed. George asks, 'May I?' then
opens the refrigerator, moves some of the contents around and
slides open the crispers.

'You've the makings for potato and leek soup.'

'Great,' we answer like chorus girls. Geez.

George cooks a more than decent leek and potato soup, and
washes up as he goes along. I wonder if, since Stash, any other
man has stood over the stove in Massy's kitchen. She watches
with serious intent, as he places the potatoes, tips in the cream,
and then ladles the steaming soup into bowls, as easily as if he
were lifting a fallen chick back into its nest. From the window sill
he pinches a sprig of dill for garnish.

Massy asks George about the pelicans, and his opinion on the
condition of the lake. She is curious, as I was, to discover what
brings George from England every year. Massy mentions gossip that
has circulated through the years of this mad Englishman walking
around Plover Lake. I find this in poor taste, and veer to summers
spent swimming the lake, and winters watching fathers ice fish.

Neither of us knows about the naming of Plover Lake, and,
as is sometimes the case, George, the non-permanent resident,

who has researched the stories of the land he is visiting, tells of the fur traders traveling along the Carlton Trail, who documented the thousands of plovers. He knows about the bird migrations that affect only this lake—things neither Massy nor I know, or if we did, we've forgotten. I am beginning to appreciate what a good historian George is.

'Remember I mentioned catching what I believe is an old Bison trail down to the lake? Well, early on in my trips out here, I was very curious about these creatures, which are unfamiliar to the British landscape. They especially liked this parkland area because of the lakes. A population of over 50 million American Bison existed in 1800. By 1885 they were almost extinct. They were largely overhunted, but some also partly blame the railway for their near complete demise. And the railway for taking away the last of the Cree Plains Nations independence by removing the last of their food source, giving them no choice but to sign Treaty Six.

'Your Prime Minister Sir John A. MacDonald wanted the land settled. He tried to bring in tariffs to control importing American goods, build a railway to connect eastern manufacturers with western patrons. He promised the province of British Columbia that if they came into confederation, he'd build the railway to link BC to Canada. First Nations and Métis tell about collecting all those bleached Bison bones. They loaded them into box cars, and sold them to be pounded into fertilizer.'

I try to imagine what a million Bison would look like grazing lazily in the spear-shaped grass, and then going down to where I had been swimming, to take a drink and cool their furry hides. The irreplaceable loss to the people who had been connected to these majestic animals.

After dinner, George and Massy settle on either side of one sofa. I sit opposite them on the other. George takes out his notebooks and begins to account for the day's findings. Massy sips wine and listens, as George talks about grebs and the pelican nests he saw earlier in the week. He writes about the movement of the storm, how much and how long the hail lasted, the amount of precipitation. Massy tells of the migration of geese over her farm. George speaks of oystercatchers, curlews, spotted flycatchers, red kites, whinchats and chiffchats, and we tease him that he is making these names up, because we wouldn't know any different. He compares the nesting of little ringed plovers at Aldcliffe in Great Britain, one of his favourite places to observe the changing seasons of birds, to those of Plover. Mostly, we sit comfortably in each other's company, occasionally lost in our own thoughts. From time to time, I look to George for a sign that our time at the lakeshore might still be resonating with him as much as it still seems to be doing with me.

When I get up to make us some herbal tea, lawyer Hall's words proclaim themselves once again. 'The money is legally yours. Your sister's letter of appeal, summing up her dreams, does not hold any legal weight.'

George raises his head from his notes. He's heard the coyote in the distance.

A breeze breaks through the back door, weaves through the house, and escapes by way of the open windows of the living room. The air still blessed from the rain.

'Would having money change your life?' It almost sounds like a board game question. "Answer yes or no."

'You mean real money?' George asks.

'Yes. So much that you didn't know what you had and it didn't matter. What would you do?'

George declares, without lifting his head from his work, 'I'm doing it. I don't mean I have pots of money. I mean I am luckier than most in that I found where I am supposed to be and I wouldn't change what I am doing. Although, I can think of a few bird foundations that I might assist.'

'Something you would want to be remembered for? A legacy?'

'I've never been married.' Is that a grin on Massy's face? 'I doubt I will know immortality by way of children. Who can deny that the thought hasn't crossed their minds about something to mark that they had traveled this way. Although I am not so vain as to expect a statue of me to be raised in Hyde Park.'

His papers will be studied, his research, and countless observations on habitat and migration will be influential in future planning, I emphasize.

'But a Dr. George Merell Bird Centre would be a solid and lasting legacy.' Massy gestures a billboard.

George laughs. 'So would an OBE.' Then thinking he has to explain, 'It's an award given by Her Majesty, Order of the British Empire, something like the Order of Canada, or President's Medal in the US.'

'Medals for service,' Massy says.

'Yes. Never-the-less, I believe one bird is soon forgotten. It is only the contribution of the whole flock that matters, the part it plays in the scheme of things.' He pauses. 'Over time, even that is fleeting. Everything is changing.' He rubs his eyes. 'But we were making wishes, not brooding about extinction.'

I point my chin at Massy. 'Your turn.'

'No idea. The usual I guess. Give some to the kids. Take a trip.' She lifts her swollen foot and adds, 'Buy lots and lots of shoes.'

'Definitely shoes,' I laugh.

George flexes his woollen socked foot.

The telephone rings. Fortunately, it is next to Massy on a small table within reach.

'He did? Oh, that's great. No, I'm fine. Margaret is here. Yes. And I have another house guest as well.' She holds the receiver away, as if to include all of us in the conversation, but when she realizes she can't make out what the voice at the other end is saying, she puts the receiver back to her ear. 'I will. You are so thoughtful. Love you, too. Oh, and Massy and George say to thank Carl again for unlocking the car.'

Massy's daughter-in-law has called to let Massy know that the baler has been fixed, and if she needs anything, to give them a call. I secretly wish for my sons to one day have partners who would call about my well-being.

Hall's words about money fizzle away and I give them no more thought. I soon excuse myself to the day bed in the small office next to Massy's bedroom where she says I can sleep, so that George can have the downstairs. I am feeling as tired as I felt at the lake. I hope I'm not coming down with something—feeling so drained and 'weak tired' as mom used to say—but I chalk it up to the swim and the rain.

'Rest well,' George says to me, patting his hand on his chest.

I don't turn on the lights, but feel my way and change into a night shirt Massy has set out for me—she jokes that I need to keep a separate wardrobe at hers—and stretch out on the day bed. A strip of light from the living room shines under the door. George is entertaining Massy with commentary to web videos of various birds singing, singing.

Massy is basking in the company of the man I had to myself this afternoon. He'd seen me in the lake, my porcelain bits. What if Carl hadn't happened along? I brush the generation Y inevitability scenario aside. Eyes closed, I slip away, listening to the rise and fall of their exchanging word song. Shirley and I fell asleep this way in the small station, listening to our parents' evening conversations. There was an air vent between our bedroom and the office waiting room, and we'd been kept awake at times when CN executives held meetings in the station. Once we even peered through to see only a shiny pair of men's shoes.

Now and then, Massy laughs in her open and natural way. I hear the words 'Stanley,' and 'house siding, organic farming.' At the mention of his name, my jaw doesn't tense the way it used to. I roll over on my side. Massy mentions 'loons', and George replies with something obscure about living near a Lune. More chuckling.

I call out 'goodnight.' The conversation in the living room hushes. I hear a muffled negotiation, 'Take my arm,' as George helps Massy out onto the deck to look up at a sky full of stars.

There is no space for patterned pre-sleep stocktaking over executor duties, no mental list making, no grudges, no grief. I slip into the vulnerable slumber that comes with letting go, trusting that others will do the locking up and keeping watch.

Through the night, satellites pass overhead, a coyote saunters through the wood shed, Massy has woolly dreams of knitting for a granddaughter, and George tosses from side to side on the bed that is too soft, but I sleep hard and full, as I haven't in one too many months.

15. Trailing

I open my eyes and see the green digits of the side table clock fall down at 4:30. I stretch and look over my shoulder at a collar of sunrise beaming through the sheer curtains. The household is still asleep. I close my eyes again, wriggle my toes, and slowly bring awareness up through my body. When my eyes let in the day, I realize I have slept more deeply than I have in months. I feel rested and clear-headed. I take in the burgundy painted walls, the faint hint of tobacco that still lingers in the collection of pipes on the shelf. The room, which can be accessed from Massy's bedroom or the narrow door just off the living room, perhaps intended as a walk-in-closet, was once Stash's study. The outer door was closed on my first visit, and my exhaustion last night had dismissed everything but the daybed along the wall.

Above the door is a wide-angle black and white aerial photo of Plover Station, set amongst the hills, the town as it once was, with station and elevators intact. The railway track snakes through the length of the picture. The previous night, I hadn't noticed frames on the walls, but now I see that certificates and awards are intermingled with pictures of Stash and Massy and their children. 'Twenty-five years of Organic farming,' 'Hockey Coach of the Year'—more than one of those—'4H Best in Show Calf', 'Agribition Award for Organic Farmer of the Year,' a smaller picture of Stan and Carl holding a trophy, and perhaps Ron beside them, tucked into the frame. I never expected to see Stash again, yet here he is, all around me.

I slip from the warmth of the covers to look closely at the photo of a group of men. I am certain I've seen it before. In an 8x10 frame is a picture of Mr. Winton, Stan's Dad, Mr. Novakovsky, Mr. Grewin, Adam, and Neal, all standing on the sidetrack beside the elevator. These were the businessmen of the town, smiling, hopeful, young, and ambitious. The same picture must have been part of Mom's collection of photographs.

I run my hand over the wooden knots of the homemade desk and note the books stacked to one side. Grey Owl's *Pilgrims of the Wild*, a farm machinery catalogue, a grain book recording the history of the crops of the farm down the years, and a book entitled Towns of the Carlton Trail. I pick up the last, and as I turn the pages, a yellowed newspaper clipping falls to the floor. I pick it up and read.

> *Plover Station (CP) Fire destroyed a 20-room hotel in this northern Saskatchewan village on Saturday morning. Owner Frank Novakovsky and his wife and three children escaped with only a few belongings. Cause is unknown. Approximately 20 volunteers could not contain the blaze due to a lack of water. Damage estimated to be $35,000. It is the fourth hotel fire in the province in the last five years.*

As if the person who placed the clipping in the book might appear and check to see if it remains where it had been placed, I page through the book looking for some shadow of dust or a crease that might indicate from where it has fallen. When I see no evidence of where the clipping rested, I open the book and insert it at random. Chilled, I go back to the daybed and wrap the covers around me.

It was the night of my birthday when *the fire in the northern village* happened. Gary Novakovsky had come running to the station and banged on the door in the night. *Mr. Novakovsky and his three children escaped with few belongings* spending the following days in the station waiting room, sleeping on makeshift beds Mother had made up. Twenty *volunteers* tried *to contain the blaze*. We'd watched from the car, where Dad and Adam said we should stay, in case the fire spread. Black and grey billowy clouds of smoke had risen over the hotel, the flakes of ash drifting down. Mom had to turn on the windshield wipers to clear them from the window. She was so afraid the fire would spread to the station. Ron Winton was small enough to curl up under the back window.

There had been a loud crackling, just before the walls of the hotel collapsed.

Cause unknown, but everyone knew who had caused the fire. Teenage Stan had been drinking, he'd caused the fire. He hadn't denied it.

The fire had sealed the fate of the station, seemingly giving the railway company the excuse they needed for shut-down, even though this was clearly all part of a national plan of closures, and then Dad had died, leaving Mom and my sister and me homeless. In due course, we'd been asked to vacate the premises. When Mom had to find work, I was left to look after Shirley, cook her dinner, make sure she'd done her homework, enforce the rules that Mom laid down. When there wasn't enough money coming in, I took up paper routes, worked in a vintage shop on weekends.

'It isn't fair that she lost her dad when she was so young,' Mom had said. 'You and I need to make sure she still has as normal and carefree a childhood as possible.'

I believed her then; I trusted that she knew best, even told myself over the years that it wasn't such a big deal, despite the fact that no one asked how I was managing.

All of those challenges and resentments erupted out of the fire. I turn on my side, stare at the aerial photo. Kick off the covers.

I will slip out of the house and drive away; it was a mistake to stay. Pretending, repressing around Massy, and then finding myself in Stan's room, his house, on his farm. I am supposed to be attending to my sister's estate, not letting myself get dragged back to a time I have tried so hard to forget. What had I read recently in some paper Jake had left lying around? Creatures either evolve or calcify.

My mind fills with racing thoughts. My leaving suddenly will upset Massy and George. There will be phone calls and explanations. The station closing had nothing to do with Stan, despite Mom blaming him for starting the fire and triggering the station closing. Stan's life really had nothing to do with mine. I've purposely made a life far away from the events of the past. Massy is my friend. Perhaps when Stan or Mom were still alive, we should have tried harder to come to some sort of clarity. *We, they.* It strikes me at this moment the impact of the we; I'd always felt it my responsibility, failure to bring resolution or unity out of the circumstances.

I wrap the trailing quilt about me and stand at the window watching the sun rise. I tell myself that I am capable of separating irrational emotion from the contents of this room. I am no longer the person that Hetty criticizes Isabel of being, someone who connects feelings with artifacts and who slows down the process of identifying and cataloguing. What I see in this room, and what Mom never knew, was a Stan beyond the one she had kept locked in a past. He had won trophies, created a successful farm, had happy grown children and a devoted wife.

This room, next to the bedroom Massy and Stan shared was a space, other than the barn or the fields, where a man could retreat to read and do his accounts. Perhaps deal with his own feelings of guilt and loss, and forgiveness. Unlike Massy, I do not set keepsakes on shelves—tokens of the life I had with my parents and then my sister. Everything is still in boxes, listed, and dated, waiting for a time when I can let go.

I wipe my face on the coverlet, at the hair that's stuck to my cheeks. I shuffle quietly to the bathroom, trying not to disturb anyone.

The dogs' nails click across the hardwood floor, as soon as they hear movement towards the door. I reach to the chair for my shirt and trousers. As the dogs wag their tails, sniff here and there for their master's scent, the space where I have slept becomes a light-filled room, and not a place meant to punish me or complicate the tasks I came to here to complete.

I open the kitchen screen door and let the dogs out, splash some cold water over my face, slip on Massy's clogs, and follow the dogs up the hill a short way. The sun is rising beyond the river. The dogs chase each other towards the pasture. There is the smell of sage in the dewy morning, and I think I see a grouse rise and fall in the underbrush. Prairie chickens, Dad called them. He'd brought them home for dinner. I walk a mile up the road, in the cool of the morning, talk to the dogs, call them to me and pat them when they obey, and slowly the painful memories that the morning's discoveries evoked begin to fade. I wander lazily back to the car, check Shirley's ashes, and take my laptop from the back seat. It needs charging. I miss my sons and want to connect with them. The morning walk, a cup of coffee, and my boys will reset my compass and set me back solidly in the present.

I set up my computer on the desk where Stan once did his books. As the computer's desktop settles all of the icons, my attention goes to the folder that I moved from Shirley's computer to my own. The folder contains an address book, emails, documents, and bookmarked sites. I transferred the folder to my computer months ago, as another task of my executor duties, and after a brief scan, assuming much of the information was private, had let it be.

I open a municipal map that Shirley has bookmarked, not unlike one I'd seen in Hall's office. I go on to Shirley's address file, and notice a group titled *Land Owners*. I've probably looked at it at some point, but I can't remember what it contains. When I open it, I notice that some of the names in this group match the names of those on the map, east and west of our grandparents' original homestead. More names in the address book, but only the names of the landowners whose land runs alongside the tracks are in the Land Owners group.

The names are unfamiliar to me. According to the dates, the emails started a year before Shirley's passing. Each name has its own corresponding file. I open the one with the largest number of emails. The correspondence, between a tspeers@ and Shirley is a series of back and forth conversations on buying back the land that had once belonged to the Speers family, but which decades ago had been sold to CN rail as right-of-way for a connecting line to go to the Yellow Head route, then rejoin the first cross-Canada CPR line.

One of the emails states they should encourage others to petition buying back their land from the rail line. In Shirley's outgoing mail and under *CN File*, I find what appears to be a copy of the letter Hall mentioned, and which his intern had finally disregarded. Shirley had scanned it and sent it to Speers. It reads: *Enclosed please find a copy of the sale of the land to CN by my grandparents. As CN has abandoned the rail line, I wish to purchase the land and rail on this line, which runs through the fifty acres which my family has retained.*

This must be what Hall singled out in his office. I search through the incoming mail files, but can't find a reply from the railway. My mind goes to the box Hall gave me. I retrieve the box from the car and spread the papers out around the floor. There is a massive amount of material. Magazine articles, graphs, and charts with statistics circled, part of a petition, even the articles on how Vancouver Island's railway struggled back into existence. There are pictures of short-line passenger systems cut from magazines, more brochures for train excursions, and business cards from companies that do feasibility studies for communities wanting to investigate the possibilities of sustaining a local rail line. Trust the lawyer's office to have made it seem as if they had done the work. I wonder if Shirley had left all of this with Hall and planned to collect it at some point in the future when she planned to go forward. Sticking to the bottom of the box is a blank envelope, seemingly over-looked by Hall's office. That would have been easy to do as it just seems to be a squashed bit of paper. I peel it off and open it to find a British Airways return ticket to London, no dates, just an open-ended ticket. It looks valid, but could have been mistaken for a receipt from another time. I put it back in the envelope and toss the envelope into my purse.

It still makes no sense. What is the point in buying back the land that was sold to CN rail so many decades ago? Could this be anything tangible to do with what Shirley had been working on? Was this why she'd said, it can be done, and it will be done? One way to find out is to drop this tspeers an email and ask. I compose a quick email.

My phone rings and I have to dig it out of my purse. I've forgotten to charge it.

'Margaret, oh there you are, I think you should get onto arranging a small reception for the advance man.' Typical of Hetty, maybe that is where I got it from. A woman who doesn't waste time on salutations.

'An old friend here has had an injury.'

'Well, who hasn't. Now, I'd prefer a small cocktail party off site, but maybe he should meet some of the regulars here.'

'Hetty, my phone's probably going to die.'

'I can send someone to the airport to pick you up.'

'No.'

'Well of course, Jake can pick you up.' Then her idea of being understanding. 'I've been thinking. Does this money of your sister's have to go to a railway? What about a donation to the museum in your sister's name? I see a large plaque with her name on it. And by the way, your displays still haven't been taken down.'

I regret confiding my dilemma. It doesn't sound like Hetty is joking. I usually capitulate, so am surprised at my assertiveness.

'Have Isabel take photos of the current windows, and slowly start dismantling the window displays of the '40s through '70s. She knows where to store the items. She is well capable of managing that, and it will all be good experience for her. And by the time she is done, I should be back.'

'Where are you?'

'Write this down, Hetty. Photos, dismantle, store. Got it? I'll call in a day or two.'

'You won't have a job in a day or two.'

I don't buckle under her threat.

'You once did this yourself. Just remind Isabel to only do one display at a time. And she'll have to do some explaining to the foundation ladies that visit on Thursdays. Get them excited about the Italians. The foundation women will have my head, if so much as a Maple Leafs jersey is out of place without explanation. Hetty, you can charm the delegate.'

'Margaret. Margaret.'

My phone dies. Lucky me.

I send a quick email to Jake, telling him about Massy's injury, and of my plan to stay at the farm until Massy is more mobile.

A quick email, as well, to each of the boys. With the emails, a photograph attached of a wheat field, half green wheat and half blue sky. I haven't had any emails from them. I take it as a good sign, and that their real lives are keeping them too engaged to write.

I desperately need a coffee, and now I am beginning to wonder if George and Massy stayed up so late that they are sleeping in. I put on the coffee, and through the kitchen screen, watch the wrens and warblers take turns at the bird feeder. I mentally review all the notifications that were attended to when Shirley passed away, banks, credit cards, utilities, the government, friends in an address book, who may or may not have seen an obituary. Was there mail from the CN rail company? Shirley's email account has been closed; there is no possible way for CN to reply to her. I feel I've been meticulous with my records. I haven't before now gone through all of Shirley's email contacts. I pace through the kitchen and notice the note from George under a fridge magnet. *Heading up to the lake, see you tonight.* How had he snuck out without my hearing? And both my rental and Massy's car are still parked in the yard.

I decide to give Jake a quick call. Despite the time change, he will be up and making his breakfast. The phone rings half a dozen times, but there is no answer.

Massy hops on one leg into the kitchen using a rain stick as a cane. She turns it over, and when I hand her George's note, the seeds of the rain stick rushing to the bottom accompany the downturn of her mouth. She pours herself a cup of coffee, and I carry it to the table for her. I hear the announcing of an email coming in on my computer.

'Just give me five minutes,' I say to Massy, as I get to my computer. The in-box has seven new messages, most of them from tspeers.

I open the first and read:

'I wondered why all the emails from Shirley suddenly stopped. Then I heard that she'd passed away. For a while, I didn't bother doing anything about buying back the right-of-way that my great-grandparents had also sold to CN. But then I thought, why not, I might as well own that land. CN doesn't need it. So, I got in touch with their lawyer and they sold it back to me for the same amount they bought it. 200$—that's a laugh. And Joe Yablowski did the same as me, and so did Frank Pankratz, and some others down the line. I haven't checked yet with all the folks Shirley sent letters to, but now that the Grain Board is gone, we're going to see about leasing or buying the tracks to get our grain to market.'

And in the next email, as if in afterthought:

'I never knew her before this. She sure kept on about the right-of-way though. I am sorry she ran out of time. At first, I ignored the information she sent about a southern co-op rail system, but last fall I finally headed down with a couple of guys to meet with their execs, to see if we can figure out how to form our own rail system to haul grain. Crazy idea, eh?'

There is a contact phone number at the end of the message.

If there is a southern co-op rail system already in place, that might do, but tspeers is talking about a system to haul grain. It would be easier to drop the money into something that already exists, but it still doesn't seem to me that was what Shirley was trying to do. Should *a rail line like the one that Dad believed in*, be in the vicinity of Plover?

Massy limps into the side office room, 'I haven't seen this many papers spread around Stan's study since he and Ron and Carl were trying to figure out how to go to organic farming.' She swipes her finger over the desk. 'Sorry, I haven't dusted. I use the kitchen table now for doing household accounts, and no one's slept in here since the kids stayed over last Christmas.' She one-foot hops back into the kitchen.

'Massy, I didn't take in last night that I was going to be sleeping in Stan's office.' I don't mention the memories that have been triggered.

Massy is flipping through 'The Western Producer,' a magazine for farmers and all things agriculturally related.

'I suppose the room might be a better fit for George, but with no door between the study and my bedroom—I hope you slept all right.' She looks over the top of the paper. 'Why do you think he took off like that?'

'I had the best sleep in months, and from what I observed out at the lake, George is probably answering a call. He'll come home to roost.'

'He never mentioned anything last night, and he didn't take the car. It's a bit of a walk from here to the lake. Maybe he hitch-hiked.'

'It sounds like he's walked all over the world. For him, this is probably a morning's stroll.'

I pick up the classified section of the farm magazine, 'Do you think there's a section in here with locomotives for sale?'

Massy doesn't look up. 'I believe what you are referring to is called rolling stock. Page 24.'

16. Goods

I am hopeful from what I have uncovered in Shirley's files, but I still need to double-check the facts. If there is anything in what Shirley was pursuing, any remote chance that I could even partially fulfill the obligation that she has imposed on me in her letter, then it is best to make sure the possibilities are sound before telling anyone else. And anyway, Massy probably assumes I am joking about searching for locomotives.

It seems to me that the morning is greener than the day before, as if the trees that delayed opening their leaves are now in a hurry to reach out for the sun's rays. West Coast cherry blossoms, crocuses, and snowdrops delight in February, and I have come to take for granted the year-round green, uncommon to most of the rest of Canada. I've forgotten how dramatic is the change from spring to summer that happens in other parts of the country.

Massy and I sip coffees on the deck and try to interpret what the geese along the river are saying to each other in their double clucking.

'It's a territorial conversation,' Massy says. 'Fighting over females, who can forage where, exchanging flying distance to the next field.'

'I suppose geese flying overhead in V-formation inspire more poetry than geese in the midst of territorial squabbling,' I offer. We'll ask George when he returns.

'What's on today's agenda?' Massy asks.

'I've got to get into Winging and pay the land taxes. I'm going to go over more of Shirley's papers. And I need to fetch some clothes from the hotel.'

We share a brunch of boiled eggs and thick slices of toasted homemade bread. Massy directs me to take pickerel fish out of the freezer for dinner, 'a treat for George,' and around 12:30, after testing the weight-bearing strength on her foot, she gives in to ice, a book, and a nap, confident that a rest will improve her ankle enough for her to soon accompany George on his studies of the plovers. As much as I am also looking forward to seeing him again, I suspect we may not see George for a few days, having witnessed his solitary contentment at the lake, but I keep my thoughts to myself.

The first phone call I make is to the lawyer handling the railway side of things in possible transfers of CN right-of-way back to the owners of the adjacent lands. The next call is to T. Speers.

The voice on the answering machine quips, 'Hey. It's all about the hay. Leave a message.' I assume the young-sounding voice in the message to be T. Speer's wife or daughter. No matter what else interests them, farmers follow the weather's dictates. Everything else waits. The third call I make is to Gerard Hall, asking his office to locate a railway contact for me. I want to speak to the person who can tell me what it will cost to buy the railway tracks from Plover to the mainline connector.

If you are reading this, it means I have not been able to see it through. I know you will finish what I started.

It would be so much simpler if Shirley had asked me to deliver her money to a designated charity. Ocean research, health initiatives, the environment, any number of organizations could use an infusion. If she had read Berton's *Last Spike*, hadn't she realized the monumental task, the frustrations, the fighting, the number of people involved? But as Adam had reminded me, Shirley didn't back down.

Some of the memorabilia for the museum comes by way of executors carrying out the wishes of their relatives, a much quicker *accomplishing* in terms of an executor's obligation, once the grieving and sorting are compartmentalized. 'My aunt wanted the museum to have these,' someone might say, delicately passing over a collection of silver tea service, war medals, or old clocks, almost as if they'd found a place for their aunt to reside along with her things. 'It isn't new,' Hetty has said, 'from the Victoria and Albert to the Smithsonian, museum collections aren't just about managing history, they also exist as part of our inability to let go. But let's keep that to ourselves, shall we. Job security.'

I don't entirely agree. After all, once a month Hetty and I take turns scouting auction houses. There are plenty of people who will let go if the price is right. My work is one thing, my obligation to my sister quite another. Going through all of Shirley's computer files and looking in depth at her railway research motivates me. I am feeling a little more in control. Why didn't it come to me sooner to apply the methods I use at the museum? Acquisition plus research equals display. Shirley has done most of the research; I just have to get the track (acquisition)—an engine and a passenger car, but I'd ask Adam about that—and then find the people to run the display, a new railway line. My equation doesn't allow for variables.

I hum along to the music on the radio, as I wash up the breakfast dishes and the wine glasses from the previous night. I glance around the kitchen for a calendar. The money from Shirley's investments will have been deposited into my own account by now. That will put a fat, if temporary, smile on Jake's face, until he learns I will be the only one with access to these funds.

When I went to the bank to take out money for my trip, the bank had set up a display for the soon-to-be-in-circulation, newly minted hundred-dollar bill. Poor Sir Robert Borden's polymer face-lift had looked out at me as if from behind a Plexiglas window. More punishment it seemed than reward for championing a people-owned Canadian railway. The new plastic money is harder to counterfeit, almost impossible to destroy, and smells faintly of Quebec maple syrup, yet it will always only represent a promissory note.

For a moment, I delve into what it would be like to have so much money that you didn't really know the amount. The countless hundred-dollar bills could buy a holiday cottage, yearly weeks on a beach, anything that we didn't have to save for. As for the boys, well, an injection of cash could pay off student loans, perhaps be a down payment for places of their own. On the other hand, I remember how Mom struggled those first years after the station to keep a roof over our heads, and Shirley in her adult years, though able to make ends meet, went without the bonus of Jake and I managing with two salaries. Why should I suddenly benefit from a windfall when they had never been able to?

'You don't have to be the protective older sister or the dutiful daughter any longer,' Jake had said more than once over the years, when Mom looked to me for support, or Shirley and I argued over her indulging my boys with spoils I wouldn't give them. Yet no matter his good intentions, he'd never fully understand why Shirley's investment wasn't mine to keep.

I rinse off the dishes and set them to dry.

Shirley's letter stated that she had no idea how much was in the account, and perhaps it really hadn't been important to her, but I still couldn't understand why she hadn't told me. Or even given herself some small once-in-a-lifetime gift.

After university, I'd felt smothered, weary of Mom's rancour, moved away as far as I could—an island seemed ideal. Shirley stayed on to be near Mom. Lived on her own for a while, but didn't want Mom to be lonely, and they had soon moved in together. When Shirley was offered the job in Vancouver, she'd insisted they make the move together. Mom had protested leaving the familiarity of place, but the negotiation and settlement was that her grandsons would be at university there, and she'd be able to see them every week.

And she had. One after the other, they had gotten to know their aunt and grandmother away from Jake and me. Shirley had slipped them a twenty-dollar bill whenever they went to visit, and their grandmother had made home-cooked dinners on Sundays when they didn't have time to get back to the island for weekends. Some of their time at university had overlapped, one son just about to graduate as the one behind him arrived, and so they had also gotten to know each other away from Jake and me. I was jealous when they chose to stay and spend time with their aunt instead of coming home weekends. It had felt that all of our lives I'd had to give in to what was best for her. And of course, even now she was extracting space and time from my own affairs. But why did I begrudge my sister these small benefits, when I seemed to have it all—husband, kids, a home to call our own.

You are forced into relationships with sibs when you live under the same roof, play together, ally against parents, cover up for each other. And in my case, partly raise my younger sister, because of the many hours Mom had to work.

After I moved away, Shirley and I never seemed to do anything together. I wish now we had both made more of an effort, that there was consolation in remembering the tilt of Shirley's head as we studied a map of the London tube, or our laughter, full of rum punch on a catamaran sailing into a tropical sunset.

I pump a drop of lavender hand lotion onto my hands. Shirley's hands, when I reached the hospital, had been limp on a sterile sheet, manicured nails, paint-stripped thumbs, so the nurses could read the oxygenation by the nail beds. When I had bent to kiss her hand, it smelled of garlic toast.

The dishes wash and dry with little effort, as is always the way in someone else's kitchen. I take the tea towel out to a small clothes hanger on the deck and drape it to dry in the warm sun.

The house is quiet, Massy asleep, dogs now in and sprawled at the foot of her bed. The items that Shirley gave Hall are organized in stacks on the floor, and I am about to look through Shirley's notes yet again. The telephone rings, and I moved quickly to answer it before it wakes Massy.

'Hall here, looking for Margaret,' he says.

'Yes,' I whisper, 'speaking.'

'I've got that information you were looking for.'

'That was fast.' I take up a pencil and paper to jot down the information.

'It seems a salvage company has offered a bid on several abandoned rail lines throughout the province, and the Plover section is one of them.'

'Are you saying they would tear them up? Is it final?'

'No, not final, but I don't see a woman and her letter standing between a salvage corporation and the CNR.'

Why does he keep doing that? Making assumptions, drawing conclusions, dead-ending me?

'I imagine you want to be on your way soon. I could arrange transfer titles in a day, if you reverse the promise on the trust land and sell the lot. Or are you going to transfer those last fifty acres of land to the VLT?'

I picture him looking at his municipal map, with coloured marker at the ready to document the change in land ownership. The Wheelers would cover over the sloughs. He would get a commission. That's what Massy had meant when she'd said Hall would get an envelope of cash. I won't be pressured by him. If Shirley was going to buy back the right-of-way, I had better own the land. What was it George had asked me at the lake? Something about my always thinking before being spontaneous.

'I have decided to keep it. I'm hanging onto it.' The words come out as if someone else were saying them.

'But—'

'Who do I have to call next?'

I write down the number he gives me, and Adam enters my thoughts. I must see Adam again. He needs to know what I've discovered.

A quick note to Massy, and I am on the road to Winging, and then back into Saskatoon and to the retirement home to see Adam. The stack of papers I've been piling up for months have turned into destinations.

Adam is doing push-ups when I arrive. '55, 56, 57. Oh, hello, just finishing up.'

'I couldn't manage five push-ups, let alone 55, and you aren't even breathing hard.'

The television is on, but the sound turned off. Some contest or other.

'One hundred every day, and a 100 sit-ups and squats.' He goes to his bathroom and wipes his face and neck with a hand towel. 'I do my fitness workout, 3BX now, and they watch me. See there.' He points to the screen where a judge is holding up a placard with 10/10. 'Get one of those most days.'

I observe that the scores could vary, but his reply is that any score is motivation, and he finds it amusing that the judges face him and not the contestants.

'Anyway,' he continues, 'the show is about the judges. I refuse to listen to their yammering. Look at those faces. Ever been to a wax museum?'

I don't watch much television. I wonder if that will change when I am Adam's age.

'Drink?' he offers.

'No thanks. I can't stay long. I have an appointment.'

He pours himself a glass of water from a small water-filtering pitcher. 'I hope the old CN hotel is living up to its past glories.'

'Yes, it does. Did. I mean, I've been staying out at Massy Winton's.'

'She married Stan.'

'Yes.'

'Read his obituary in the paper. Jean ever let go of all of that business?'

'No, not really.'

'Sometimes it's easier to get through things than over them.' He seems to wait for me to respond. 'I hope her anger didn't affect you girls.'

I shift gears to why I've come back to see him. 'I've been going through some of Shirley's files. Did she ever tell you she was going to buy back the CN right-of-way land on our grandparents' old homestead, and that they might have thrown in the tracks?'

'The last time she was out here, I was away somewhere. I received a few letters from her, but she mostly wrote about your mom and dad.'

An aide comes by offering tea and coffee. Adam declines, but I accept a Styrofoamed black coffee.

'There are quite a few emails going back and forth between Shirley and her potential co-conspirators, and a conversation with a T Speers.'

'Not computer savvy. Couldn't really help you there. But Speers... Speers... he might have been one of the farmers along the line.'

'My lawyer says the tracks are going for salvage, Adam. How fast can that happen? What should I do?'

'I can get my hands on a locomotive.' He gets up and shuts the window. 'How are the tracks looking?'

'Weedy.'

'Gonna need a mower, and a ballast regulator. I can probably put a crew together to clear the tracks. Give me a couple of days.'

'There won't be any tracks to clear.' Standing in the small room in a place where residents have come to watch game shows on TV, I stop. My morning's optimism fizzles. How impossible this all is, foolish really.

When he sits down again, Adam places his pinkie fingers on either side of his mouth and draws it down into a frown. 'Just like when you were a kid. Your face would take on that exact same look, and we'd know you were riveted. Jean and Neal couldn't get you to come up for air if you were busy with your John Glenn scrapbook or some collection or other. Still have all those Beatles bubblegum cards?'

'I wish,' I say, as I exaggerate a smile and raise my eyebrows, thrown a little by his recollection of me as a child. Adam pulls a pen from his shirt pocket and an address book from a drawer and begins to make a list.

'Okay,' he says, 'since I last saw you, I've been asking around to see who is alive and kicking. Lemme give you the goods. I know a conductor, and Gib knows a young-ish engineer.'

He doesn't seem to be listening to a thing I am saying. How old would this crew of his be? I picture zombies in black-striped overalls staggering down a railway track. Probably from some movie one of my sons watched. Wouldn't there be regulations we'd have to meet? If it is anything like the museum, the red tape will be endless. The furrows in the corners of my mouth reflect in the mirror. 'That's my resting neutral face,' I defend.

Adam is completely absorbed in his notes, talking to himself, counting on his fingers, saying something about batteries. His expression turns to one of pained bewilderment and then he says, 'I'm going to make some calls. Say, do you remember Chester? He was a good friend to your Dad too.'

'The Cree drayman? Adam, he passed away years ago.'

'No, no, he's got a granddaughter.'

We seem to be going in circles.

I suddenly feel guilty for bringing my executor responsibilities to the doorstep of this dear man. It's been so wonderful reconnecting with him, I didn't notice on my first visit. There is the possibility that he is dealing with some form of dementia.

He hands me a slip of paper with a list. 'This should help.' His television show is back from commercial; a singer is mouthing some words, and then the camera returns to the judge's faces.

'Till tomorrow,' Adam says, shutting off the television.

He whistles, about to uncap a Löwenbräu. He's had another union brother deposit since my last visit I guess.

'Wait, wait,' he stops, mid-uncapping. 'I found a couple of books I want you to have. This one shows the most beautiful stations in the world.' He flips to some turned corners. 'Here's the Gare du Nord in Paris, the Kuala Lumpur Station, just look at this Chhatrapati Shivaji Terminus in Mumbai. Lots of them. Might inspire you.'

'I'll be sure to check them out next time I'm in the vicinity,' I reply.

'And I thought Shirley was the funny one. Keep it. This one isn't really a book, but a compilation of short lines in England that have been recaptured. Look, see this one at Mountsorrel in Leicestershire. A branch passenger train, joins a double track main line. All accomplished by locals. There's talk of others too, Fleetwood, Leven's railway in Scotland. Good models for us.' He forces the books into my hands.

I tell him I will try to visit before going home. I catch myself about to speak a half octave higher, 'Remember. Two before lunch,' and stop myself. He may have minded me when I was younger, but that is no reason for me to be treating him now like a child.

I slip the list into my pocket, and from my rental car, make a couple of phone calls, one to Alan Tachuk at the municipal office in Winging asking him to arrange a meeting with the municipal councilors, and another to tspeers, asking if we can meet tonight or tomorrow. Then at 3:30, I find myself on the top floor of the highest building in Saskatoon, on my way to the office of the assistant manager of CNR's operations for the Prairie Rail Division.

While I wait, I read over the one page that I've written and am about to present. I organize my words for the elevator pitch, in case the meeting is brief. I probably should have waited to meet with him, come up with tactical strategies to convince him, but from what Hall told me, there was no time to lose. I rehearse. 'I will immediately pay cash for the purchase of the forty miles of rail line tracks from Plover to the Saskatoon connector. Turning those rails over to salvage would be a travesty.' I wish I'd worn the business suit I'd arrived in, but it is now rolled up at the bottom of my suitcase. A quick trip to the bathroom; at least I can touch up the lipstick.

The assistant manager of operations looks barely thirty. He hasn't put on his suit jacket to meet with me; it hangs on the back of his chair. My eye goes to the crisp ironed line down his blue sleeves. No ring on his left hand, tattoo on his right thumb. I made the appointment by my name; perhaps he thinks I am a journalist looking for an interview to cover a story.

'Thank you for seeing me on such short notice.'

He is attentive and curious about my wish to buy the tracks and preserve them, but he also looks like he might burst into laughter at any moment. His polished black shoes strike a note that I can't identify.

'I'm assuming by your coming here that you have worked out several details, that there is a considerable groundswell behind this. Have you set up a corporation or a foundation of sorts?' he asks. 'Do you have a website that I could view?'

It is the reference to a website that throws me. I'm not used to this kind of scrutiny, considering my position at the museum.

'Well, as we are fairly new, the Plover Railway Line Inc.' (Inc. might make me sound on top of things) 'is still in the process of designing its website.'

Do I have any idea of the cost involved, that an offer has already been made? Have I consulted a lawyer? Do I know that several farmers along that line have already bought back the right-of-way bordering their farm properties? Have I estimated insurance costs? Carried out green studies? What about service structures and maintenance crew?

'Would you at least submit my proposal for consideration? Today please.' I pause to ground myself, and face him with a look of determined control, when the whole time my brain is scrambling for another angle. I sit forward and invoke the tone I use to negotiate with the museum's board, and pull from my bag of tricks the word *envision*.

'Those tracks were laid over a century ago. They are a part of the land. It will take—someone like you to *envision* their future.' I quickly try to evaluate his demographic, and hear desperation turn to stupid as I point to his thumb.

'They are our national tattoo. As important as that is to you. You wouldn't cut that out.' And then I run out of steam. That's it, I sigh. It's all I have.

He hands me his card, says he will look into it, but is fairly certain that the board of directors may have little say in the deal.

'After all, this Canadian rail line is now a subsidiary of an American rail company. Follow up with a letter.'

My gut tells me he is smirking all the way back to his office, either out of amusement or mischief at being flattered. As I wait at the elevator, I notice that most of the cognoscenti occupying the glassed-in offices are the same age as the young man whose card I now hold in my hand. Not much older than my sons. Great. In minutes, I imagine, they will all be making toot-toot noises, pulling air whistles, and making jokes about the 3:30 appointment who fell off the rails, is off the beaten track, or some such.

As I enter the elevator, two of those young men slip in before the doors close and ride down the first two floors with me. They show no interest in me, whatsoever. By the sounds of it, they must be young fathers of toddlers, and are preoccupied in a discussion on who is the best engine in the *Thomas the Tank* series. The first says it is 'Emily,' the other says it is 'Ryan,' but before they exit to their floor the young men agree that 'Rex' is the best. 'Oh yeah!'

17. Coupling

For some reason, the elevator stops on every floor as it descends, and at each stop, the automated voice announcing the floor level is fighter Shirley, her turn of phrase encouraging me that down is not out. *Ding*—seven—you're going to have to go over his head. *Ding*—six—it'll take more than a few edgy questions to finish us off. *Ding*—five—you should have slapped on a little more lipstick. *Ding*—four—*our national tattoo?* toot, toot, drink o'clock. Three, two, ground. Ejected out into the street. Alone once more.

A small tornado of swirling air caught between the city buildings throws dust in my face, adding injury to insult, and I cough, try to grab at a loose hair tickling my tongue. The smallest things, a hair on the tongue or an errant eyelash demand our fight or flight attention, while not until prolonged wretchedness manifests in ill health or broken relationships do we pause and take stock of bigger things, more important things, if even then. I spin round—cannot remember where I've parked the car—and note the mall entrance façade of the former Canadian National station that I'd ignored when entering the mall. It won't be in Adam's book, the mall franchise marquees have defaced its history and most of its dignity. Perhaps his book notes railway stations the world over gone from bustling centres of travel to malls or markets. The light changes at the intersection, and as I hurry across the street, I feel the firm touch of a hand at the small of my back. Before I can move away, I recognize the voice.

'Might be another storm coming.'

'George. What are you doing here?'

He lifts a bag, and points back in the direction of the shop. 'Buying chocolates.'

We cross the street, neither of us really knowing where we are going, but carrying on in the same direction.

'I'd forgotten that Dr. Simpson and I were meeting this morning to examine the plover nests. He wanted to upload my pictures onto his system, so we came back into town together.'

He must have slipped out of the house before dawn to walk all the way back to the lake, likely before I was blubbering to myself in Stan's study.

He hesitates before adding, 'I planned to telephone and say I'd stay at the hotel tonight.'

Perhaps it is the crowded street, but my hand automatically goes to the crook of his elbow. 'Oh no you don't.' I am going to hold him to his promise of cooking dinners. 'There is a plate of very fine pickerel fish waiting to be fried.'

'There is?' He rests his hand over mine and says, 'I am parched. Ale, or perhaps a shandy?'

'Pub up ahead,' I note. 'The Dickens.'

'Prairie Blighty,' he tells me. 'No one in Lancashire believes me when I tell them this place exists.'

'Post-colonial confection is everywhere. Victoria boasts three Oirish bars.'

Lancashire, he said. So, is that where he lives? I assumed he might be Oxbridge as I hadn't noticed a pronounced northern accent, though, now that I think about it, at the lake I'd noticed the odd 'im' and 'er' rather than 'him' and 'her,' and his a's were more Canadian than posh 'ah.' I reach into my purse.

'As I recall, you provided the tea last time. My treat. And look, I've got my keys.'

It isn't a quick ale. It is two pints of Boddingtons, a shandy for me and a large plate of well malt-vinegared chips to share. The Dickens pub is dimly lit for an afternoon, and the seats smell faintly of purple gas, the tax-exempt fuel I've read that farmers are in danger of losing. The original pub owner's decor has been lost to several owners since, despite a picture hanging above the bar of a younger Queen. Dickens book-title posters at the entry are now a palimpsest for small batch brewery advertisements. Deer antlers hang above a smoke-stained *Tale of Two Cities* and fishing rods are nailed criss-cross over *Great Expectations*.

Guinness is on tap, alongside Molson and a local beer called *Whit Ale*. The bar maid, who has streaked pink through the ends of her hair, says she has never heard of a bitter, but tells George she can throw a shot of tequila into a Guinness if he'd like. With the exception of a couple of lost-looking souls playing the lottery machines, we have the place to ourselves.

George takes a big swallow, wipes the foam from his top lip, and bites into a chip, 'Mash tastes the same everywhere, but chips never do.'

'Someone in New York once told me you can't get a good pastrami sandwich west of Colorado. The water effects the taste of the bread.'

I relax into my chair and wonder if this is a watering hole for the executives I've just left behind. I take some satisfaction in knowing they are still shut up in offices, while I am having a drink with this handsome man.

'I don't remember ever being in this place.'

'I've been coming here for as long as I've been visiting the province. Heard a rumour that Prince Philip once graced the premises.'

'Really?'

'Probably an urban legend. Although, they have visited this city a few times.' He sprinkles more pepper. 'Mind?'

'No.' I sprinkle on more malt.

I am happy to once again be alone with him. As when we were at the lake, I am more than just comfortable with him, I seem to trust him. I tell George about re-examining Shirley's computer files, in light of the request in her letter, and the possibility of several farmers alongside the Plover tracks now taking back the ownership of the railway's rights-of-way. I tell him how unprepared I was meeting with the young executive.

'I was so optimistic this morning, but his face spelled defeat.'

George encourages. 'Don't read too much into his demeanor.'

'What if local train lines in this country really are a romantic notion of the past? With only a few here and there exceptions.

Either corporate nationals for hauling grain and freight, or a mechanism for monied tourists to see passing landscapes.'

'Do you think romance was the reason your sister was so determined?'

I see Shirley's *Boulevard of Broken Dreams*. 'She wasn't so easily corrupted. I just don't understand. We've plenty of tracks and lines, why don't we serve the small communities the way Great Britain does?'

'And pay billions in subsidies?'

My shandy has almost disappeared and I'd really like a second, but I have to be able to drive, and so sip on the unrequested water the bar maid has delivered.

George sips his beer. 'Sometimes we try too hard to answer the big questions. It seems to me, if you don't mind my observations?'

'Of course not. Go on.'

'Just that you may have to ask yourself the smaller, or rather more immediate question of why you want to do this. It may be for reasons different from your sister's. Not just carrying out an obligation to her.'

'What did you mean? It's my duty as her executor. I'm being loyal to her request.'

'Ah. Queen and country.'

'I suppose, if you put it that way.'

'Do you think your father would have wanted to be remembered for a train once again running from your home?'

'Home? Haven't you heard? Once you leave, there is no going back.'

'And yet nearly 40% of the world's birds migrate each year.'

'Maybe the ones who return adapt to change.'

I could argue and remind him that that figure may continue to decline according to his studies of habitat affecting migration, but the afternoon does not warrant politics and evolves away from debate. I tell him instead about Adam.

'His body once knew that track so well, he could walk it with his eyes shut. And now, well, despite seeming very vital, I've probably just confused the dear old man.'

'Your description puts me in mind of "The Signalman".' George points to a pegboard. 'Ever come across the stories?'

I look to where George points, but can't quite make out the row of letters, some of them so badly scratched away. The letters seem to spell Nuby Unct—something or other. I've ignored all of the reminders for my yearly eye exam, but make up my mind to have my eyesight tested when I get home. Time to forgo vanity for vision.

'It used to say *Mugby Junction*, also one of Boz Dicken's,' says George.

'I don't know it, but I did study *Great Expectations* at university.'

'Dickens once made part of an American railroad journey to your Niagara Falls. He wrote his rail stories after a train he had been on derailed. I'll try to locate a copy for you, if you'd like.'

'Not something I would have associated with Dickens.'

'Perhaps your sister was a little like him.'

'Charles Dickens?'

'He may have had his own romantic notions of trains, but he was also curiously fascinated by the technology of the future.'

'I really don't know if Shirley cared about technology.'

Conversation evaporates; there is no awkward silence. We are in a local pub, but for all that we notice, we could just as well be on the Las Ramblas or alongside the Rialto.

'My apologies. I haven't properly conveyed my condolences. I'm sorry that your sister has passed on. I'm sorry for you both.'

'Thank you. Do you have brothers or sisters?'

'I have a brother. Nearly twins, born just 9 months apart. He's a photographer. Years ago, we pooled our pounds sterling and bought a London flat, though neither of us lives there.' He opens his wallet and shows me an antiquated looking key. 'If you ever felt the urge for a walk along South Bank, you'd be more than welcome.'

A lottery machine lets out a series of bells, signaling a win, and a woman in a furry hat turns and smiles towards us, giving a thumbs up.

I swirl the dregs in my glass. 'Perhaps I should take a trip to England or Europe—maybe ride the Eurostar for some fresh insights,' I say half-heartedly.

'The Eurostar wouldn't tell you about local lines, but if it's the Virgin at 'off peak' to Lancaster, I'm your man.'

My cell phone rings. I consider not answering it.

'George? No, this is Margaret? Are you sure you have the right number?'

George grimaces, and in a poor charade, writes a number symbol on a napkin, indicates himself, and points to me.

'Yes. I'm Margaret.'

I switch to speaker phone.

'George tells me you are interested in some old railway lines or stations? My usual ramble goes by the old Quorn and Woodhouse station up here in Leicestershire. I walk up to where they're restoring the Mountsorrel line. What is it you are wanting to know?'

'I'm not sure.'

George leans in. 'Hello Tom? George here. Do you know if this came about with private funding? How many folks did it take to get it off the ground?'

'In part, but also some government monies as well as endowments. When you back here? We need someone to give a talk on night migrations.'

'Won't be long now. I'll call as soon as I'm back.'

'You can tell your lady friend I'll go by the Mountsorrel rail restoration and gather some more details from the person in charge.'

After Tom hangs up, George explains.

'Sorry, last night after you went to bed, I emailed some of my birder friends. Massy gave me your phone number. I thought it might be easier if they contacted you directly. I apologize, I should have said.'

I reach out across the table and touch his hand. 'That was so thoughtful of you.'

We stare at each other and I pull my hand away.

'If there are government monies here to be had as well as donations, there might be enough to initiate a study, or even lay some groundwork.'

'A couple of years ago, an ornithologist friend and I had lunch on the Gwili steam train in Wales, and I know there are plans for expansion. They rescued their trackbed, that much I know. Not entirely what you're after, but you might also get a call from someone named Anna, over in Aberystwyth.'

'Do you think we could find out how they went about taking over the track? Aber where?'

'Aberystwyth. Wales. Last time I was there, they were filming a detective TV show.'

We look up to the ceiling and see above us another set of antlers dangling precariously, and without saying a word, he picks up our near-empty glasses and moves us to a back-corner booth. We sit in meditative silence for a long while. Dickens no longer features in our mood. Sibs, books, and trains slip away. George goes for his second pint, sips, and then takes out his camera. He leans in close to show a picture of me that he took at the lake. I am standing near the shore watching the approaching storm clouds. The picture looks almost black and white.

He looks at it for some time, then says, 'You are beautiful.'

I feel myself blushing. Most women counter to deflect a compliment. I'm no different, but this time I don't.

'Dr. Simpson pointed out that you are the first woman he's ever seen in my photos.'

'Am I really?'

'Yes. Yes.'

Those cool grey eyes.

'Your hair still smells wonderfully of the lake.'

I tuck my hair behind my ears. 'I'm so glad I went for a swim. And watched the storm. How clever you are to keep a tent there.'

He reaches under the table and takes my hand.

His look seems to be asking for my permission, and I look at him, wondering what it would be like to kiss him. He slides even closer to me in the booth and then breathes a kiss onto my neck.

I lean back into the cushion behind me, feeling my heart beating in my chest, while he is still holding my hand. And then I lean in and kiss him.

I'm as surprised as he is. We open our eyes briefly, smile, and then let go. This time it is a long, deeply satisfying exchange.

I look up and realize that though we are in a secluded area, this is very much a public space. He immediately agrees.

'I always keep a room at the hotel across the street. As a home base,' he says.

'But I'm there too. I haven't cancelled my reservation to stay at Massy's.'

We don't hold hands crossing the street, but we are as close, side by side, as two people who want to be together walking down a street can be.

He walks me to my door. 'I'll just pop up to my room for a couple of things and be right back.' He pulls me in close and we share another indulgent kiss. Then he places his palm on my pounding heart.

It is the fastest shower I've ever taken, but I don't wash my hair. I slip into the robe that offers surrender, and I wait at the door.

There is a knock. I anticipate his arms pulling me in.

'Jake.'

'I thought I'd surprise you. Massy said you'd probably be here gathering up your things to stay at hers. I'm on my way to Toronto to the conference and I've got a 3-hour layover, so I just grabbed a cab and dashed over.'

The stairwell door down the hall opens, and I watch as George stops short.

'How long did you say your stop over was, dear?' I say loud enough for the entire floor to hear.

'Just long enough for a quick drink.'

Jake pecks me on the cheek and enters the hotel room. I look down the hall at George, my head heavy on the door. He lingers for a few seconds, and then backs away into the stairwell.

I quickly put on some fresh clothes, while Jake pours us each a half glass of wine from the mini-bar.

'Has the money been deposited yet?'

'No. Not yet.'

'I could probably slip over to the lawyer's for you right now.' He looks to the bedside clock.

'Not now, Jake.'

He changes the subject to landscaping, or some repairs or other around the house that he's tackled, while I fuss with some make-up. I can't make out through the partially closed bathroom door much of what he is saying. I spend most of his time with me going in and out of the bathroom, at one point sitting on the toilet almost breaking down, feeling like a bungie jumper in free fall suddenly yanked back to reality. And then I walk him down to the cab. If he thinks I am acting a little off, it is no more so than I have been for the last six months.

There is a cool obligatory hug goodbye. 'See you soon.'

'Travel safe.'

From the lobby, I ring George's room.

'I'm sorry,' I tell him.

'Don't. Please, don't apologize.'

'Before, with you, I was only thinking of what I wanted in that moment. Now all I can think of are consequences.'

'I don't want you to feel guilty about anything. And you need to know, I'm not looking for a quick shag.' I may not know a lot of British slang, but I get what he means.

'Massy will be expecting us. She'll be very suspicious and disappointed if we don't both go back. I'll be in the lobby in twenty minutes.'

'Of course. Alright. I'll come along in twenty.'

George suggests stopping for some wine. The drive back to Massy's is uncomfortable, at least for me. I feel foolish, and when George touches my hand, he quickly senses my discomfort. Neither of us speaks about our feelings. George notes some birds or other.

When we arrive back at Massy's, the yard is still, the dogs nowhere in sight. Massy's car is in the driveway, but she doesn't answer when I call out.

We go up the stairs and George puts the wine we've bought into the refrigerator. The house is a cool haven from the warm June day. I slip off my shoes, hold them in my hand as I pour a glass of water, then turn up the radio, the way I would if I were at home. It is a way to avoid any awkward conversation, non-coupling analysis, but George senses this and remains quiet. He comes towards me only once, but I walk out to the deck, and, from the front of the house, look left and right towards the river and neighbouring pastures. If she is nearby, Massy will have seen the dust on the gravel road and know that someone has arrived.

'I'll head in that direction.' I point east with one shoe as I put on the other. 'I might run into her coming back, though I can't imagine she's gone far with her ankle.'

'She may have gone off with her son, or even a neighbour. We have time to talk.'

George washes his hands and stands drying them, staring at me.

'Can you do dinner?' I ask.

'Yes. I see there is some wild rice. I'll start that to go with the fish.' He shrugs. He seems diminished.

Sage and wild mustard scent the early evening air, and I follow a well-worn path running parallel to the river. Everything feels stripped away. Hours ago, I very nearly made the worst mistake possible in a marriage, but I don't blame George. He hadn't tried to take advantage. There had been something real between us. A longing? But for what? I have love in my life; I am loved. I'm not reckless, desperate, or unfulfilled. As for him? I can't say for sure.

This side of the acreage looks as if it has never been disturbed with tilling or planting, plentiful with short grass and sage. Farther along, I can see a barbed-wire fence, whose posts are slanting to the side. A time ago, it might have been to keep cattle in the pasture. I'm slowly meandering, trying to put distance between George and me.

Within minutes, Massy's aging canine best friends approach, panting and tails wagging, from around the corner of some Saskatoon berry bushes. Massy limps with a walking stick, one foot in a flip-flop, the bandaged one in a fat slipper.

I wave, and as soon as we make eye contact, I explain in one long breath that I've seen Adam and met with the executive who told me the rails between Plover and the Saskatoon connector are to be salvaged.

'He may have been all of thirty years old. He asked me if there was a *groundswell* and if we had a website. I made up a name, called us the Plover Railway Line, Inc. but honestly, I think I just made a fool of myself.

'Oh, and Jake stopped by on his way to Toronto. I was just grabbing my things to bring them out here.'

Massy stops and flexes her foot, taking the weight off her sore ankle.

'Did you get my note?' I ask, when Massy looks away without replying. She is withdrawn. Something has changed since the relaxed evening of the night before and our morning of coffee.

'Do you remember Adam, the section man?'

The dogs' tails smack against my legs. I bend to acknowledge the dogs, with a scratch behind the ears, and a pat on the back, and then they are away.

'Of course I remember Adam.' Massy sits down on the grass, and begins to rub her ankle. 'He came to Stan's funeral.' She looks towards the house.

I follow her gaze. 'Guess who else I ran into in town? George is putting on some wild rice. He said the pickerel looks great.'

Massy doesn't speak. Maybe she really has become used to her own company, and is now regretting inviting guests to stay. Perhaps it is the mess in Stan's room. Honestly, I don't know why I am still hanging around on her farm.

'I am sorry about leaving papers all over Stan's room. I'll clear them up before dinner.'

'Papers?'

'I sorted through some more of the stuff Hall gave me.'

'Somewhere in that room is a clipping about the Plover fire. It says cause unknown.'

She might simply be stating a fact, but I doubt it. I know better than to react in the present with the emotional blinders of the past, but it has been ingrained in me. Old habits die hard. I instinctively rise to defend. I can choose any number of responses, but caught off-guard I counter, and then calculate how long it will take to pack up the car.

I try to be off-hand. 'But Massy we know how it started.'

'She should have moved on.'

That *she* was my mom. 'She did. Right out of the station and into a rental.'

'He was a good father and husband.'

Why is all of this coming out now?

'She was a good mother.'

Take my Queen; I will take your Knight. We avoid eye contact. I blame myself for being swept along in the joie de vivre of our visit, feeling sorry for her being injured, and not sticking to my commitment to stay at the hotel. If I'd just called and told her I needed to stay in town, told her to get her son or daughter-in-law to stay over.

'I've been sitting around all day going back over how their whole family was ostracized after your dad died. As if Mr. Winton was somehow also to blame for that.'

'I wasn't there to see.'

'I was.'

Perhaps too many years have passed without a proper redress of past hurts. I've misjudged this easy reconnection, and allowed myself to get caught up in things that are not related to why I am here in the first place. I see George moving about the house. Feel my neck where his lips touched. When I glance at Massy, she too is watching George go back and forth from kitchen to dining room. It comes to me that the papers scattered around Stan's room might not be what has prompted this slip into pouring salt on the circumstances of the fire, or the station closure of so many years ago.

'George was buying chocolates for you when I ran into him.' Massy looks at me, as if in disbelief.

'You did say he could do the cooking, and I'm starved.'

'Your note said "running a couple of errands." I would have gone with you.' Her tone softens.

'You were asleep. I guess I was in a hurry.'

'So you and George met in town.'

Massy undoes the clips of the elastic bandage and lets it fall away. She loosens it and rolls it up to use again. I crouch down beside her, take up the bandage, gently rub the pressure lines on her ankle, and began to rewrap.

'Why are you out here?' I ask.

'I got sick of just sitting around, and the dogs needed a walk.'

'I ran into George accidentally. You saw his note. It said he was heading to the lake.'

'And then you disappear. As if it had been planned. Did you stop off for a drink?'

'Well, yes, but a very, very quick one. And no, it wasn't planned. Why would you even think such a thing? I was seeing Adam, and then I had the meeting. It was a long day. Dr. Simpson was out at the lake, and they drove into town to upload some pictures or something. We actually did just bump into each other on the street. It's a small city.'

'By the way, Terri called.'

Terri? I don't know a Terri. Massy is full of surprises today.

'Speers? We sat all morning, and you never once mentioned that you had been sending emails to Terri Speers.'

'Shirley exchanged emails with a T. Speers. I thought the T stood for a Tom or a Ted.'

Massy had most of the day to look through my computer files, but I don't believe she would do such a thing.

'I probably should have shared what I put together from Shirley's files, and that box Hall gave me, when you and I were having coffee, but I didn't want to talk about something that may not amount to anything. Anyway, how was I to know that you know tspeers, and how did this Terri find me here?'

The tensor bandage is now wound around Massy's ankle. I apply the clips to hold it in place.

'Thanks.'

The dogs bark and chase each other back to the house. George appears on the doorstep, waves a bottle of wine, and goes back inside. He is either back to his pleasant-guest self, or is putting on a good act.

'Someone saw you in Winging, and word got around that Shirley's sister was out staying with me. I could have told you Terri tried to push some hair-brained scheme of a truck co-op to haul grain. You could have asked me.'

'Ask what? Shirley left orders to build a rail system.'

'Okay. Okay. What did George say?'

'What do you mean, *what did George say?*'

'Well, of course, you and he might have more in common. I'm just a plain old farmer's wife.'

How many times over the years have I heard that retort? From the safety and distance of the West Coast, I've often just looked out the window, and let the seconds tick by until Massy went on to another subject.

I smooth back my hair, in the way I once caught it up into a pony tail. I shade my eyes and look towards the setting sun. 'You are not, and have never been a plain old anything.'

I pull on my watch. The sun is aiming for the hills. The June solstice pending, the day with the most light, and then the days will get shorter. Massy fidgets with her bandaged ankle and then throws her fluffy slipper in the direction of the pups. They immediately come running to fight over it.

'I don't know where the other one is anyway.'

I pick at a mosquito bite on my arm. 'I should charge my phone.' I am looking towards the house, towards George.

'Margaret,' Massy exhales. 'Life is short. If you are interested in George, go for it. Jake wouldn't know the difference.'

I hoist myself up and walk a circle around her.

'I beg your pardon? What are you talking about? What makes you think I am interested in George? We accidentally ran into each other. I told him about meeting with the CN kid and he listened. We had an innocent drink, purely coincidental, and he didn't *say* anything.'

Massy wraps her arms around her knees, and looks like she doesn't believe me.

'You didn't see the way he was looking at you last night,' she says.

I stand there with my arms folded.

'He pointed out a pair of blue jays on the way back here. Said something about them and chestnuts. Honestly, my mind was elsewhere.'

Massy tugs on my trouser leg, motions for me to sit back down beside her.

'I can't compete with you.'

'There isn't a competition. And why would you say that about Jake.'

'Margaret, face it. He's always taken you for granted.'

'Massy, you're the one who says Stash used you like a crutch. The weight of that.'

'Other people's observations on marriages, other than their own, are opinions based on just that. Observation, not lived experience.'

'So Jake's taking me for granted is your observation.' I air quote.

I've never revealed details about my marriage to Massy, despite her being completely unrestrained about Stan and her. Probably something ingrained in me by my mother.

The once fluffy slipper is now strewn about as clumps of cotton, and the dogs have tired of it. They sit panting and waiting for the next challenge.

'You wouldn't notice if George was interested.' Massy half laughs.

If only she knew.

'Okay. Now you are starting to piss me off.'

'Can I just say this one thing?'

I feel my back teeth grinding, but remind myself I am a guest. Massy pulls up blades of grass one at a time.

'We've known each other a long time. Let me change my wording. Wouldn't you agree that after all these years, we know just about everything *about* each other? Are more than aware of each other's best and worst character traits.'

'Of course.'

'As in, you know I can be too spontaneous, that I'm a hard worker, but I can be absentminded, sometimes a bit irritable, and maybe a *little* selfish.'

'And now suddenly self-aware.'

'Well, with respect to you, sometimes your head is so far up your arse.'

'Thanks for the backhanded compliment.'

How am I to respond? She is being cruel and funny. Over the years, I admit I have, now and then, been sometimes oblivious, or maybe it's just been preoccupation, or avoidance. Hetty would probably second that. We each take a deep breath and rest back on our elbows.

She eventually offers, 'You used to blame Shirley for taking your things, messing with your collections of this or that. Petty stuff that you amplified.'

'But she did.'

'Everything isn't always black and white.'

'You really have been stewing all day.'

'We are angry with them for dying, angry with ourselves that we didn't sort things out when we had the chance. Feeling guilty for being left behind. And now, on top of everything you did for Shirley, she's stuck you with this railway thing. When we should be concerned with our own legacies.'

She sounds as if she is spouting some pop psychology.

'That's a whole lot of anger,' is all I can muster.

George comes down the path holding out two glasses of wine.

'Anyway, he's probably more your type.'

'Have you been paying any attention to why I am here?' I whisper, sensing George's nearness.

And then he is at my elbow. 'You seem to be having such a wonderful time together, I thought maybe you'd want to sit out here with these.' He offers the wine.

Massy asks, 'You do have mosquitoes in England, don't you?'

'As a matter of fact, we do.'

George hesitates, then turns to go back towards the house. 'Well, the rice is ready. I'm about to cook the pickerel.'

On second thought, he hands the wine glasses to me and says, 'Alright then, let's avoid the mosquitoes altogether. Up you get. Margaret give her your shoulder, will you.' He slips his arm around Massy's waist, and her arm around his neck. Massy hugs my shoulder, and I try not to spill the wine. If George senses that something is wrong, he doesn't let on. Massy looks at me, an impish smile running ear to ear. Her assumptions about George and me hopefully spent.

I reply by twisting my features into the tightest arse face I can muster, and in a statement that couldn't have been further from the truth, and because I know I can get away with it, I give myself the last word.

'I think you've packed on a few bushels there, Combine.'

18. BUSTITUTION

We eat our dinner with little conversation, despite George having set the dining room table with a linen tablecloth and candles he has found. I wonder if he really means them for the three of us, or if he is trying to send some sort of message to only me. Massy's inflamed ankle has unleashed all kinds of past resentments, in her and me, and then George interrupted our sparring. And she was making assumptions that I was interested in him. Or had suspicions. My manner resorts to one of courteous formality.

I turn my thoughts away from George, and to what my next move will be if the young railway executive replies with, 'Sorry, the rails have been sold.'

Would it be possible to build new rails? What might that cost?

Massy twirls bits of rice with her fork. George pours more wine for himself and Massy, but I decline. Last night's dinner had been so much more enjoyable, everyone in the same temperament, talking and laughing over our soup. Tonight, we move the the pickerel around our plates, while Stephan Grappelli plays in the background. This trip has had more surprises than I ever thought I could handle.

'Margaret, I noticed that a light on your phone is flashing,' George says.

I retrieve it from the charger.

A voice message from an unknown caller. I bring it back to the table and listen. Then replay it for the other two.

'George, George you there? It's Anna here. Would you get a bloody mobile, dear chap. I'm at Heathrow, just back from Bardsey, counting puffins, and I'm on my way to NEW FOUND LAND, and they say our place names are difficult to pronounce, to help them set up cameras to document their puffins. I thought I might make a side trip out to you, to see this SASK AT CHE WAN you are always going on about. Yes, I volunteered for a time for the Teifi Valley Railway helping lay some new track. Things are a bit, um, challenging up there at the moment. I won't go into that right now. But folks do love to sign their sleepers. Alright, are you there? Hello? Call me and let's fix some dates. Hwyl.'

'You will love her. Energy of a hummingbird.'

Massy asks, 'What does she mean by sleepers?'

'You call them railway ties, we call them sleepers.'

'I don't know about signing them, though, might be danger- ous, people wandering the tracks looking for their names,' I add.

'I best soon get in touch with her,' George says, 'I've got a meeting I've got to get back for.'

Massy thrums her fork on the side of her plate. 'Terri Speers is going to stop by later.'

'Terri Speers?'

She explains to George. 'Margaret's sister, Shirley, had been communicating by email with a T. Speers. Seems they discussed farmers buying back the land easement and rails that pass through their property. The original land owners sold it to the CN in the '40s for this northwestern route.'

I nod in agreement. 'I didn't connect the two—that Massy might know this person.'

'If all the landowners along that stretch owned the track and rails. Hmmm.' Massy's look is one of moving puzzle pieces in the air.

George says, 'Shirley certainly kept all of this close, at once so ambitious and autonomous.'

'The three of them were good at the autonomous part,' Massy blurts, then embarrassingly adds, 'I'm sorry, Margaret. That was uncalled for.'

I think of my dear sister and her grand scheme. 'Shirley just needed more time.'

'You'll figure it out,' George says, as he pats my arm.

Massy attempts lighthearted flattery. 'Has she told you what she does at her museum, George? She has probably catalogued more Canadian historical artifacts than anyone in Canada.'

I bristle at the pointless flattery. Massy trying to make up for her previous impetuous comments.

I say, 'And yet knows nothing about reviving a railway. Managing real heritage.'

'I'll have to take a trip out to this museum of yours.' George begins to clear the table, trying to sound casual and indifferent I assume. 'Been a while since I saw Pacific Orcas. Now, what is the itinerary for this evening? I mean before or after this mystery woman arrives. Would you like to hear about the digestive system of pelicans?'

'No.' We laugh in unison. His easy manner dispels some of the tension.

He retreats to the kitchen. 'Where did I put those chocolates?'

'I was rude and insensitive,' Massy speaks in a hushed tone. 'It's a poor excuse, but I blame this bloody ankle. I've never been good at sedentary. When my body breaks down, I split hairs.'

George turns up the volume on the radio, and begins to wash up the dishes.

Massy continues. 'I really have tried to put all that business behind me. I was sitting in the kitchen while you were gone, and this energy started to percolate inside me.'

'I suppose it was bound to happen. For both of us.'

'You're probably right.' She rises from her chair, limps to my side and plants a kiss on my head. 'I've been saving up all my crankiness for your arrival.' Then whispers in my ear, 'Do you think he's involved with this Anna?'

I am not in the mood to guess at George's past romantic liaisons.

She pauses, appears to hesitate. 'Since you are already angry with me,' and then Massy leaves the table, and goes to the study where I slept. She places a cigar box in front of me.

'Open that.'

Inside are a few random items. A velveteen barrette, like the one that Shirley had stolen, some Beatle cards, a few marbles, and a yellowed Toronto Star clipping, which, when I unfold, bears the headline, *John Glenn is Brought Aboard the Destroyer Noa After Landing in The Atlantic Ocean.*

'You?'

'I pilfered your treasures, and I was the one who ripped things out of your scrapbooks. Me. Not Shirley. Just silly childhood pranks.'

'Why?'

'I don't know. Maybe because when we first met, all you ever wanted to do was spend time with your sister.'

'But I blamed her for stealing my things. My relationship with Shirley was formed out of my believing that she had always been taking things away from me. That she had hidden things from me. That she had intentionally been chipping away at my identity for her own ends. You have no idea how your actions created a chasm between us. Do you understand that?'

'I found these after Stan passed. I'd truly forgotten. I'm sorry beyond words.'

'And, you maintained this deception throughout all of our grown lives?'

First she attacks Jake and our marriage, and then hands back my property as if it had been some, some minor oversight. But worst of all, my sister had gone away knowing only my accusations, and thinking that I believed her to be a liar. What kind of friend maintains such lifelong malicious treachery?

'And I blamed Shirley.'

'She knew she hadn't done any of those things. She had a goodness in her. I'm so sorry. Please, say you forgive me.'

'Just like that?'

'It's good to see you finally standing up for yourself. But, yes.'

George brings in the box of chocolates, gift wrapped, and hands them to Massy. I can't look at either of them.

'Almost forgot about these. The prescription for sprained ankles.' Massy tears at the tissue paper.

'I'm hoping you will share,' George says. 'My preference is cashews.'

'George, how thoughtful. Thank you. This, and that one, look like covered cashews, and you may have them both.'

George pops both of the small chocolates into his mouth, and sensing friction, retreats to the kitchen.

'Have one.' Massy holds out the box to me. 'Please. Have one.'

I reached for the darkest chocolate, and then another, and then the last one. I know these are the ones she likes. I go to the door and throw them as far as I can. Childish, petty, but in these tight quarters it gives me some small measure of satisfaction. I am not about to embarrass myself in front of George.

'Feel better?' Massy leans against the table and asks. 'Please, say you forgive me.'

'Why? It isn't about the barrette or the cards, or these.' I pick up and let the marbles roll across the table. 'It was that Shirley said over and over, she hadn't taken any of my things, and I never believed her. What a fool I've been.'

'She loved you and looked up to you. People mattered more to her than things. I don't believe for a minute that she let any of this come between you.'

I love you, my bossy marvel, she'd said in her letter.

'Can we change the subject?' Massy looks towards the kitchen. 'Tell me about Shirley's research. Please.'

'So, you're sorry?'

'Of course, I'm sorry. I've wanted to put this behind us for a long time.'

I look down at the box of stolen possessions of long ago. They are like the inanimate objects in the museum display cases. They aren't mine anymore. I am no longer connected to them. I have no desire to reclaim them. What would staying angry solve? Massy is partly right, Shirley never attached herself to *things*. Even when we'd sorted Mom's property, she wanted none of it. Her reaction had always been to shrug off my accusations. Knowing, as Massy said, of her own innocence, her own self.

'The papers in Stan's study. What did Shirley come up with?'

'First. I'm taking back that John Glenn cutting.'

Massy throws back her hands in surrender, and then brings them together in a Namaste.

Then, I slowly relent. 'She was actually in touch with a short line railway down South.'

'It was probably in the papers when they started out, but I can't honestly say I've heard of it. South of Regina is a whole other Saskatchewan. Someone must know.'

I roll a marble across the table to her. 'Were the Winton's really ostracized?'

'What?'

'Before. When we were outside, you said the family was blamed.'

Massy picks up one chocolate, then puts it back.

'Do you really want to keep doing this?'

'Tell me. I need to know."

'Your dad didn't just serve as the station agent. He managed the skating rink, served on the school council. That station waiting room was a gathering place that unified the town. Even the village priest took his own confessions to the waiting room. When Neal wasn't there anymore, everything fell apart. Mr. Grewin made it his job to remember every little detail of every disagreement that anyone had had with your dad, especially Stan's dad. He reminded Mr. Winton senior that he had blamed Neal for CN cutting train service down to two days a week and implementing a slower trucking service to deliver goods. Blamed him when someone else wanted to use a bus as substitution for a train. All the town friendships fell apart when the CN closed the stations along this line.'

'I suppose it was too intangible to blame the railway for what happened to the town.'

'You and Shirley and Jean moved away. The hotel and pub site was covered over in gravel, and even before the stores closed, Plover became a ghost town. Everyone avoided the Wintons because of Stan. He should've never confessed to starting the fire.'

I look towards the east windows. The sun's rays show the streaks of filmy residue, where someone has been trying to wipe clean the glass.

'All I knew was that I no longer had a dad. Later, I hoped that by getting as far away as I could, I would forget about everything I'd lost and move on.'

Massy swirls her tongue around chocolate toffee stuck in a back molar.

'These days corporations have psychologists. Get everyone to talk about how they feel.'

I return to the windows that look out at the river. Would my so-called friend's revelations, had they been made years ago, made a difference in my relationship with my sister? For years I felt Shirley was a thieving magpie, and so she'd also take my boys from me. But she hadn't. How utterly ridiculous.

George pokes his head around the corner. 'Ice cream anyone?'

I turn to face him. 'Yes, please.' Today someone kissed me, with a kiss that felt again like the first time I'd ever been kissed, and it had placed me so solidly in the present that it left no room for my grievances with Massy. I realize now that the things she took from me, when she took them from me, she needed more than I did.

'The dessert dishes are on the second shelf in the cupboard left of the sink. George, I so appreciate your cooking and washing up.'

George is standing next to the table now. 'It's always easier in someone else's kitchen.'

Massy says, 'And George… I need to apologize to you too.'

'Whatever for?'

'I haven't been my best today.'

I turn and point. '*She* is a dove.'

George tilts his head, perhaps about to spout something on doves, but says instead, 'If I'd met you both at some function, I would have thought you sisters. Besides, it's boring to always have to be on your best behavior, and neither of you is boring.' He claps his hands once, and says over his shoulder as he goes back to the kitchen. 'Right. I'll tell you later what I once said to a BBC interviewer that ended up in my being banned from the airwaves for a decade.'

He sees the car, before the dogs start barking.

'Someone is pulling into the driveway. Maybe I'll set out four dishes of Neapolitan.'

After the introductions are made and we are settled on the deck with our dishes of ice cream, I say to our guest, 'I feel silly. I assumed you were a man.'

Terri's brunette hair is gathered up in a clip at the back, and she looks as if she is still getting used to farm life. Her hands are soft looking, and she is dressed in beige trousers and a lavender-coloured sweater, suitable for casual Fridays.

'Everyone else around here assumed so too, but I'm not my brother.'

George asks, 'Has your family also farmed here for generations?'

'My grandparents auctioned everything off thirty years ago. The land was rented, and then divided between the beneficiaries of their will. Those beneficiaries are slowly getting rid of sections, and I've bought a couple at a very good price. I worked in government finance for ten years, never really spent much time out here.'

'I vaguely recall the name Speers, but never knew the family,' Massy admits.

'My dad went to school in North Battleford. My grandparents thought he might get scholarships if he was in a bigger place. He eventually went to McGill and met my mom, and we lived there most of my early life, before they moved back to Saskatoòn.'

'I swear,' she raises her right hand, 'I just woke up one morning and felt I had to be here. As soon as I walked the land again, I knew this is where I belong. I don't want to spend the rest of my life in an office.'

Terri waves her spoon at one of the dogs who comes over to her knee. For a second, I think she is going to let him lick the spoon.

'You'd like some of this, wouldn't you?'

'Sit,' Massy commands.

'I'm slowly taking over from the renters, but I have no idea what I am supposed to be doing next. Learning as I go. It's hard to explain, or maybe not, but something about being back on the farm just feels completely right.'

She places her ice cream dish on the deck and the happy dog slobbers up the dregs. 'I'm really too young to retire. When work started to reorganize, I took what they call a temporary release.'

'Does that mean you may go back at some point in the same capacity?' George asks.

'Actually,' Terri says, 'things have picked up a bit, and I've made an arrangement to do some contract work from home. But, yes, with some money they released to me and some savings, I bought a tractor.' There is pride in her voice.

She leans towards George. 'Drives like a Bentley.'

'How did you ever connect with Shirley?' I ask.

'I think she might have gotten her hands on a municipal farm map and just sent letters or emails to all of the farmers with land adjacent to the old Plover rail line. When she sent me a copy of the sale of—I guess it would be your grandparents'—land to the CN, I went back through the few papers my dad had kept and found the same kind of offer. They sold it back to me for $200. I just emailed her. I went around to most of the farms I suspected she might have mailed, and I tried to convince them to do the same.'

'Did you ever meet?' I want to know.

'No. At first, I thought her ideas were out to lunch. May have even deleted her emails initially. Well, she was your sister, she must have had your ear in all of this?'

'I wish I could tell you that I knew what she wanted to do, but I really didn't. I've been playing catch-up.'

Terri doesn't let my feelings penetrate too deeply into her own train of thought. 'I was disappointed when her emails just stopped. I eventually found her obituary online.'

She stands and paces back and forth on the deck. 'I took her to mean she really wanted to get moving on a rail system. With the grain board gone, the more I thought about it. I started to do some investigating of my own. When I read about a co-op rail system down south, I headed down to meet with them.'

'And what did you find out?' George asks.

'Took them about four years to get it all in place, but it seems to be a success. They did get some kind of a government loan or grant. I didn't bring that information with me, but it looks like they sold shares initially, and the train they have put together is hauling local farmers' wheat. I think it's a fantastic idea.'

She grows more animated by the moment. I quickly conclude that Terri's kind of enthusiasm needs acres, and not a cubicle in a stuffy governmental department. Still, I know from experience that it takes more than enthusiasm to get a project from start to finish. Hetty must be up to her ears with the Medici visit right about now, working overtime and fuming that I am not around. I'm actually impressed with myself that I haven't given it much thought.

'Would anyone like tea?' George asks.

'Tea? Wouldn't have any beer, would you?' Terri asks. 'I've run out.'

'There should be some in the refrigerator,' Massy offers. 'I keep some on hand for my son.'

'Alright if I just help myself?' Terri turns, and heads around the deck and into the kitchen, her voice trailing off. 'Through here? Nice place you have. I've never been out this way.'

The screen door slams, and the three of us smile at Terri's straightforwardness, and the way she doesn't stand on any grounds of formality.

'Anyone else?' we hear her call from the kitchen.

George throws back his head. 'Yes. Why not. Would either of you like a cup of tea, or coffee, water?'

'I cannot keep ordering people around.' Massy hops up and gently puts weight on her bandaged foot. 'Not bad. Really.'

She meets Terri coming out of the kitchen as she is going in. 'How's chamomile, Margaret?'

'What I can't seem to get my head around,' Terri says, 'is how Shirley came up with this idea.'

'Our dad was the station agent in Plover,' I explain. 'We lived there for many years. Do you know anything about trains?'

'Me? No. I've never even been on a train.' She takes a long pull on the beer. 'Unless you count the narrow-gauged kids' one at the city park.'

'Can I get you a glass?' George asks.

'It comes in a glass.' Terri holds the bottle in the air. 'Bad, I know. Something my dad used to say.'

George has the dogs under his feet now, panting from the day's heat, and he is alternately stroking their backs. 'So you say you've been down to the southern part of the province and seen this operation.'

'They've got four engines, cover around seven hundred miles of track."

'Seven hundred?' I am surprised.

''Bout that. The train stops at fifty sidings.'

'Is there a passenger service too?' I ask.

'No, definitely not a passenger service. Anyway, if you want to see them, I have some of the stats on the system down south.'

'Is there the possibility of a passenger service?' I assume that if there is a track and a freight train, perhaps there could also be a linked commuter service.

'I'm a little confused here, but to be fair, a lot's happened since your sister started this. The cost of shipping grain used to be subsidized through the federally legislated Crow Rate. That's long gone, and now the grain board is as well. I think farmers are open to options now. They need a way to get their wheat to market.' She takes a quick short sip of beer. Inspecting the bottle's label, she says, 'Good. Initially, I was going with a fleet of trucks.' She speaks openly, without any emotion in her voice. 'Course, we need to find the money first.'

I wonder if this is the time to mention my sister's money. Massy shakes her head.

Before I can ask Terri if she knows how many farmers have bought back the rails on their easements, and if she knows anything about the rest of the rails going for salvage, she says, 'There is only one slight problem. Just a small one.'

'Only one?' I ask, anticipating she'd of course be saying 'money.'

'There's a couple who bought the farm next to mine. I had no idea it was for sale. Sold privately. Anyway, when I ran the idea by them, they said they were completely opposed to a train running adjacent to their land. Seems they moved out to go *off the grid*. City dwellers.' She takes another gulp of beer, without acknowledging that she has also been a city dweller.

'They will not contribute to noise pollution and global warming by diesel fuel. Said they'd lobby to prevent any such thing.'

'There are many statistics on rail vs. cars and airplanes with respect to carbon emissions,' George offers.

'I think my Carl could explain the diesel fuel. And, he's been farming organic for years.' The kettle keeps whistling as Massy takes a while to get to it. She returns with two mugs, the herbal tea bag strings wound around the handle of each mug. 'No,' she cautions the dogs when they spring up to greet her. I see the possibility of another tumble and hurriedly take my mug from her.

'There must be statistics on one train engine vs. hundreds of trucks hauling wheat a long distance.' Massy eases herself into the Adirondack.

Terri settles back into her chair as well. 'Someone I used to work with is an expert in grant applications.' She opens her telephone and is immediately engaged, her eyes moving up and down.

We drink our tea, or beer, waiting for Terri to say something about what she is doing. I reach into my pocket and pull out the rock I picked up from the tracks on the day I arrived.

I hold it up for all of them to see. 'Fool's gold.'

Terri doesn't look up. 'Cool.'

'May I see?' George takes it from my hand, almost stroking my fingers as he does so. 'I don't think so, although I have occasionally seen what you refer to as fool's gold on that stretch of rail track.' He looks at it closely and then he scratches at the surface. 'This looks like schist with mica fleck.'

Massy blows on her tea. 'Do you know about rocks too?'

George downplays his response. 'Not entirely. Many birds nest in rocks; it's just incidental information gathering. Nice specimen.' He gently places the stone back on my palm.

I avoid looking at George, and turn my attention to Terri.

A rail line like the one that Dad believed in. What kind of a rail system did he believe in? Was it a freight service? Was it a passenger service? Would it still be one that he believed in if there are no small towns connected along the line? If it served only to haul grain? Or a nostalgic weekend steamer? Neither Shirley nor Neal can give me the answers, and in any case, as Terri has said, so much has changed.

I don't yet have all the answers either, but I wish Shirley were here with us on this deck, right now. Her thorough research might be paying off; her emails had inspired Terri to move ahead with investigating and planning. There is nothing autonomous about this.

And if there had been a chasm between us, it had been one of my making, and only I could change that now.

Terri makes several more calls, and our motley crew watches the sun go down, golden.

19. YARD

The telephone rings and rings. It is odd to answer another's telephone, but also unreasonable to expect Massy to run for it. As I reach the kitchen, she limps up behind me and George is dashing up from the spare room.

'Hello, hello.'

'Beeching. That was the guy's name.'

'Adam?'

'The guy in Britain. The one who caused the shutdown of over four thousand miles of track and closed over two thousand stations. Were you heading out? Look, I've got a kid giving me a lift out to Plover Station and I was hoping you could meet us out there.'

I blink away sleep. 'Where are you now?'

'About five miles out.'

'I don't understand.'

'Can you meet us there?'

I look at Massy and George waiting and watching me, point to the receiver, and mouth *Adam*. George eyes the coffee pot. Massy crosses her arms in front of her thin nightshirt.

I squint at the clock. 'I suppose so. Yes. No, I wasn't heading out the door. It might take me thirty minutes or so.'

Adam says, 'No problem. She says she'll be here in thirty minutes or so,' to whomever is next to him in the car. 'That'd give you some time to sort out some charge points.' Before I can say anything more, Adam hangs up.

Massy has the coffee water on the boil and coffee in the press.

George knuckle rubs his eyes. Even so, he wears the cheerful alertness that is himself. Is this how he would have looked if we'd woken up together?

'Adam wants me to meet him at Plover Station. Says some kid is driving him out. I better change.'

George offers, 'I'll throw on some toast for you. Do you want company?' I sense a slight plea in his tone, but not pressure.

'Have a leisurely breakfast, or get some more sleep, and I'll be back, whenever, I guess.'

I arrive at Plover Station to see Adam down on his knees in the yard examining the tracks, while a young man, I guess in his late 20s, seems to be doing something with what looks like a magnifying glass.

Adam gathers me up in a fatherly hug. 'Margaret.'

He presents the young man with a flourish. 'This is Sam. Sam meet Margaret.' The young man shakes my extended hand.

'He's been making some modifications out at the Museum Station. Finishing up a PhD.'

'Post doc. Actually.'

'Sorry, son,' Adam laughs, 'we wouldn't understand all of that scientific stuff anyway. Well, maybe Margaret could. Please. Just the newspaper cutting version.'

'My project is batteries, specifically battery-powered locomotives. They're trying it in the US. I couldn't believe my luck when someone told me about the rail museum east of the city. I asked them if they'd help me out, and well, they've been letting me experiment on one of the old diesel locomotives.'

'He was out there the other day. And that little track we built connects to the line that connects to this one.'

'I remember. Pleased to meet you, Sam. But Adam, I don't see what this has to do with anything.'

'Shirley's train. Dayliner. From here. Take folks right into Saskatoon via the connector.'

A bench was once positioned on the platform, near this spot. Mom had held us either side of her, to save us getting swept away by the force of the train's passing. Shirley had formed her first sounds from what she'd heard. From the last steam locomotive, slowing in front of the station, 'ph, ph, ph,' to the diesel, speeding up and away, 'ch, ch, ch, ch, ch, ch, ch, ch.'

I look up and down the empty street, the boarded-up buildings.

'Ahh. And these folks needing to zip into the city.' I present the empty main street with my right hand, 'They are?'

'Well, obviously not here. Not now. But once this thing is operational. Commuters. Local folks needing to take a day trip into town. Moms and strollers. School children. All this space is a bonus. Lots of room for a car park.' He spreads his arms wide open. 'Think of the future.'

Sam raises his palm, 'I only said this spot would be a good point of charge.'

'Like I said, Adam. There are no customers here.' I remember the behavior I witnessed, the last time I saw him. 'But forget that. There is no station.'

'Simple covered shelter would be enough, buy tickets onboard. Or, since the town of Winging already owns the area around the tracks, we could start the pick up there.'

'Permission for all this?'

'One thing at a time.'

'One thing at a time?' I know why, as a child, I had liked him so much, but that was with a child's ability to leap at possibilities, not as an adult hampered by practicalities. 'I had a meeting with a railway executive yesterday and he tells me that the remaining tracks are going to be sold for salvage.'

'What time was that? Because I called up some of my union brothers last night. Heard them tell the same rumour. Thing is, it's not decided. A fella I called, called another fella, and he found out they have to accept other proposals. Heard there are some other legal issues. Like I said, not a problem.'

'Oh, Adam. There is so much more to this.'

'I know. I know. It will be a lot more money, and so I've decided to auction off the posters, and give you the money.'

'You don't have to do that,' I say.

'Done.'

'No really. Apparently, Shirley made some crazy investment and left eight million dollars.'

'Well I'll be.'

'The thing is, in her letter to me, Shirley asked me to put her money into reviving a rail system like the one that Dad believed in. I'm not sure what that means.'

'You know what that means.'

'Look around, we can't just run a train back and forth as if it were an elaborate—toy.'

'Toy?'

'Last night I met with this Terri Speers. Remember? I told you that Shirley had been corresponding with a Speers, and she says that without a grain board, farmers are looking at options for hauling their grain. There would have to be a feasibility study to see who would support this. We can't just throw money away.'

'Did you look at the list?' asks Adam.

'What list?'

'I gave you a list. A list of people who could help you carry out your executor duties, give Shirley what she wanted. Bring a community together the way your dad used to.'

I feel in my pocket, and then realize I must have set the list down somewhere.

'Alright. Freight. I mean grain, if we have to at first, then eventually, or maybe on alternate days, a commuter. Don't you see? It doesn't matter, so long as you get a working train back on these tracks.'

He is adamant.

All of this time, Sam stands fidgeting beside Adam, his eyes darting from me to Adam, as if he is trying to decide whose team he is on.

'I'm just going to take some measurements.'

Adam watches him go. 'This kid really knows his stuff. He was telling me on the way out here, that—'

'Can we sit down please?' I turn to go back to the car. Adam plunks himself down in the June dandelions, unzips the light jacket he is wearing and spreads it out for me to sit on.

'Take a seat. Wait a minute. Damn my brain.'

He jogs back to the car he and Sam have traveled in, faster than I think he is able, and waves a newspaper in the air.

I fold my legs under me and stare at the tracks. Station and elevators gone, as when our sons had taken all day to build a Lego city and then dismantled everything before dinner—sides of buildings, chunks of roofs—so that the sections could all fit handily back in the case.

'You've made the papers.'

'What?'

'Only the third page, but still.'

He opens the paper and I read the headline:

MUSEUM CURATOR RETURNS TO CHILDHOOD HOME TO REVIVE ABANDONED RAILWAY.

My bio and a picture of the old Plover Station follow with an excerpt taken straight from the museum's brochure. Below that the journalist opines on outreach and engagement playing a more vital part in the future of museums. Apparently, he has his own opinions as well on Beeching and Hall cut backs. The article ends with 'Watch This Space For Updates.'

'Good God. What have you done?' I cup my head in my hands.

'I knew you'd like it. I figured you'd be a little busy so I went ahead and had a chat with the head nurse, her son's the editor of the daily, and he called me and I told him all about the plans. But see there, that's his own doing.'

'The plans?'

Adam says, 'Time zips by a lot faster as you get older, but you wouldn't know anything about that yet. Sometimes the movie in my head plays in slow motion. Neal giving the baggage man what for, Jean in the bay window, lowering the semaphore, and Shirley running around making trouble. I am over there,' he points to where his section house once was, 'with a life, and next thing you know, I am wondering why I am the last one to leave the theatre.'

The flies buzz in the heat as we watch Sam, now running his hand along the tracks. He waves at us, pushes aside the weeds and disappears down the track. A truck comes down off the highway and drives through town, leaving a trail of dust.

'See,' Adam says, 'and you said there were no folks around. For all we know, he could have been our first customer. This is just a short line, it could pay for itself, and so what if it needs to be subsidized.'

I shake the paper. 'Am I the only one who is still skeptical?'

Adam rests back on his forearms.

'Aren't you the one who went to see the executive? You're here, aren't you? Not in some apartment overlooking the Arno?'

'Florence? What does that have to do with anything?'

'Shirley wrote and said you'd sent her a postcard from there. Conference maybe? Years ago. Said if you won the lottery, that's where you'd go.'

'I did?'

'Maybe Shirley saw something that she knew you would see too. She missed her dad, but she was too young to remember the day to day workings of this place. You got it in you. And let's not beat around the bush, you are every bit as stubborn—or shall we say, determined—as Shirley was. Plus you've got a head full of howtodo museum stuff.'

'Do you actually believe there is any possibility of making this work?"

'You saying we aren't as determined as the Brits? Their rails got tore up in the '60s, turned them into walking trails, but they've reversed some of that damage. Rebuilding the rails, and are putting the trains back. I got magazines that prove it. Hell, yes.'

This isn't the disorganization of someone whose functioning is fading away. Here is a resilient and robust man. We sit waiting for Sam to reappear. A few starlings flit about. The heat waves shimmer over the rails. Their dispatches as mystifying as the way in which messages first traveled by telegraph.

'A lot of narrow gauge mind you, for their days-out steam train excursions. Geez, I better tell Gib there's no Ghan trip for me this time 'round.'

He squeezes my hand, and I wish we could just pack up and take off on any such excursion. Jake. Jake and Adam. That might be something I can arrange.

Adam looks pleased. 'Kid's a genius.' He waves at the young man now balancing on the rail. 'I told you it would be a good spot.'

'Now you go back and look at that list.'

When I arrive back at Massy's, egg-salad sandwiches, fresh radishes, and lemonade are laid out for lunch, awaiting my return. George is seated on a high stool with a towel draped over his shoulders and Massy is giving his head of hair a fresh buzz cut. George sits serenely as Massy lightly runs her hand over his scalp, letting the clippings fall to the towel. I can see them as a couple.

'Shedding some feathers,' he winks.

'Is Adam alright?' Massy asks. 'Are you?' I know she is also sheepishly referring to what had happened between us the night before. I nod.

'It seems Adam has an engineer who wants to test a battery-operated train engine. Sam's his name. He's going to ask his supervisor at the university if he can arrange to have a section of track cleared by way of permission between the university and Canadian National Railway.'

Massy blows lightly on George's neck and then takes the towel from his shoulders and shakes it over the deck.

'It seems they are benefactors of the university. They are interested in innovation and projects like his. He says he is certain they will fund this. Oh, goodness, and take a look at this.'

George hands me a glass of lemonade and then reads the short article in the paper. 'That is some good PR news.'

'News that will likely get me fired.'

Massy has been reading. 'Wow.'

'That's it?' I ask her.

'My ankle is much better.'

George chuckles. 'That too. And. Anna called again. She'll be here next week. She's got some practical solutions for the problems that will come up in restoring a rail line. And Tom's faxed over a few pictures and details of Mountsorrel.'

Massy lays out plates and napkins for our lunch.

'Terri called and said that we should form a conglomerate. I mean, you should.'

George closes the section of paper he is reading and corrects, 'Corporation.'

'Yes. She said she will either figure in or bypass the green family's right-of way if the corporation buys the whole section of track. Try to get back the sections some farmers have already taken back. Her friend is also putting together the papers for a government grant for said corporation.'

George continues, 'Apparently since the changes to the Transportation Act, competition is a good thing. There is national funding available.'

'It's almost too much to take in,' I sigh. 'In a good way. As if this was getting organized before I arrived here.'

George cautions, 'Don't count the chicks as part of the flock unless they return with it in the spring.'

Massy passes around the sandwiches, and George takes from the refrigerator some pickles that he has sliced. I wash my hands at the sink.

Massy says, 'And Terri says we should decide on a board of directors for the Plover Railway Line.'

'She's right. Feels like Monopoly. Sure, why not. Massy? George? A working mission statement. Do you swear allegiance to the Plover Railway Line, which will be built through the efforts of good people for the good of all people?'

Massy frowns, makes a face. 'We? I don't know anything about being on an executive board.'

'I'm sure that's how most of them start,' I say. 'You know about this area, the farmers, your son knows about shipping grain, maybe I should ask him too, and George you know about protecting the habitat, and you've been on many trains.

'Of course,' George laughs. 'Riding the TransPennine Express does make me an authority.'

'You should ask Terri, too,' Massy says.

'Of course,' I agree. 'And Adam.'

George adds, 'This is good. This is momentum. You are beginning to make this happen.'

Massy nods her acceptance, already looking as if she is seated at a long board table, seconding a motion.

It sounds flippant, but it isn't meant to. Gerard Hall comes to mind. I'll have to consider making him a member of the board. That would have been Shirley's idea. Save money on legal advice.

Massy reads from the notes she has written down while speaking to Terri: 'There will be a meeting next week in the Winging municipal office. I will ask (that is, Terri will ask) Alan Tachuk to invite the core members of the town councils of three neighbouring municipalities as well as the grain growers' association, the farmers adjacent to the tracks, and any and all to attend and I, or you (she means herself or you) can tell them about the plans. Make sure there is support for an independent short-rail system to haul grain. She also said she thinks we should sell shares for the rail line.'

Maybe it is time to tell Terri about the money.

20. Points

George, Massy, and I arrive in Winging and discover cars lining both sides of the main street and nowhere to park. It is the date of the regularly scheduled council meeting, but Alan Tachuk has reclassified it as imperative, and asked the meeting be moved to the village hall. As Terri has asked him to do, Alan has invited core members of the town councils of three neighbouring municipalities, the grain growers, small shop keepers who still exist in the villages along the route, and any and sundry.

I don't recognize anyone in the packed room other than Alan. He processed my tax payment on the fifty acres. As I look around, I can't help but take in a young couple standing against one wall. They are wearing Wellingtons, jeans and jean jackets, looking as if they have stepped out of a Ralph Lauren ad. A bit too high fashion for farmers. The young man is holding a book under his arm, the woman a notepad and pen. Terri's nemeses.

Alan introduces two mayors and the head of the Grain Growers Association, and then turns the floor over to Terri Speers. I let her take the lead.

'Welcome everyone,' Terri says. 'Thanks for coming out. I know it's a busy time of year. I see some of you have come straight from haying. Nice to see a few wives too.'

'So, the Crow Rate subsidy is gone and now the wheat board that negotiated marketing of grain is dismantled too. Some of us are looking forward to doing our own marketing of our grain, and some of us are not. Either way that means hauling our grain quite a distance from our farms. Time away from farm work, cost of gas, yada yada. It's seems to me, and no doubt to many of you, that a lot could be gained by figuring out how to go about this together.

'Alan here and I have gone over the municipality maps and most of you have been invited here because you own the land adjacent to the old Plover rail line, or like me you've also bought the easement land on which the tracks lay.'

A farmer steps forward and raises his hand. 'I'm just in the process of reverting that land to my ownership, and I plan to join my sections on either side, once the rails are gone. It will add to my tillable land.'

Terri puts up her hand. 'Let's just start at the beginning OK? A while ago some of you received letters from Shirley, the daughter of the last railway agent at Plover station, maybe some of you remember Neal Harris. This is her sister, Margaret. Margaret, can you stand up please. Some of the folks at the back can't see.'

I stand and wave. 'Hello.'

'That's fine, you can sit back down now.'

She leafs through her notes. 'A few of us have had discussions amongst ourselves about how to proceed, now that the federal government has dismantled the grain board, and the nearest grain elevators take half a day to get back and forth from.

A young man steps forward. 'I like the idea of a fleet of cooperative trucks.'

'Well, that was just some preliminary brainstorming we did. But now, a few other things have come to light. With a rail line still in place, this is the smarter alternative. I've visited the seven hundred mile reinstated short-line rail down south. Some of you have probably heard about it. I invited their chairman and treasurer up to tell us about its success, but it was a little short notice. They will travel up here in the next week or so. Those people who bought shares at the beginning of the redevelopment of that line have now sold them for double the purchase price.'

A few mutters go through the crowd. I think this a slightly misleading ploy.

'Let's see now, um, George,' Terri calls out. 'Since the fellows from down south can't be here, I'd like to invite Dr. George Merell to say a few words about communities in Great Britain that are rebuilding their rail lines.'

Someone shouts, 'How many pelicans you seen this year?'

'Yes,' Terri goes on to explain, 'several of you know that Dr. Merrel has worked with Dr. Simpson on keeping track of the pelicans at Plover Lake, and we really appreciate him coming all the way over here every year. But today, George, can you please tell us what you know about a rail line going forward in England. It's not one for hauling grain, mind you, but—well, George, why don't you go ahead.'

A few people shuffle from front to back, some give up chairs so others can sit. A couple of farmers who've gotten to know him over the years, acknowledge George with a nod or wave.

George puts his hands in his pockets and begins to speak. At once he has everyone's attention.

'First of all, and I'm happy to finally have a chance to say this,' he begins—

'I seen you on TV, doc.' Another enthusiastic interrupter.

George smiles and waves it off. 'I'm lucky in that I've gotten to see bird conservation areas all over the world, but the ones I know best are in Britain. Several of them are on National Trust lands, actually both Canada's and our National Trust, and some AONB. Sorry, that's not a place, it represents Areas of Outstanding Natural Beauty. Plover Lake is like those, but it belongs to you, the wildlife in this area, as well as resident and migrating birds, and so it is also a globally significant ecosystem. It is contaminant free, the whitefish are thriving, and yes, the pelican count is up this year. And thank you for letting me use your telephones, boating me up to the island, and feeding me on occasion.' A few chuckles.

'As Terri mentioned, I've spoken to a few friends who have seen first-hand the replacing of tracks and trains that were dismantled back in the '60s. The lines were torn up and done away with. Up in Leicestershire—that's in the East Midlands of England—they are in the process of rebuilding an entire section of track. The locals didn't want to just stand by anymore, they wanted to preserve their railway and rebuilt it themselves. Their section, similar to the Plover Line joining the Saskatoon line, was a part of the Great Central Railway, going down to London, and, just as your railway served these farms, that railway was important in hauling out granite from their quarry. I'll pass these pictures around, and you can see the before, after, and now.

'It's taken hundreds of volunteers, a lot of money, and determination, but you can see from those pictures that they've rebuilt the entire rail bed and track. There are many more like it.'

'That's something we would not have to do,' Terri says. 'We're lucky to still have the Plover Line in place. The whole point being that that community took control of their rail line. Just as you will hear from the fellows from down south next week.'

'That's right,' George says. 'I'm heading back to England soon, and I plan to visit this project, check out a few others, and get an up-to-date first-hand look at them.'

He looks around the room, and then says, 'Margaret,' calling on me to speak. Terri is about to rise, but George sends her a look that says, Margaret's got this.

At first, I'm hesitant, trying to put words together without prep notes, nervous about people who don't know me thinking I've come to tell them what to do, but then the words begin to spill out. 'Terri has very feasible ideas for putting together a plan. She knows how to handle the business side of things, form a cooperative and maybe sell shares.' I hear myself sounding like Hetty. In front of me are ordinary folks who want the truth, not some museum-speak.

'Look. This is a very costly venture and the benefits may not be visible for years to come. Terri can explain in great detail how this might be managed, but you—we—need to ask ourselves if we can rebuild a short-line railway with money and a whole lot of commitment. This railway would be for you, for the community. If we can revive a train system, it might reduce the costs of shipping grain, it will allow you to fill the boxcars directly and get your grain to market. There is the possibility that down the road, if the demand is there, and we have the ability, that we could run a commuter car into the city. I'd like to think a rebuilt line might also provide opportunities for the next generation. Maybe in ways we can't see yet. And before you ask, I have access to funds for getting the whole project started.'

Terri can't hold herself back any longer. 'An additional option for funding would be a public campaign. My research suggests asking individuals if they would like to buy their own railway tie. Course they wouldn't own it, but for anyone who was interested we could issue a certificate with their name and the mileage marker of their tie. We could even post a list in a newspaper or something.' She looks around the room and comes back to me.

I add, 'My sister, Shirley, found there are additional government funds available for green transport, reducing carbon emissions, environmental protection.'

'That's a whole lot of line to repair,' someone says.

George volunteers, 'I've walked the old Plover Line, over a two-day period. You would need an engineer to inspect the entire line, but there is not one bridge or trestle over the entire distance, and I think, maybe, only one switch. That should keep costs down. An engineer would need to inspect the ties, of course, and project a cost of repairs.'

I look in the direction of the green couple who are listening intently.

One farmer steps forward. 'I own the land now, the land that the railway bought from my grandparents. Are you going to buy the land from me now?'

Terri speaks confidently. 'I think the corporation would have to decide that. Obviously, we would like to keep costs down, but yes, that may be possible. I'd like it better if you donated it Nick, you know the newspapers like to read about people who do generous things like that.'

Nick scratches his head. 'We'll see.'

The door opens, and Adam and Sam enter. I've been so caught up in phone calls with Terri and this meeting that I have completely neglected Adam. A couple of farmers seem to recognize him, maybe from years ago on the section gang, and one of them pokes the other to shift and a seat is presented for Adam.

When the room settles again, Alan Tachuk speaks. 'I'd like to volunteer to go over some of those grant proposals.'

Terri Spears starts up again. 'About the southern line. The shares run in the three to five-thousand-dollar range. If we did this thing, we could sell a limited number of shares. Just so we are all on the same page.'

'Are you saying the share owners would own the rail line?' someone asks.

'Yes, that's what I'm saying. It will all need to be sorted.'

'What about you?' One of the wives points her head in my direction. 'Margaret, what guarantees do we have that you aren't going to just splash the cash and high tail it out, or buy the bulk of the shares? Why do you want to rebuild an abandoned rail line, when you don't even live here?'

George stands to come to my defense, but I say, 'It's OK, George. I grew up here. As Terri mentioned, my father was the last railway station agent. He believed that a railway brought a community together. But the railway that was here before was installed and also run by a corporation that needed to take profits. If this railway is rebuilt by this community, to serve this community, and we are all stakeholders, not just me, we can make it work the way we need it to work for this community. And yes, I have some cash as you put it. My sister invested in potash back in the day, and in her will she asked me to help revive—this— line. And I won't own any shares. I have a job that I have to get back to, but I will be part of the Board of Directors and will come back here as often as I can, to do whatever I can.'

The door opens and the young thumb-tattooed CN executive I'd met with a few days ago enters the hall. He is holding onto a computer bag with one hand and cell phone in the other. He must think he can slip anonymously into the back somewhere, but everyone stares at him when he enters. The room buzzes with the locals wondering who the fellow is.

'Something else,' I shout over the din. 'I met with the CN representative who is the liaison between the local rail branch office and the American rail company that owns all of the tracks in Saskatchewan, and this is the young man.' I point him out. 'They want to rip out all the tracks for steel salvage.' There are several groans.

'I'm here like everyone else,' the young man says, 'to hear about options. But I have to tell you, the owner company isn't completely closed to what the local office recommends.'

The Ralph Lauren couple summon up their courage and step forward. The man sounds likes he's rehearsed his script. 'Tearing up the tracks would be a commitment to making sure we do not use the fossil fuels that a diesel engine requires. And in so doing, will also preserve in perpetuity the beauty of this area. We have Wordsworth on our side.' He waves his book in the air.

'Where's he at?' someone asks. 'I'd like to hear what he has to say.'

George steps forward and explains, 'This intelligent young man is referring to the poet William Wordsworth and his opposition in the 19th century to a rail line running through his community. In his day, he, like this young man, was concerned about nature.' Before he steps back, he adds, 'I believe Wordsworth may have been trying to protect his Windermere.'

There are a few snickers. George smiles in amusement.

The young man's partner comes to his aid. 'If that rail bed could be turned into a walking and bicycle trail and connected to a Trans-Canada trail, everyone would benefit. Think of the birds and flowers that could come back to this length of track.'

I wait for Adam's response. Several farmers look from one to the other. If you are going to try and sell the benefits of a bicycle trail through his land to a farmer when he has no competitive way to get his wheat to market, you might as well give him a ticket to Mars.

George will not be out-birded by someone in untested Wellingtons.

'I know the birds of this track very well. The sloughs and lakes in the surrounding area, as well as the containment areas in various sections offer good protection and nesting places. There are ways of implementing wildlife habitats, and protecting animals such as beaver and deer. Of course, someone would be appointed to study and encourage the diversity of wildlife along the Plover Line. Maybe look at past bird surveys. And you are absolutely correct, there is a challenge here. We need to consider the impact of our actions on bird populations and migration. How to balance the needs of humans and wildlife.'

He is considerate and gentle in his response. I wish that I had positioned myself nearer to him.

A cell phone rings several times before the CN executive acknowledges it.

Alan looks around the room and asks anyone who wants to, to introduce themselves again and to speak freely.

Only a few are brave enough. They want more information, some guarantees, and wonder if a bank will lend them more money to back such a project, on top of what they already owe on farm machinery and expenses. Terri assures them there will be more information to come.

When it comes around to Adam's turn, he directs his attention to the young couple preoccupied with trails and pollution.

'Excuse me, I didn't catch your names?' he says.

'Oh. I'm Justin, and this is Justine.'

'Nice to meet you. Must have come in after you introduced yourselves. Can I just ask you this? If I could tell you that this new train system would not be using fossil fuel, would be quiet as a kitten, and the air around it only smelling of the flowers alongside the track, would you support it running beside your farm?'

The couple look at each other. 'It could be years away,' Justine challenges.

As he pulls Sam next to him, Adam says, 'This here young man has come up with a clean way to operate a locomotive, and you can come up to the train museum—I'll tell you later how to get there—in fact all of you are invited, and you can see for yourselves what it can do.'

A look passes between Adam and Sam, and then Adam says, 'Some of this is secret science, you understand.'

Sam speaks, 'I can point you to some readily available published papers,' he says, 'but the emissions are less than those from cars. I've based my post-doctorate on my research.'

Adam adds, 'It's already been done in the US, and Britain is looking at its own variation. Look, the simple fact is we lost the train through here because a big company was losing money. But we don't need to fill fat cats' pockets. We have a chance to rebuild it, take it back. Damn it. This is worth doing. Let's not louse it up.'

I touch the watch around my wrist. When the room begins to hum again with conversation, I look towards Adam. He nods and gives a discreet thumbs up into his chest.

Finally, the young CN executive introduces himself as the district supervisor.

Before he can get a word out, spurred on by Adam's fervor, I address the executive, whom I now relate to a shiny-shoed man who told Dad the station would be closing.

'As you can see, there is a considerable groundswell here. Just tell us who we have to go to next, because you are not going to sell these tracks for salvage, and, even if you do, despite our now owning the land, we will build a new set of tracks. This railway isn't going to belong to some suits back east holding a monopoly of shares. It is going to be ours.'

The room breaks out in applause. The room is very hot, and I have to push my way around people to get to the front door. I can't breathe, I need air. My head is down; I can't take in all these people. As I excuse myself through the crowd, just outside the front door, standing away, are four men and a woman. Even if he hadn't greeted me in a whispered voice, I would have recognize him anywhere. Ron. The boy who could once fit under the window in the back seat of a car.

Everyone in the meeting room is talking at once now. I can barely hear Ron introduce the woman.

'This is Chief Mary Stead, she's Chester's granddaughter. You remember Chester. He was your dad's drayman. She's married to our MP.' I can't hear the names of the others.

Adam makes his way to me, and I feel his hands on my shoulders. 'Thanks, Ron,' he says, and then he shakes hands with everyone in the small group. 'Good of you all to turn up. Come inside.'

Adam asks everyone blocking the entrance to make way, and he leads Chief Mary Stead and her group into the room. I hang back with Ron.

'Not a fan of crowds,' he says. 'Can we take a walk?'

I don't realize how important the people are that Adam is taking inside, but I desperately need some fresh air, and I follow Ron
up the street to a small bench. It is strange being in the presence of
someone I'd only known as a child. It is his voice, the way it still
sounds the same, that immediately connects me to him. I sit down
beside his thin frame and smile. I want to jokingly ask if he still goes
after gophers with a slingshot, and if what Adam has told me is true,
that Shirley once punched him in the face. Maybe, since he knows
about organic farming, and Massy has led me to believe he is
informed about such things, he can reassure me that the Very Land
Trust is really a worthwhile cause. I haven't seen him since we were
children, and being with him again sends me back in time.

'Adam filled me in,' he says. 'He always seems to think I
have all the answers and then he gives me a list of things to do.'

'You've kept in touch?' I ask.

Ron looks up and down the street. 'No. Not really.'

I'm not sure what to say or ask. He seems fragile, in a way I
can't pinpoint. 'I saw a picture of you and Stan in his room, and
the trophy for organic farming.'

Ron turns away and looks at the cars down the street, as if it
is difficult for him to look me in the eye. I don't want to make
him uncomfortable, and so sit quietly and wait for him to speak.

He turns then and says, 'Carl tells me you are out staying
with Massy.'

The cacophony from the village hall has died down, and I
can faintly hear a woman speaking.

Maybe if we start way back with some innocent memories,
we can make our way up to the present. I vaguely remember him
running down the track at Plover Station behind his brother
Stash, trying to keep up.

'Do you ever run into the Plover kids? Karen and Theresa,
or Gary, or the Grewin girls?'

He hesitates for a moment, looks at me questioningly, and
then his face softens.

'Massy doesn't know this.' He leans over onto his knees,
clasps his hands in front of him. 'Stan—we used to call him Stash,

so people didn't confuse him with dad—made me his executor a year before he died, and he made me swear never to tell her, or anyone.' He looks at me now, his hands trembling slightly. 'If you make a promise, you gotta keep it.'

A hurrah and another applause comes down the evening air from the meeting. A cat pads slowly across the street, and a group of teenagers standing near one of the parked trucks are passing headphones back and forth.

'I know a little about promises,' I answer.

He looks over his shoulder, takes a deep breath, and blurts out, 'I started the hotel pub fire.'

'I beg your pardon?' I just don't believe him.

His words come rushing at me. 'Stash didn't want me to be punished. He was my older and tougher brother, he said that he'd take the blame. He scared me, telling me I'd be sent away. I believed him and I let him take the blame. I didn't think it would have to be for our whole lives.'

My mind is racing, trying to put facts together, trying to go back to that night, and the days and months afterward, but all I can remember is a scared boy holding something in his hand.

'I don't understand.'

He sighs.

'The night the Plover hotel burnt down, I'd snuck into an open window in the pub to try to steal some cigarettes. I wanted to show Stash I was as tough as he was. Mrs. Novakovsky had left candles on the counter to try to clear the air of all the cigarette and beer smell. There was a bottle of rye in an unlocked cabinet. It would be a bonus if I could take a bottle out the window with me. Give it to Stash and his friends.

'I knocked the candles over, and everything went very fast after that. Stash was checking out the outdoor sauna Mr. Grewin had just built, when he noticed the smoke, and he saw me trying to climb back up to the open window.'

He lifts his sleeve to show me a scar on his forearm. He hadn't been holding something in his hand that night. He had been hiding his arm.

'A nail on the sill caught my shirt and was tearing at my arm as I tried to lift myself back over the sill. Stash pulled me to safety. Told me to run home and wash up, and then he climbed back inside to try and put out the fire. When he realized he couldn't stop it, he yelled "fire" to wake the Novakovskys, and when he could hear them scrambling upstairs, and was convinced they'd escape, he got out and ran to get away as fast and as far as he could.

'I used to hear Massy nag Stash he should contact your mom, and ask her to forgive him, but he always said there was nothing to forgive. Years ago, I looked up your mom's address. I wanted to tell her, tell everyone it was me, but Stash said it was pointless. Why start now, he said. It wouldn't do any good.' He looks at me, his eyes pleading, 'He didn't betray me. I want you to know, though. I need someone else to know.'

The night of the fire, Dad and Adam told Mom to gather the town kids and shelter them in the car; Ron had crumpled up across the back window, and kept asking where his brother was.

We sit here, staring blankly at the teens across the street. Ron looks towards the municipal hall and says, 'I've always wondered if Adam knew, but I've never asked him. I wondered if Stash told you, 'cause he said you found him hiding out in the skating hut days later, when he decided to come home.'

I am having a difficult time processing Ron's revelation. My mother had blamed Stash for everything. Her anger and frustration were laid at Stash's feet. Wrongful suppositions and speculations, because a kid had never admitted or denied starting the fire. Stash had been unaccounted for the next day, and when he'd turned up covered in scratches and skin burns, there had been so much grief and anger, his parents had quickly sent him away to a boys' school, partly to punish, and partly to protect. My mother had died having based a life time's worth of resentment on something that hadn't happened. What a waste of energy it had been, the decades of useless grinding on her psyche, mine, and everyone else's.

I can read from his earnest demeanor that he is looking to me for something. What? Forgiveness, permission, acceptance, direction?

I say, as sincerely as I mean, 'You were just a child. It was an accident. It wasn't your fault or your brother's.'

It is probably the mother in me, maybe on autopilot, partly hoping to see a weight lift from him, but even as I say these words, I know the years of feeling guilty and keeping secrets, like those in Massy's cigar box, will not immediately vanish. All the while, in my head, I am also turning back time, trying to rewrite the script, and wondering whether, if my mother had known that the younger Ron had set the fire and not Stan, she would still have felt exactly the same, because who started the fire would have changed nothing. Searching for ways to leave the past behind might have made all the difference. Yet, who was I to judge how difficult it was to lose a husband and their combined dreams when my mother was still so young.

I'd thought that settling my sister's estate and her ashes would have been easier than this. All of the confessions are unsettling. At the same time, I feel removed from them, but not in a repressing way, as years ago. I don't feel harmed by those secrets, or that I need to own or carry them around now.

Ron picks up a rock, tosses it up and down in his hand, before dropping it back down into the dirt. I feel he wants to avoid any more discussion of the matter.

'It'd be great if you could get this train thing going,' he says. 'Stash and me used to love to run down the street and throw a penny on the track just before the train arrived. And your dad. He'd always help us find it, where it had flown into the ballast. You know, I kind of had a crush on Shirley when we were young. She punched me in the face when I called you a sissy.'

I watch him blush. I wish Shirley had known.

I've forgotten about everything going on inside the meeting. 'Who are those people you brought to the meeting?' I ask.

There is a hint of pride in his tone. 'They're from the Chief's Cree band, and her MP husband's riding. They've been developing some ideas for tourism, historical sites, tours, courses on the old ways. They're keen on trying to figure out a way to make use of the abandoned rail lines through their unceded territory.' He bends to retie a shoelace. 'I've written a few of their grant proposals. A year ago, they received funding for a feasibility study. They've just been waiting. Adam called me, he does every few years, and asked me if I knew anything about abandoned rail lines. He told me to talk to Chief Mary Stead, Chester's granddaughter.'

I reach into my pocket and find the piece of paper with Adam's list. I pull it out and read his hastily scribbled words.

—*No time, you look up the numbers*
—*Call Chief Mary Stead, ask her for Ron's number*
—*Contact Prof. Jem at U of S engineering dept. and tell him you need a battery-powered locomotive*
—*Call Gib at the museum and ask him for the retired engineers association*
—*Ask Alan for a new municipal map*
—*Call the head nurse who works here and get her son's number—he's the editor of the Saskatoon paper*

Massy appears on the street and calls to me and Ron. We start to make our way towards Massy.

'Should I break my promise? Should I tell her?' Ron asks.

What difference would Ron's confession actually make? I turn to him, want to say something more to ease his pain, but also wonder if in Massy's eyes this would vindicate Stan or just make her relive the whole thing again. Should Stash's children know Ron caused the fire and not their father? What would happen to the relationship they have with their uncle?

'I can't tell you what you should do. I'm sorry that you've had to carry this secret for this many years. Maybe someday the time will seem right to share it. Sometimes, we have to just make up for the past by going forward.'

He nods.

I tell him, 'From what Massy's told me, you mean everything to her and Carl and Kelly. Stash would be very glad of that.'

I put my hand on his shoulder. 'I want you to meet a birder from England. He'd love it if you showed him some northern swans.' We walk towards Massy.

'The CN rep says the rest of the rail will be left in place, and there is something in the original 1940s legal paperwork,' Massy says breathlessly. 'It stipulates that the easement must be returned, if possible, to the bordering original farm owners or their descendants if the rail line is abandoned. At no cost. Silly corporation never bothered to update any of the old legalities.'

The three of us make our way to the door where several farmers have come out for a smoke. We go back inside in time to hear Terri shouting, 'Couple of more points. I've got a proposal here that you can all sign if you will give your support to a Plover Rail Line Cooperative. And to finish up here, if you haven't seen the article in the paper, I've got several copies.'

From a corner, Justine's voice peeps, 'I'd like to be part of the ecology team.'

21. Loop

A few days after the town meeting, Terri insists on a follow-up gathering at Massy's of the major stakeholders. Chief Stead can't make the start of the meeting, but has sent a message stating she is confident of the purchase of the rails. Her note states that this venture is also a way of taking back control over what was long ago imposed. The day before, I drive out to the Very Land Trust property and the fifty acres I am going to hang onto. It seems a good time and place to take stock of everything that has happened. Ron has told me, 'Jean showed great foresight in turning the land over to the Very Land Trust. There is plenty of land left to grow crops, and it does the world good for some of the old homesteads to be left to return to natural habitat.'

I watch the warblers dart among the grasses, and am grateful for the rest of the birds and wildlife that can freely come and go, and now I know Mom made the right decision. Maybe it was her way of giving back. What had steered her leaving the bulk of the land to a trust, I will never really know. It is a mystery. For those left behind, death leaves many questions unanswered. Perhaps some of them don't matter.

The wind in this province is an ever-present companion, and as it meanders through the birch trees, I laze in the car.

I am wakened by Hetty. 'Haven't I always treated you fairly and given you every opportunity to contribute in your own independent way?'

I am too dozy to argue. 'Of course.'

'And yet, after all these years, you completely ignore my appeal to return and do your part on one of, no, let me clarify that, *the* most important exhibit we are about to mount, plus leaving me to answer for that publicity stunt you carried off that made its way into the papers.'

'I didn't—'

'At least I am doing you the courtesy of telling you to your face. If it was left up to me, you'd be fired on the spot. Suffice to say, you are no longer working for my department. Report to the Board of Directors when you decide to mosey on home. Expect something more than a reprimand.'

'Hetty, be fair. I love my job. And you need me.'

'We'll see about that. Turns out Isabel speaks fluent Italian and she and the advance delegate have accomplished above and beyond what I requested. She's moving into your office as we speak. Perhaps the Board will give you the option of resigning rather than being let go.'

I look at myself in the dash mirror as if I will find an explanation there. I love my job. This must be just a misunderstanding. When I get back and can talk to her in person, surely things will sort themselves out.

I dial home and when there is no answer I realize that I don't know how long Jake was planning on staying in Toronto.

Ron, and Mary Stead, Alan, Adam and Sam, Terri, Massy and George are ready to get to work on what has to be done next. We gather around the table until after midnight, planning who will do what, and for the time being, I forget that the career I have devoted myself to has disappeared. Terri is a natural leader, with unbounded energy, and that is what this project will need going forward. I place a call to Hall and ask him to gather the necessary requirements to incorporate. That is where it will start. Terri and I will co-manage the finances. George, the community of Plover Lake, and a Cree advisor will oversee environmental concerns, as well as extended feasibility, and future planning. 'I'll get Justine on board. Maybe get her to do a flower count over the next year,' he adds.

Ron and Mary Stead, and Alan, will explore the tourism possibilities. Ron is also keen to assist Adam and Sam in acquisition of rolling stock, moving the battery-operated engine, and the necessary cars for transporting grain. Ron has knowledge of the university's benefactors and companies working in conjunction with innovation projects. Massy will keep meticulous records of it all, and assist Carl with community involvement.

The next day George heads out with Massy's car to meet Dr. Simpson, and she and I make a trip to the lawyer, visit the CN official, and take an introductory meeting with university engineers. We dine at the Bez together, and we walk across the Broadway Bridge.

'I've been fired,' I tell her.

'No. Can they just do that?'

'I'm pretty sure Hetty can,' I answer, but I want to put off the unemployment issue. We order Irish coffees.

Massy offers, 'Maybe you should keep some of that money.'

We eventually get around to George. 'He's an interesting and very attractive man, but I don't really think he is my type after all,' Massy confesses. 'Though I am looking forward to everyone working on this project together, there just isn't any chemistry between us. My soon-to-be grandchild is going to take priority once they come along.'

It's hard not to be drawn into her cheeriness and that smile.

'When I return, I want to come here by train. I want to see the Rockies from the Dome car of VIA rail's *Canadian*. After the railway line cooperative is legally established and the funds allocated, I'm going to buy myself a ticket out of the monies, a one-time travel expense. If that's allowed?'

Massy doesn't hesitate. 'Book yourself into a cabin. Heck, if it was me, I'd throw in a few spa days too.'

I want to breathe the ocean; I want to roam through the camus along Beach Drive, swim in the Pacific again, get lost in the thick of the forest. George's voice is clear and alive in my head. 'When I hear the fells calling me, I fly back.' Maybe I too can learn to migrate.

One day Adam calls. 'With the crew I'm putting together, we're aiming for track readiness and a first run of the Neal Plover Locomotive as soon as next fall, long as Terri's grants come through. Sam's conversion of the locomotive at the train museum outside the city has excited the university so much that they are ready to give him whatever funds he needs for the next step, in exchange for the patents. They want to keep him in their employment now that a newspaper article on his work has come out and he's had several offers from European developers. And they will secure the connector line.'

'Thank you, Adam. For everything. I want to visit you before I head back to the coast.'

'I'm out at Plover most days. Stop by.'

I am ready to go back and plead for my job, but now that this project is needing more attention, I begin to cling to my days here as well.

Terri arrives with the budgets for the financing, and explains how the shares will work. 'I've had over a dozen calls and a few people have even brought signed checks to purchase shares in the short line. We need to decide how many shares, before I speak to the reporter next week.'

Terri and Shirley would have worked so well together. It grieves me to contemplate the future experiences and joys that she will not claim, but I tell her.

'*You sure lucked out in finding that one. Terri'll be good.*'

Russ emails in answer to the one I'd sent. Before his PhD is to be completed, he needs one more project. Jake has told him about Shirley and the possibility of rebuilding the Plover Line. 'Is there any way I could spend some time out there and conduct an environmental political study?' asks Russ. I thrill at the privilege of getting to share some of this plan with my son.

Marvels.

Jake picks up before the end of the first ring.

'I need to tell you something,' I start.

'Oh, that you've lost your job? Yes, Hetty called. That Cersei Lannister of a woman couldn't contain her delight in telling me. There's an official-looking letter with the museum's logo sitting on the landing.'

'I'll open it when I get home.'

'I have no desire to read the mail stating that you have got the sack. Do you think that's also something Shirley would have wanted?'

I'm not going to argue with him.

'The money is in an account in my name only. Shirley's money is going to be seed money for the initial phase of a rebuilding of the Plover Line. I may need to come back here and I don't know for how long.'

It might be the 'coming back here and not knowing for how long' that softens his demeanor. I know that he loves me and hates to be away from me. If I know anything about Jake and myself after a decades-long marriage, it is that we haven't stepped aside before, for even the most serious of disagreements, and have always found ways to come back to the love that first brought us together. Still, what he says next is somewhat out of character.

'I'm sorry for the hostile way I said what I just said. I couldn't help making some plans for us with a bit of extra money, and now you've lost your job there will be even less coming in. I'm sorry I'm such a worrier.'

He gathers his thoughts. 'I've been doing a lot of thinking. It's been a rough few months. We've always been able to talk things through to clear the air, but lately it doesn't seem to be working. Maybe this is a good time to reevaluate how we go forward. Maybe I'm no longer the one you want to do that with.'

I start to say don't be ridiculous, then stop. All I know is at the present moment, in light of all that has happened, I need my life to go beyond grief in new ways.

'Make us a dinner reservation at that place we love,' I say. 'I have so much to tell you.'

'Really?'

'It's a start.'

'If you do have to go back out there, I promise no more surprise visits. I'd want to visit, though, and see how it all takes shape, 'cause you're good at this.'

'Do you mean that?'

'Of course. You don't need me to tell you that.'

No. I suppose I don't.

George invites Massy and me to walk a five-mile loop along the track easement and back for a preview glimpse of the detailed sectional assessment of grasses and birdlife that he plans to carry out, but Massy's daughter-in-law needs help for the upcoming weekend market, and George and I take the walk alone.

His friend in Leicester has sent him more of the area's rail revival plans and time lines, and he has suggested inviting a few of their members out on an excursion. We discover a patch of big bluestem, one of the original prairie grasses, and George says he will ask Massy if she can try to reproduce it in her garden.

'Anna is arriving in a few days, and in ten days I will be going back to England, briefly. I have to attend the yearly meeting with a colleague who is the co-coordinator of the British Trust for Ornithology's Wetland Bird Sanctuary for Morecambe Bay.'

He puts his arm around my shoulder, and we make our way back to the car as if we have been companions for longer than the past few weeks.

'I'm leaving in a couple of days,' I say.

'How would you feel about visiting the Lune estuary? I could introduce you to England's own once Great Western Railway, now the Great Western Main Line that I take up from London. It will be a quick trip.'

I am uncomfortable with his suggesting future plans for the two of us. We've done nothing I can't tell Jake, and yet I feel a nagging old-fashioned sense of disloyalty, more because of what I feel for George than what I've done.

'If you've learned anything about me, it is that I value loyalty above everything. I'm not ready to leave Jake, and I don't think I am the affair type.'

'There you go thinking again.'

We both laugh.

'My sister and I weren't as close as we could have been, because of a lifetime of misconceptions. We were both affected by my mother's bitterness and disappointment, probably me more so. I wish we had talked everything over and over and over until we both had a deeper understanding of each other. I know we loved one another.'

We stop, and he steps forward to face me. 'Everything about you, that I have come to know, is caring and decency. And whatever your past relationship with your sister and mother, as

you said, you loved one another, and out of that love grew
loyalty and strength. I firmly believe that how we grow after a
certain point has more to do with our own determination and
evolution. We can pick away at the past or let it be.'

'Sounds like bird talk.'

'I was defaulting to Lennon and McCartney.'

He pauses and I see him looking ahead the way he studied
the storm from inside the tent. 'I want to be a part of your life.
If it is just part of your rail line troupe so be it, but I think—that
blasted word—you know I want more.'

More. I look away, and then back to him. 'I know.'

He pulls me close. 'I wandered to that part of the lake that
day, and you were swimming there, because we were meant to
meet. I believe that with every fiber of my being.'

He wraps his arms around me, I rest my head on his shoulder, and we hold onto one another for a long time. This brief
holding on, for me, the space permitted between a couple daring
to try out a new love and one staying the path of tried and true.

When we part, he slips a key into my hand, 'If you should
feel the call of the fells.'

It rains for a day, rain that the crops need, but as soon as it
stops, George goes off to check on his pelicans, and to walk the
rest of the track with Dr. Simpson from Plover to Saskatoon, in
his detailed study of the bird habitats that might have settled in
the interim decades. He appears to me almost on the verge of
tears as he sets out. I want to go with him, but return to the hotel
on my own to pack up all of my belongings and get ready to
leave for home.

I drag my suitcase out to the car and drive the short distance
to Plover Station. Not a cloud in the sky. I run my hands through
the long grasses. Adam and a small crew he has assembled are
working in short sections. I might be back to see the summer
unfold. Days before, Justine collected the stocks of weeds along
the track and set them in boxes to dry and to save the seeds. They
have set up a small awning for her work. The men are setting fire
to small areas of weeds along the track. Flames rear and die back

down into puffs of smoke, as the four men carefully make their way along the track, extinguishers at the ready.

Adam spares a few minutes to say, 'I knew there was a reason for me to keep up my morning exercise regime. Still, I'll be leaving the tearing up of old ties to them youngsters. Bloody hard work. And I thank you for it.' He limp-sprints back to his crew, waving over his shoulder. 'See you soon.'

I take the box containing Shirley's ashes from the back seat of the rental. The box is heavy and warm.

'Sorry you've had to wait so long for me to get around to this.'

I open the box and pull the bag of grey silt carefully away from the sides. I set the plastic bag down on the railway tie and with cupped hands, push aside the stones. I open the bag and gently tip the ashes onto the rail bed. Some settle in the ballast, others are gathered up in the wind and taken away, just as a few drift to the smoky haze of Adam's track clearing.

I reach into my pocket for the stone I've carried since the day I arrived, and place it back in the rail bed with the others.

22. Eight and Sand

At eight o'clock on the appointed day of my meeting with the Chairman of the Board of Governors of the museum, I search first for Hetty, but she is nowhere to be found. I sit near the totem poles for a few moments, waiting, as the Coast Salish elder once told me, for my spirit, still provinces away, to catch up with my arrived physical body. Kindled by thoughts of George walking along the sand beside the blue lake, Massy in her blooming garden, and Adam doing his pushups, I wonder if any of my words are resonating with Ron and the rest of the Plover community. I miss them, but it isn't with a sadness like the one I have carried for the last few months. Missing Shirley will be omnipresent, rising and receding in seasons, artifacts, memories, perhaps diminishing down the years, or until my own recall withers, but as I look up at eagle on one of the totem poles, I am happy and courageous at the unfolding purpose of her legacy.

The doors to the Renaissance exhibit are locked and I don't have my master key, choosing to avoid my office and any clearing out before my meeting of reprimand. Nervously holding the official request with the appointed date and time of a meeting, I run my fingers over the letter's embossed logo.

'Thank you for meeting with me, and I'm sorry I could not forewarn you about the subject of our discussions.'

The chairman is a man with perfect posture, who always seems to smile from some inner happiness. Our brief encounters at fund raisers have always left me grateful for his dedication to the museum. He invites me to sit across from him on one of the two rococo settees, that I know were brought up from storage. In a glass cabinet, keeping their place in time, are a few upper and lower Canada bits and bobs we've added to the décor.

'I am quite aware of your recent activities in Saskatchewan, as the local story was syndicated to the press here.'

'I'm so sorry if that was inappropriate. I assure you I had no knowledge of it.'

He brushes away my protestations. The man wants to get me out of his office as soon as possible.

'You have been with the museum for quite a few years now, Margaret.'

'I love my job here.'

'And have shown diligence and creativity in your position, but nothing like you have displayed with this boldness in rebuilding an abandoned rail line.' He opens the smaller windows on either side of the arched window.

'It came upon me quite unexpectedly.' I infer from his quick intake of breath that it is best to keep silent.

'In light of this, and after discussions amongst members of the Board, discussions, which had to be kept secret for obvious management reasons, I would like to propose that you fill the newly created position of Executive Director of Outreach. This museum, as all museums, if they are to survive, must move away from only storing and displaying dusty relics and get involved in changing communities in a much more proactive way, and I, and my fellow directors, would like to offer you this position. Salary commensurate of course with responsibilities, a budget for field research, two to three staff, access to the film department, and whatever your needs might be to enhance our museum's growth and assist with your project.'

The letter I have been holding falls to the floor. As I reach to pick it up, a faint cackling enters through the open windows. The chairman takes a thermos from his briefcase and pours his morning coffee. 'Margaret. Will you accept the offer?' Through the office's wide window, geese flying in V-formation rise on the air current created by the flock. The tired lead moves back into formation allowing a new one to take her turn and push on ahead.

Railway terms

BALLAST—Track ballast forms the trackbed upon which railroad ties (sleepers) are laid. It is packed between, below, and around the ties. It is used to bear the load from the railroad ties, to facilitate drainage of water, and also to keep down vegetation that might interfere with the track structure

SIGNAL—A mechanical or electrical device erected beside a railway line to pass information relating to the state of the line ahead to the engine drivers

EXTRA—A train not included in the normal schedule

DIVISION—The trackage area under the jurisdiction of a railway superintendent

JUNCTION—A point at which two lines or separate routes diverge from one another

SWITCHMAN—A railroad worker responsible for assembling trains and switching railroad cars in a yard

DRAG—A long heavy freight train moving at low speed

TOKEN—A physical object given to a locomotive driver to authorize use or a particular stretch of single track

BUFFER—A device that cushions the ends of rail vehicles against each other

TURNTABLE—A section of track that rotates to let locomotives and rolling stock turn around or access several engine maintenance sidings in a small area

GAUGE—The width between the inner faces of the rails

Branch Line—a secondary railway line that splits off from a main line

Boiler—A cylindrical container adjacent to the the firebox in which steam is produced to drive a steam locomotive

Siding—A section of track off the main line

Trailing—A turnout where both routes merge in the direction of travel

Goods—The products which are carried

Coupling—The mechanical connector at either end of a railway carriage, allowing it to couple together with other carriages, cars to from a train

Bustition—A portmanteau of 'bus' and 'substitution', the product of replacing a train service with buses as a temporary or permanent measure

Yard—An arrangement of tracks where rolling stock is switched to and from trains, freight is loaded or unloaded

Points—The articulation of rails that determine the route to be taken

Loop—a second short distance parallel track on a single-track railway line, allowing one train to pass another

Eight and Sand—A term used to wish train crews well and a quick uneventful journey. Comes from notch 8 (the highest power setting of modern locomotive throttles), and to apply sand to prevent wheel slipping

Acknowledgments

Thank you, Chris Needham, and everyone at Now Or Never Publishing. You took *Sleepers and Ties* off the siding and brought it into the station. A special thank you to a national treasure, Connie Kaldor, Coyote Entertainment, Quebec, Canada, for permission to use her lyrics to "Margaret's Waltz," taken from her album *Wood River*, melody based on "Margaret's Waltz" by Pat Shaw. Thank you to my peers at Lancaster University for your critiques and camaraderie. Your varied expanding accomplishments make me very proud of our collective. Thank you to the Irish writer Conor O'Callaghan who mentored the early chapters. Your attention to detail helped shape the work, and your own fine writing sets the bar high. Thank you, most stalwart and kind members of the Victoria Chapter of the Professional Writers of Canada, especially Kathy and Thelma, my writerly cohorts and friends. Thank you to my first readers, Catharine, Katharine, Margaret, Jamie, and Amy. It meant so much.

To say that a writer needs to believe in their work, sometimes for years, cannot be overstated. It helps immeasurably if you are sent, whether by chance, fate, or faith someone to champion your work and invest their heart and energy in your protagonist's story. David Llewelyn, you are the definition of a scholar and a gentleman, and I count my lucky stars you came into my writing life. Thank-you for reading and guiding Margaret's journey over many drafts, and for your gracious hospitality and writing cabin in Wales.

I would be remiss if I didn't acknowledge the railway men and women, among them Nap and Jean, who operated the railway stations and contributed so much to the vitality of village life, and those now working to rebuild the rail lines in their communities. Thank you, Jim, for your patience and support, for appreciating the need for time and space, and for your enlightening analysis when I pose questions. Our living story gifts me with much contentment when the craft challenges.

Above all, to Paul and Amy, my eternal gratitude for your constant encouragement and love, and for inspiring me through your own writing, and your creative and gracious lives. This one is for you.